I0599935

CAPTURED LOVE

THE CRESTWOOD UNIVERSITY SERIES
BOOK 3

EMERY PAIGE

EMERY PAIGE PUBLISHING

Cover Illustrator and Designer: Andra Murarasu

Editor: Chrisandra's Corrections

Proofreader: EAL Editing Services

 Created with Vellum

To those who've been forced into a box just to fit in:
To hell with that.
Never dim your light.
Never doubt your worth.

AUTHOR'S NOTE

Thank you so much for taking the time to pick up Captured Love.

I wanted to take the time to also give you a list of content warnings.

This book isn't dark, but your mental health is important and I want you to make the best choice for you.

Content Warnings:
Mentions of body image and insecurities
Some violence (not between the heroine and hero)

PLAYLIST

run for the hills - Tate McRae
Bed Chem - Sabrina Carpenter
Too Sweet - Hozier
Me, Myself & You - Perrie
Eye of the Tiger - Survivor
After Hours - Kehlani
APT. - ROSÉ, Bruno Mars
Little Things - One Direction
Dancing in the Flames - The Weeknd
Motivate - Little Mix
LEVII'S JEANS - Beyoncé, Post Malone
Please Please Please - Sabrina Carpenter, Dolly Parton
Begging - Dua Lipa
Cross Me - Ed Sheeran, Chance the Rapper, PnB Rock
22 (Taylor's Version) - Taylor Swift
You can check out the playlist on Spotify

1

SELENE

I'm convinced that I'm preparing to walk into the lion's den. That's the only way I can describe the feeling that is pulsing through my veins. I should be comfortable, being that I'm in my element, but calm is like a foreign word to me.

Even though I'm blasting music that is supposed to make me feel like I can take on anything, it's not working the way that I want it to. Instead, I'm standing in front of my mirror, fiddling with the hem of my green top—which is supposed to make my green eyes pop—trying to decide whether it looks good enough. It's tight, but in a way that's supposed to make me feel powerful. I adjust it again, trying to force my nerves to settle. This is not the time to feel self-conscious. It's time for me to own this.

I rub my hands down the front of my leggings just before I flash myself a smile in the mirror, and it's obvious to me that it's fake. However, I hope it reads like the confident woman I show the world on a daily basis.

Beneath this whole persona, I'm still me. The me that worries about not being enough. The me that wonders if this is all just one big mistake. But I push those thoughts away. I can't let them ruin this.

This is the start of something. I don't know what exactly, but I can feel it. Like I'm standing at the edge of something that could either be amazing or disastrous, and I'm just daring myself to take the leap.

Tonight, I'm going to see Knox Sanchez.

Alone.

In his bedroom.

The guy all my friends say is trouble. The guy who's as emotionally unavailable as he is annoyingly hot. The dude who, for reasons I can't quite understand, I can't seem to stay away from.

The day that he and I met still lives rent free in my mind. Jade Samuels's words still play on repeat in my head. She warned me by saying, "Knox has a bit of a reputation. He's not exactly known for his long-term commitments, if you catch my drift."

Hailey Reed, her best friend, agreed. Not to mention that her boyfriend, and hockey captain of the Crestwood Red Wolves, told her the same. Both of them made me wish that I could push the urge I had to get to know him more out of my mind, but I would be lying to everyone as well as myself.

I even managed to tell them that I wasn't looking for anything serious anyway—to get them off my case.

Which is true. Or at least, it used to be true.

But that's something I can't dwell on right now.

Because he does seem to be interested in me. The night we met, we exchanged numbers. While it took a little bit of time, I feel as if he's warmed up to me.

We've been texting for weeks now, and each message from him sends a little jolt of excitement through me. Not that I let him know that. I play it cool, like this is no big deal. Like he's just another guy.

But it's a lie. I know that, and maybe that's what scares me the most.

My music takes the opportunity to switch to "Run For the Hills" by Tate McRae. Is that a sign that I'm about to ignore?

Probably.

I grab my phone and silence the music. I thought the sudden silence would help, but it doesn't. The music had been on to help drown out my thoughts as well as hype me up, but what I didn't need was for it to call me out as well.

Before I set my phone aside, I swipe over to my messages and scroll through old texts with Knox. The first conversation that catches my eye is from a few weeks ago, where I sent him a screenshot of some cheesy reality dating show. I told him in all caps that he had to watch it with me just so we could quote, "dissect, and mock every second."

It was a brave thing for me to do and I can admit that I did it after I'd taken a couple of shots of tequila in my room.

Cause who does that to another guy you aren't already friends with. I remember how he teased me for even suggesting it, making me thankful that he didn't make it weird or just ignore me.

I keep scrolling. There's the time he sent me a late-night text with a meme about Brewed Beginnings, our local coffee shop because of a recipe I shared with him. Then there was that message where we spent half an hour arguing about which '90s song was the ultimate throwback. Not to mention the innuendos that could go one way or the other.

It's not like these messages are dripping with romance, but it still feels like there is something else there. I thought I might have been overanalyzing the situation too much, but when he invited me over to his place, I knew where this was heading.

And I can't wait, even though the nerves are still very much here, shifting me back to the present. I think about turning the music back on and just switching the song, but instead I just stand there, staring at myself in the mirror.

I trace the outline of my lips with my fingertip, wondering if adding a red lip would make me look more daring or like I'm trying too hard. The rest of my makeup is subtle, the kind that's supposed to look like there's barely any on even though it took me a good thirty minutes to perfect. I want to look like myself, just a bolder, more confident version than I usually pretend to be. The kind of girl who can handle a guy like Knox Sanchez without getting in too deep.

"Who are you kidding?" I mutter to my reflection. It stares back at me with wide, doubtful eyes. Green as a forest after a good rain, Mom used to say when I was a kid. Sometimes I think they're too honest for their own good, giving away every fear and insecurity I'm trying to hide.

I take a deep breath and close my eyes, imagining what tonight could be. Maybe we'll just talk. Or maybe he'll open up about something real, something deeper than the casual banter we've been trading via text messages. Maybe he'll kiss me, and it will be one of those life-altering kisses that makes everything else fade away.

Ha. Chances are very high that I'll chicken out and turn around before I even knock on his door.

My phone buzzes on the dresser, breaking into my thoughts. I snatch it up quickly, half hoping it's Knox with some excuse to cancel and I can take all of this stuff off. Or find a party to go to and drown my sorrows.

It's not him. It's my best friend, Isla Johnson.

> Isla: I'm so nervous about dinner this evening. Send good vibes!

I hesitate, mostly because the thoughts I'm having are traveling at a thousand miles an hour, but also because what I'm about to do, I've been keeping from the woman who knows just about everything about me. If I tell Isla where I'm headed, she'll freak out. Not that she disapproves of Knox. She barely knows him, but she probably has taken Jade and Hailey's words to heart. Then again, I also don't know what Asher, her on-again, off-again boyfriend, might have told her about Knox. Maybe at some point I'll want to know, but tonight isn't the night.

Still, I can't just ignore her. She's the one person who's always been there for me, through every single thing. And me for her. So I find something to say that hopefully makes me sound normal.

> Me: You'll be amazing. Don't stress! Your parents and Asher's mom and sister are going to get along wonderfully. Let me know how it goes. Xx

I set the phone back down and take a deep breath. I'm fucking terrified. Not just of tonight, but of everything that seems to be changing around me. Isla and Asher are back together—again—and this time it looks like it might actually stick. She's spending more time with him, which I get, but it's left me floundering a bit on my own. It's like I just got her back because she was in New York for years. Then there's school in general and working part time.

And Knox. He's the wild card in all of this. The X

factor that has the potential to throw my already precarious balance completely out of whack.

But I can't not see where this leads. And I'm not sure if that's a good thing or a bad thing, if I'm being honest. I grab my purse and keys, making a last-minute decision to ditch the heels I'm wearing for a pair of flats. The shoes tone down the outfit just enough to keep me from looking like I'm trying too hard. Or so I tell myself.

After staring at myself for a few more seconds, I leave the comfort of my dorm room to face whatever is waiting for me at Knox's place.

The walk to Knox's house is shorter than I want, but cooler than I expected. With every step, I run through potential scenarios in my head: him opening the door shirtless, me tripping over the threshold and landing in his arms, us sitting awkwardly on his couch with nothing to say. Why I've painted this to be some romance in my head when he's indicated anything but is beyond me. Let's be real, it'll end up being a booty call.

I'm not opposed to that either, but it doesn't mean I'm not nervous. All of this isn't something I normally do, but I can't say I'm not excited by the idea of it. By the time I reach the house he mentioned he rents with some of the other guys on the hockey team, my heart has dropped to my stomach.

The place is a typical college guy house: slightly rundown but with a certain charm. There's a hockey stick propped up against the porch railing and a battered couch on the front lawn that I don't remember seeing the last time I was here.

Strange.

I stand at the bottom of the steps for what feels like an eternity, clutching my purse so hard my knuckles are white. The flats were a good call; my feet would have been killing me already in the heels I'd thought about wearing. I glance up at the door, half expecting it to fly open and for Knox to be standing there, wondering why I'm staring at his door like a lost puppy.

No such luck. The door remains closed, the house eerily quiet for what I imagine a jock's haven to be.

I fish my phone out of my purse and check it again, just to make sure I got the time and place right. Still nothing from him. A part of me is relieved—if he's forgotten or if this was some elaborate prank, at least I'll have an out. I can slink back to my room, put on pajamas, and watch terrible reality TV while eating ice cream straight from the container.

But another part of me—a growing, annoying part— will be disappointed.

Selene, just go up and ring the doorbell. Or, hell, text him and tell him you're here.

I take a deep breath and steel myself, walking up the creaky wooden steps to the front porch. My hand hovers over the doorbell for an agonizingly long second before I mash it with more force than necessary. I can hear the chime from where I'm standing, and I step back, biting my lower lip.

Nothing.

I wait another few seconds, shifting from one foot to the other, then knock on the door. Hard. The sound of my fist against the wood is almost desperate, and I wince at how eager it must seem. I take a step back and glance around the porch, half expecting one of Knox's roommates to burst out and tell me he's not here.

I sigh and start to turn away when I hear the sound of a lock disengaging. My heart lurches as the door swings open slowly, almost tentatively. Knox stands in the doorway, his hair tousled like he's just woken up from a nap. He rubs his eyes and gives me a sleepy half-smile.

"Selene," he says, his voice rough around the edges. "Hey."

"Hey," I say, my voice higher than normal. "I wasn't sure if you were here."

"Yeah, sorry. I crashed after the game and lost track of time." He runs a hand through his brown hair, and I can't help but notice he's wearing a soft-looking shirt over a plain white tee. I catch myself staring for a couple of seconds before he speaks again. "Come in."

With those simple words, he moves out of the way, and I step across the threshold, unsure of what waits for me on the other side.

2

SELENE

"Nice place you have here." I almost slap myself on the forehead as a reflex. *Nice place you have here? Really, Selene?*

"Come on. It's a couple steps above a shithole, but I can't complain," Knox throws out there.

I snort before I can control myself. I take a moment to look around the living room and notice that it's surprisingly neat for a common area of a house with guys living in it.

Knox breaks my momentary trance. "The guys aren't here right now, so it's just us."

Just us. The words hang in the air like a low-hanging cloud. This is what I'd been hoping for even though Knox is definitely red flag central. Between the warnings I've already received about him and the interactions we've had with one another so far, I'm mentally preparing for how much of a mistake this will end up being.

"That's...convenient," I say, trying and failing to sound nonchalant.

He starts up the stairs and I follow, my eyes inadvertently tracing the muscles in his back as they flex with each step. We reach the landing and he pauses, turning to look over his shoulder at me.

The tension that has been brewing between us reaches a new high. I swear I stop breathing as I wait to see what he's going to do next.

"You sure you want to do this?" His voice is low and I can sense the seriousness in his words.

No. Yes.

I'm not sure.

A thousand answers swirl around in my head, each one contradicting the last. The rational part of me is screaming to run, to get out before I dive into something I can't easily climb back out of. The other part—the larger part, the part that has a mind of its own when it comes to Knox—is already imagining what his sheets will feel like against my skin.

Finally I'm able to voice my opinion. "Yes, I do want this."

"Why? Why did you come here? I'm sure you've been warned about me."

His smugness catches me off guard. The fact that I wasn't expecting him to say those words has to be all over my face because I feel my eyes widen. But somehow, I manage to say, "I'm here because..."

Because I can't stop thinking about you.

Because bad decisions make good stories.

Because I'm lonely and you're here and maybe we can fill some void for each other.

"...I need this. Whatever this is," I finish lamely.

Silence fills the space between us. Knox's eyes search mine, and for a moment I think he might tell me to leave, that it's better if we don't start something we can't finish. But then he nods, and the tension breaks just enough for me to take a breath.

I follow him as we walk down the hall. He pushes his door open and stands aside, allowing me to enter first. His room is exactly what I imagined: sparse but functional, with a bed that looks like it was made by someone who rushed to get it done, an old desk cluttered with binders and textbooks, and several hockey posters taped to the wall.

I walk to the center of the room and turn to face him. He closes the door softly behind him and leans against it, crossing his arms over his chest. The posture looks casual, but there's a guardedness in his eyes that makes me think he's bracing for something.

Great... because I feel the same way.

I take a step toward him, then hesitate. The knot in my stomach tightens as I try to read his expression. This is it. It feels like the point of no return. Once we cross this line, there's no going back to the safe distance we've maintained since we met.

"We don't have to rush," he says, uncrossing his arms and taking a step toward me.

I nod quickly. "I know."

Knox reaches out and brushes a strand of hair from my face, his touch softer than I expected. My skin tingles where his fingers make contact, and I feel a warmth start to spread through me. He's so close now that I can see the different shades of brown in his eyes.

"Why do you make me feel so nervous?" I blurt out before I can stop myself.

He raises an eyebrow. "Nervous? You always seem pretty confident to me."

So my act has been working. However, I decide to flip the script back on him because I hadn't planned on admitting this anyway. "This doesn't make you feel similarly?"

Knox takes a deep breath, and for a moment I think he's going to deny it in an effort to play it cool. Dread rises up my spine as I wait for his next move.

"Maybe," he admits softly.

That confession swirls around us, making everything feel more real, more dangerous. This is not what I expected. I thought it would be simple: come here, fuck, and leave. But now I'm starting to see that this might not be that simple.

He steps back and runs a hand through his hair,

messing it up in that way that makes him look even more attractive, if that's possible.

"Look," he starts, "I don't want to fuck this up before it even starts. We can take our time."

Take our time? Does he mean he wants something longer than just tonight? The thought both excites and terrifies me. Not to mention, why did that pop into my head?

In an effort to stop overanalyzing, my gaze drifts back to his. I can see in his eyes the moment the dam breaks. He closes the gap between us within a second and his hands land on my cheeks, pulling me toward him.

Our lips meet and it's like nothing else matters. The kiss is hungry, desperate, as if we're both trying to consume the other in one breath. My hands find his waist and I pull him closer, needing to feel every inch of him against me. His body is strong and hard, just like I imagined.

He breaks the kiss first, but keeps his forehead pressed against mine. We're both breathing heavily, our chests rising and falling in unison.

"Selene," he says as he takes in a rugged breath. "If you change your mind at any point, just tell me."

I don't trust myself to speak, so I nod. He captures my lips again, this time slower, more deliberately. It's as if he's memorizing every detail about them. A shiver runs through me, and I clutch at his shirt, bunching the fabric in my fists.

Knox's hands slide down my neck, my shoulders, then trace the outline of my waist. He finds the hem of my shirt and pauses, as if asking for permission. I lift my arms, and he pulls it over my head in one fluid motion. The cool air in his room hits my skin and I stop myself from shaking like a leaf. I already feel as if I've bared my soul to him and we are just getting started. He takes a small step back to give himself room to pull down my leggings, and soon I'm pushing them down my legs and stepping out of them.

The urge to cover my body is real. Although I still have my underwear on, I feel completely exposed. It's as if he can see every curve, every bit of cellulite that I want to wish away.

Knox's eyes trail over my body, taking in every inch with a slowness that makes my skin prickle. He doesn't move, doesn't reach for me. He lets out a shaky breath before he says, "Holy fuck. You're so beautiful."

I freeze in place at his words. It's the last thing I think that Mr. Bad Boy Knox Sanchez would utter, but since I decided to take him up on his offer to 'show me a good time' I feel as if I've been having an out of body experience.

None of this feels real—the way he's touching me, the way he's looking at me. This was supposed to be a simple fling, an easy distraction from everything else in my life. But now there's a dangerous tenderness in the way he's handling me, like I'm something that could easily break.

Hell, maybe that's true, but that's not what I need to be focusing on right now.

"Don't say things you don't mean," I whisper, more to myself.

"I never do," he replies, his eyes searching mine.

Before I can process his words, he pulls me closer to him and bends down to kiss my neck. I swear a jolt of electricity flies through my body. My hands tangle in his hair as he works his way down to my collarbone. Every touch feels like it's setting me on fire. He reaches behind me and unclasps my bra with a skill that speaks volumes about his experience. It slides off my shoulders and he catches it before letting it drop to the floor gently.

I expect him to dive in, to take what he wants like the cocky bad boy he's supposed to be. But instead, he just looks at me, taking in every detail with an intensity that makes me squirm. I was already feeling self-conscious about my curves before I came here, but now I swear it's increased tenfold.

My thoughts come to a screeching halt when he lifts me and carries me to the bed with an ease that makes my heart race even faster. Laying me down gently, he stands over me and removes his shirt. His torso is chiseled, each muscle defined like a work of art. He unbuckles his belt, and I prepare myself for what's coming next, but he pauses.

"Do you want this?" Knox's voice is just above a whisper, and it almost sounds like he's barely controlling himself.

He's giving me another out. I could still leave and save myself from whatever complicated mess this might turn into. But we both know I won't.

"Yes," I say, more sure now than just a few short minutes ago. "I definitely want this."

He nods, as if he's just convinced himself of something, then kneels on the bed beside me. His hands are gentle as they run up my thighs, stopping just short of where my body wants him most. He leans down and kisses my stomach, my ribs, then moves to one breast, taking my nipple into his mouth. A moan escapes my lips before I can stop myself, and he switches to the other with a deliberate tenderness that has my body moving involuntarily.

Just when I think I can't take any more of his teasing, his hand slides between my legs, over my panties. He applies the lightest pressure and it's enough to make me gasp.

"You're leaking through your panties already, picosita. You couldn't deny how much you wanted me if you tried."

I heard what he said, yet it was as if the words missed my brain completely. I'm not sure if he's waiting for a response from me, but there was no way I was going to be able to respond. To say he's left me speechless is an understatement.

His fingers trace lazy circles along the thin fabric of

my panties. It's not enough. My hips lift toward him, seeking more of his touch, but he holds back, making me whimper in frustration.

"Patience," he says against my skin. "I'm taking my time and savoring this."

My mind is a whirlwind of thoughts and emotions. This is supposed to be just physical, something simple and uncomplicated. Yet this feels like anything but.

"Knox," I manage to breathe out, not even sure what I'm asking for. Relief? Reassurance? All I know is that I need him in a way that I don't want to begin to do a deep dive into.

He looks up from my chest, his eyes dark with desire. "What is it?"

I bite my lip, hesitating. "Nothing. Just... don't stop."

A slow, wicked smile spreads across his face. "Wasn't planning on it."

With the slowness of a snail, at least to me, he hooks his fingers into the waistband of my panties and slides them down my legs. He pauses for a moment, just looking at me, and I can almost see the wheels turning in his head.

Then, without warning, he lowers himself between my legs and kisses the inside of my thigh. My hands clutch the sheets as his lips move closer to where I've been dying for him to take me. When his tongue finally flicks against me, a cry bursts from my lips. He grips my hips to hold me in place as he begins to work me. Him taking his time was worth it.

It doesn't take long before I feel that familiar tension building, something I haven't felt in a long time. My breathing becomes rough and ragged. My body is trying to keep up with the sensations he's causing, but it's no use. All I can do is hope that I can hold on just a little longer. His hands knead my thighs, his touch both firm and gentle. I'm not sure how he's mastered exactly what I want without instruction, but I'm not about to complain either.

"Knox," I rush out, not able to take it any longer. "Please."

He slows, then stops, pulling back to look up at me. His lips glisten and his eyes burn with an intensity that takes my breath away. "Please what?"

He's torturing me, and he knows it. Asshole. But I play along because at this point, I'll do anything he asks.

"Please... make me come."

He smirks, clearly pleased with my begging. "As you wish."

Before I can prepare myself, he plunges two fingers inside me while his mouth returns to its task. The sensations send my body into overdrive, and I explode almost instantly. I scream his name, not caring if his neighbors hear.

Knox continues until I've ridden out my orgasm and then slowly withdraws. He kisses his way up my body, but I can't move. I'm completely spent, at least I feel that way until his lips land on mine. I can taste the remnants of my own pleasure on his lips. My hands find their way to his shoulders, tracing the lines of his muscles, then down to his chest. His heart is pounding as hard as mine.

He backs away and I immediately miss his warmth, but it only takes a second for me to figure out what he's doing next. His hands make their way to his jeans, and I watch as he undoes them and takes both his pants and boxer briefs off in one quick motion. My eyes widen once they land on his cock, and I can't help but wonder how it's going to fit.

I can't deny that I'm also a little excited about the challenge. It's something I'd heard whispers about on campus since we exchanged numbers, but never something I thought I would actually witness.

He reaches underneath the pillow next to me and pulls out a condom. I watch as he tears it open with his teeth and rolls it on. There's something incredibly sexy about how practiced and fluid his movements are. *He's probably done this a thousand times before*, I remind myself. *You're just another notch on his belt.*

Sliding back over me, he positions himself at my pussy. He waits, searching my eyes for something—permission, maybe? Reassurance? I don't know what he needs from me, but I give him the most confident look I can and nod. That's all it takes.

He eases himself into me and my body tenses up, causing Knox to halt his movements.

"Relax," he says as he brushes a strand of hair from my face. "I don't want to hurt you."

His tenderness surprises me, but I don't say a word. Instead I take a deep breath, forcing my body to relax, to allow him in. He moves slowly, inch by inch, and the initial discomfort starts to give way to a growing pleasure. Each thrust penetrates deeper, making me gasp and clutch at his back.

"Fuck, Selene," he says through gritted teeth. "You're so tight."

He starts to move with more intention, setting a rhythm that reignites the fire that had just barely cooled. My nails dig into his shoulders as he drives into me to the point where I can barely contain the moans fleeing my lips.

"Damnit."

I look into his eyes when I hear what he's muttered. "What's wrong?"

"I'm close," he warns, but I can already tell from the way his muscles are tensing, and his thrusts are becoming more erratic. "This wasn't supposed to happen this quickly."

For someone who I thought was very experienced in this area, I'm shocked by his words. I smirk, pleased that I have this kind of effect on him. "It's okay," I whisper, running my fingers through his hair and pulling him down to kiss me. "Come for me."

With that permission, he lets go. His thrusts become

desperate and forceful, and I find one of my hands gripping the headboard as his body slams into mine. The sound of skin against skin fills the room, mixed with his ragged breathing. With one low animalistic groan, he stiffens and buries himself deep inside me, his body shaking as he reaches his climax. I can feel the intensity of his release, and it sends a final shiver through my own body.

For a moment, the world is silent except for our heavy breathing. He collapses on top of me, careful not to crush me with his weight, and I wrap my arms around him, savoring the closeness for a moment. This isn't what I expected. It's more intimate than I ever imagined, and a part of me is scared by how much I'm enjoying it.

Knox rolls off me and lies on his back, staring at the ceiling. I turn onto my side to face him, propping my head up with one hand. He looks different in this moment, but I can't exactly place why. I want to say something, but I'm not sure what. Thanks? That was amazing?

Before I can decide, he speaks. "You were... incredible," he says, though there's an almost reluctant tone in his voice, as if admitting this costs him something.

I smile, stupidly pleased by the compliment, but I can hear a 'but' there that I'm trying to ignore. "You're not so bad yourself."

We fall into another round of silence. This was supposed to be uncomplicated, no-strings-attached sex. But now that it's done, everything feels a lot more tangled.

"Don't get any ideas," Knox says suddenly, turning his head to look at me. His eyes are hard again, the softness from earlier wiped away. "This doesn't change anything."

And there it is—the gut punch I knew was coming but hoped would hurt less when it landed.

"I know," I say, though my voice sounds small and distant to my own ears. "I wasn't thinking anything else."

He sits up and swings his legs over the side of the bed, running a hand through his tousled hair. "Good. Because the last thing I need is drama."

I watch as he stands and walks to his closet in all his naked glory. It doesn't take much for me to figure out where this is going. Why did I think this would be a good idea? Because I'm an idiot, clearly.

I slide out of bed and search for my clothes. My clothes are a crumpled mess on the floor, but I pick them up and throw them on.

I have just enough time to pull my leggings over my hips before Knox turns to face me, having put on a fresh pair of boxers and a t-shirt. He pauses, as if he might say something to soften the blow he just delivered, but I don't give him the chance.

"I'm going to take off," I say.

Knox shrugs. "Do what you need to."

"You're the biggest asshole I've ever met, you know that?"

"Wouldn't be the first time I've heard that."

Part of me wants to stay and argue with him because

he can fuck all the way off, but I know it's a waste of my time. Instead, I grab his hoodie from the chair by his desk and slip it over my head. It's far too big on me, hanging down to my thighs and swamping my hands in fabric, but it smells like him and for some stupid reason, that comforts me. I throw him a look, almost daring him to say something about it. He doesn't say a word, saving us both the trouble, and within seconds I leave his room, closing the door behind me.

I try to contain my emotions as I look up, but apparently that wasn't in the cards. My heart skips a beat when I find Isla and Asher are standing there. I can feel the heat rush to my cheeks. Crap. This is exactly what I didn't want. I'm sneaking out of Knox's room, and of course, I run into them. I can see Isla's eyes widen as she takes in the scene—my flushed face, my slightly messy hair, and the Crestwood Red Wolves hoodie that's definitely not mine.

I freeze, trying to mask the anger bubbling up inside me. "Oh, um... Isla! Asher!" I stammer, feeling completely flustered. "How are you? How was the game?"

"Fine...but what are you doing here?" Isla asks, raising an eyebrow.

"I was just... helping Knox... with something. But I'm leaving now." I try to sound casual, but it's clear I'm not fooling anyone.

"Right. Helping. But why do you look pissed?" Isla's skeptical look doesn't help me at all.

Asher wraps an arm around Isla's waist, and when I glance at him, his expression matches hers. They both know exactly what's going on, and it makes me want to scream.

Before I can come up with any kind of response, Knox's voice calls from inside the room, "Selene, did you forget something?"

My face flushes an even deeper shade of red. "Fuck you," I mumble under my breath before giving Isla and Asher an awkward wave and practically bolting down the hallway.

"Wait—" Isla starts to say, but I cut her off.

"I need to calm down. I'll call you later, okay?"

I don't wait for her response. I just need to get out of here. This whole situation is fucking crazy, and I can't handle it right now. I just need space from what feels like a massive car crash that has become my life.

3

SELENE

hat the hell was that?

I still find myself saying those words as I make my way into the library to start my shift. I've replayed the scene in my mind again and again over the last week. However I still can't make sense of how Knox could be so callous. Yes, we'd agreed to keep things casual, but with how quickly he ran away from me after we had sex, you would have thought I poisoned him or something.

I wish I could stop thinking about it, but the whole thing still feels like something out of a bad movie. For now though, it was time to focus on the reason I was here.

I hang my coat on the rack behind the circulation desk and take a seat at the table. Being here, even this late at night, usually comforts me, but not today. Sure, being here this late at night can suck, however I'm mostly a night owl and I make sure that my work schedule doesn't interfere with my ability to party on weekends.

I have priorities and all that.

The library is nearly empty, as it usually is during my late-night shifts. A few die-hard studiers are working quietly and I'm sure there are several people on the upper and lower levels. My head snaps to look at this guy I might have seen on campus a few times before because he yawns so loud I can hear it from where I sit. With a quick shake of my head, I open my philosophy textbook, determined to do some homework until someone needs to check out or until I need to lock up the library. I end up staring at the first line of the assigned reading for a few moments before closing it again.

"Selene, you look like shit," a familiar voice says.

I look up to see Isla Johnson, my beautiful blonde best friend standing in front of me.

I roll my eyes and cross my arms across my chest as I stare her down. "Well hello to you too. I had a feeling you would show up today."

"Well you gave me no choice since you've been dodging my texts and calls."

She has every right to call me out on that because it's true. I didn't want to have to deal with explaining exactly what she saw at the hockey house last week.

"I still don't even know how to tell you what happened."

Isla's nails tap out a random rhythm on the circulation

desk. She cocks her head to the side, her expression softening just a fraction. "Babe, you don't have to tell me. I saw enough." She pauses for a second before she continues. "Although I would like to know the details."

With a heavy sigh I rub both hands across my face before tossing my hair to one side. Isla has seen me in every conceivable state—drunk, heartbroken, ecstatic—but this feels different, more raw. But that could be just because of how recent this all is.

"You sure you want to know?" I say, though I know Isla is never one to back down from the gritty details of my life —or anyone else's for that matter.

"Spill it," she says, as she walks around the desk and drops her bag at the other desk. "Are you working alone tonight?"

"Yeah, Seth called out tonight."

"Excellent." Isla pulls up a chair and sits in it backward. She rests her arms on the top of the backrest. "I mean, only tell me about what happened if it's going to make you feel better. If not, we can just talk about something else."

I appreciate her effort to be understanding, but I know she's dying to know. Heck, if it hadn't happened to me, I would want to know too.

"Okay, well," I say, and it's followed by a short pause. I lean closer to her in an effort to keep this all quiet. "When you, Asher, and I ran into each other in the hallway, Knox and I had just gotten done having sex."

Isla raises an eyebrow but stays silent, encouraging me to continue.

I take a deep breath, bracing myself for her reaction to the next part because if anyone will understand how deeply it hurt me, it's Isla.

"It was... I thought it was great. Like, really great. But then he just got up and walked to his closet to get dressed and told me not to get any ideas because this doesn't change anything. No cuddling, no chatting—nothing."

Isla's eyes widen. "He what?! What a dick."

"Right?" I say, feeling a small surge of relief that she's on my side because she easily could have thrown out the fact that she told me so. "I wasn't expecting things to end that...abruptly."

"And cold," Isla adds. "What the hell...I know Jade and Hailey said he was an ass, but I didn't think he would do that."

I shrug, not wanting to admit that I thought the same thing. Knox and I had been talking and texting for a little while. It wasn't like we'd hooked up out of nowhere, not to mention my best friend is dating one of his teammates. This means we'll probably run into each other. But what hurts the most is realizing that maybe he never actually cared at all.

"He's a guy," I say, attempting to keep my emotions at bay. "Maybe I just misread everything. At least now I know where we stand."

"Where you stand is that you're done with him," Isla

says firmly. "You deserve someone who actually gives a shit, not some hot-and-cold douchebag who only wants you on his terms."

I want to believe her. No—I do believe her. But knowing something and feeling it are two different things.

"So that's why you've been hiding?" she asks. "Because you're afraid to run into him?"

"No, I just didn't want to hear 'I told you so.'"

"Selene, come on," Isla says a little louder than she should. "You know I'd never rub it in like that. I'm your best friend first and foremost."

A wave of guilt washes over me. Isla's been nothing but supportive, even when she has her own stuff going on. I glance around to see if anyone is paying attention to us before letting out a long, deep breath.

"I know," I say quietly. "I'm sorry. It's just...hard right now."

Isla leans over to give me a big hug. "We love you, you know that, right? Me, Asher...we want what's best for you."

After a few more seconds, Isla pulls back, and her eyes search mine. I can see the concern for me in her gaze. "So what now?" she asks.

"I don't know," I admit. "I guess I'll just ignore him if I see him on campus."

"And delete his number," Isla says with a small nod, as if she's already made the decision for me.

"Yeah, that too," I lie.

The thought of erasing Knox from my phone feels weird, but I know she's right. Keeping his contact is just holding onto false hope. And it sucks because our conversations were actually entertaining.

I unlock my phone and pull up Knox's contact, staring at his name for a long moment. My thumb hovers over the delete button, but I can't bring myself to press it. Instead, I lock the screen and slip the phone back into my pocket.

"I'm here for you," Isla says, her tone softening. "You're not alone in this."

I nod, grateful for her friendship even if I'm not ready to let go of Knox completely. Why is it so hard to move on from something that wasn't even a real relationship?

"Enough about me," I say, desperate to shift the focus. "How's Asher? Are you guys still good?"

"We're great," Isla says with a smile. "He's been busy with practice, but he still makes time for me. We had the cutest date night a couple of weeks ago. He cooked dinner at his place, and we binge-watched a couple of old horror movies."

"That's awesome," I say, genuinely happy for her. Isla's relationship with him when we were seniors in high school ended with him breaking up with her, so seeing it be more stable this time around makes me believe that maybe it's possible for the rest of us too.

Isla's smile lingers and I assume she's thinking about her boyfriend. I can't help but feel a pang of jealousy—not because I want what she has with Asher, but because I long for that kind of stability and warmth. Something consistent, where I don't have to question how the other person feels.

I force a smile even though I am truly happy for her. "I'm really glad you guys worked things out."

Isla's eyes soften. "I've learned that relationships take work. It's not always easy, but if both people are willing...it can be worth it."

I nod, digesting her words. Relationships take work. It echoes in my mind like a mantra I need to believe in. Maybe that's what I had been hoping for and that has mixed with my thoughts about Knox. Maybe we could have put in the effort and made something worthwhile. But that made me do something a little foolish and hope for more.

And hope, I realize, is the real enemy here.

"Do you want me to grab you a drink? I think I'm going to refill my water bottle."

Isla's voice brings me back to the present. "Sure," I say, handing her my empty bottle. "Thanks."

While Isla walks away, I pull out my phone again, unable to resist the urge to check it. No new messages. Part of me hopes that Knox will text with an explanation or even an apology, but the rational side of me knows better. He's probably already moved on to the next girl.

"Here," Isla says as she returns, handing me my water bottle. She quickly covers her mouth as she yawns. "I'm not sure how you manage to stay awake to work here this late."

"It's a gift—much like me in your life."

That makes Isla snicker. "Now you sound more like yourself."

I smile, taking a big sip of water. "Seriously though, you can head out if you're tired. I know you have an early class."

Isla hesitates. "Are you sure? I don't want to leave you alone like this."

"I'll be fine," I assure her. "Plus, I need to finish up this reading anyway and we are probably going to end up making too much noise in the library if we keep this up. I'm glad you stopped by."

She studies me for a moment longer, then sighs. "Okay, but text me if you need anything."

"Absolutely," I say, standing up to give her a hug.

Isla gathers her things, and I watch her walk toward the library's exit. The silence that follows is both a relief and a weight. I glance at my phone one more time—still nothing from Knox. Not that I was expecting anything, yet I'm still annoyed. Sighing, I open my textbook and try to immerse myself in the words, because right now, it feels as if it's the only steady thing in my life.

4

KNOX

I sit on the edge of my bed, staring at my phone screen. Selene's name glares back at me, taunting me. My thumb hovers over the text message icon, debating. A few quick taps and I could pour out everything I'm feeling. But I can't. I won't.

With a frustrated sigh, I toss my phone aside. It bounces on the mattress and lands face down, her name disappearing from view.

Thank fuck.

This is all for the best even though I still can't get the time we spent together out of my mind. It was supposed to be a quick fuck, nothing more than casual sex, yet I keep replaying the moment as if it were a movie.

The way she looked at me when I left my bed is burned into my brain. Something told me getting involved with her, even temporarily, was a bad idea. Yet I let it happen.

I rub my temples, trying to prevent the headache that is already forming. This is the last thing I need.

I get up and pace my small room, glancing at the poster of the hockey legends that cover the walls. I wish things were as simple as going out with Wilder when he asked. I'm sure he's still out doing who knows what. I assume he'll roll into the house in a bit, but I'm kind of jealous that he's living the life I should be: uncomplicated, fun.

Fucking a, I'm starting to sound like an old man. My old man, nonetheless.

My phone lights up and I freeze. For a split second, I hope it's her. Maybe if she reaches out first, it'll be easier. But I can see from here that it's just a notification from social media. I walk over and pick up the phone, turning it slowly in my hands.

She's not even my type. Too smart, too ambitious. Girls like Selene want more than I'm able to give. They want a future, or at least someone who can stick around long enough to see where things go. I have one and a half more semesters, and then it's do or die for my career. There's no room for a real relationship.

Plus, I refuse to let my heart get fucked over again.

But damn if she didn't make me laugh. And not just laugh—I felt something when I was with her, something deeper than the usual hollow satisfaction I get from screwing around.

I shake my head trying to clear the thoughts from my mind. I need to use this anger and confusion and turn it into something productive on the ice.

My duffel sits by the door, packed and ready for this early morning practice, but I can't bring myself to leave just yet. Instead, I flop back onto my bed and stare at the ceiling. It's cracked in a few places, the kind of thing you expect to see with college housing. One of the cracks looks like a lightning bolt. Another like a hockey stick.

I imagine the stick coming loose from the plaster, floating down, and smacking me in the face. Maybe it'll knock some sense into me.

What the hell am I even thinking?

A loud knock startles me from my daydream. I get up slowly, hoping it's not Blaise. It's rude to think that and I know he means well, but I'm not in the mood for a pep talk.

"Yo, Knox." Blaise stands in the hallway with his own hockey bag in tow. His blond hair looks messy, but I'm sure mine looks the same. "You ready? I can drive us."

I pause. If I tell him no, that I want to go alone, he'll know something's up. But if I go with him, maybe talking will help get my mind off Selene.

"Sure," I say, grabbing my duffel.

His car is a couple of years newer than mine, but that comes as no surprise. His parents are pretty loaded, not that he flaunts it much outside of the sick computer setup he has in his room. He unlocks the trunk, and we toss our gear in before sliding into the front seats.

Blaise fiddles with the radio as he pulls out of the parking spot. He settles on a rock station, then glances at me. "You okay?"

"Yeah," I say, but it comes out too quick, too defensive. "Just tired."

Blaise shrugs, not pushing it for now. He's a good friend, better than I probably deserve these days. The kind of guy who will wait until you're ready to talk, but who won't let you suffer in silence too long either.

As we drive, my thoughts drift back to Selene despite my best efforts. To the night after the party when we talked for hours before anything physical happened. To her ridiculous theories about aliens and the genuine passion she had for her job at the library. To the way she fit so perfectly in my arms as I fucked her.

Fuck.

"We killed it last game," Blaise says, breaking the heavy silence. "If we keep that up, scouts are going to take notice."

I nod though my mind is only half present. Hockey has always been the one constant in my life, the thing I could throw myself into when everything else went to shit. Now even that feels tenuous.

"Wilder said you bailed on him last night," Blaise adds casually.

"I wasn't feeling it. Did he come home yet?"

Blaise gives me a quick nod. "Yeah, he was headed into the shower just before I knocked on your door."

"So hopefully that means he won't be late for practice. Last thing I want to deal with is hearing Coach put his foot up his ass for delaying things."

"Touché, but what's been up with you?"

Ah. Now it's time for Blaise to start pushing, I guess. "What do you mean?" I know my attempt at deflecting won't go unnoticed.

"Just that you've had a bigger stick up your ass for the last week than you usually do."

I let out a sigh, long and exaggerated. He probably deserves an explanation, but I'm not sure I can even articulate what's going on in my head.

"I'm just stressed, man. School, the season, everything. I'm bracing for a fight so don't be surprised if it happens... on the ice of course."

"Everything?" he asks, raising an eyebrow. "Does 'everything' have a name?"

How the hell did he figure that out? I stay silent, watching the snow that has accumulated on the sides of the road. Blaise is perceptive; he probably has some idea already. Have I really been more grumpy than usual?

"Look," he continues when I don't answer. "All I'm saying is that if you need to talk, I'm here. Or if you just want to bitch and moan, that's cool too."

"It's nothing," I say finally. "Just trying to figure some shit out."

We pull into the rink's parking lot and Blaise kills the engine. He doesn't move to get out of the car yet, and I know we're not done. Great.

"Knox," he says, turning toward me. "You know I've got your back no matter what. But you've gotta stop internalizing everything or it's going to eat you alive. I don't want what happened between you and Asher to happen again. We've got to keep everything together."

I think about what happened between Asher and me and how we almost came to blows because I called him out on his feelings about Isla. Now look where I am. Except it was obvious Asher loved Isla.

That is not the case here. I'm convinced the sex was so good that she has my brain scrambled. Not to mention I came faster than I ever have in my life.

"We're good," I tell Blaise, even though I'm not sure if we are. "There's nothing you need to worry about."

He nods and opens his door, cold air rushing into the car. I follow suit and grab my bag from the trunk.

Inside the rink, the familiar smell hits me, and I feel like I'm home. It's comforting in a way that almost makes me believe everything will be okay. The scraping of blades on ice echoes through the hallways as we make our way to the locker room.

Most of the team is here and my eyes land on Levi and Asher, who are talking to one another in front of the stalls.

I'm willing to bet they are talking shit like usual. Levi gives me a smirk as we walk in, and I just shake my head. Idiot.

"Sanchez! Dalton!" Coach Johnson's voice comes from the doorway. "Nice of you to join us."

"We're early, Coach," Blaise says, but Coach is already walking away.

"Wilder better not mess this up for all of us," Asher says as turns to look at us. "Where the hell is he?"

"I'm right here, sweetheart."

I roll my eyes and feel the distinct urge to grab the bridge of my nose. The headache I thought I stopped from forming is preparing to come back with a vengeance. "Nice of you to join us, Wilder."

The best way I can describe Wilder walking into the room is to say he sauntered in with his hair still damp from the shower. A cocky grin is plastered on his face, and I can already sense what he's about to say next. "Don't get your underwear in a twist, Knox. I'm committed."

I shoot him a look that says I very much doubt it, but I keep my mouth shut. No point in starting another pissing match with him right before practice. At least we don't have to deal with extra drills because one of us was late.

We change into our practice gear, and just as I'm lacing up my skates, Coach comes back into the locker room.

"Listen up!" Coach Johnson says, commanding the attention of the entire team. Even Wilder, who usually is ready to toss out a joke, stays silent.

"I don't need to tell you boys how important the next few weeks are. We're doing well, but we need to continue to do well. If we don't, you can kiss the playoffs goodbye."

I scan the room, looking at my teammates. We've been here before—this place of uncertainty where one bad game can cost us everything. We always find a way to pull through, but this season feels different. Harder. Could also be that it's our senior year, but whatever.

"Get your asses on the ice," Coach finishes. "We're running systems today."

The team files out of the locker room, and I hang back for a moment. Blaise notices but doesn't say anything, just gives me a look that says he's still thinking about our conversation in the car. I grab my stick and head toward the tunnel.

It's time to get to work.

5

SELENE

I adjust the strap of my bookbag and then knock on Isla's dorm room door. A few seconds later, the door swings open, and Isla gives me a big grin. She's wearing fuzzy socks, which make me smirk. "Hey, Selene," she says, stepping aside to let me in. "Thanks for stopping by."

I'm not surprised she said that. When we hang out at each other's places, ninety-five percent of the time, we are at my dorm because Isla and her roommate, Tessa, don't get along.

Isla has tried to keep the peace, but I would have probably ended up getting hauled off to jail if she'd said the things she said about Isla the last time I was in this building. To mock someone for a condition, let alone an invisible illness they can't control, is cruel. If I hadn't reminded myself what was at stake if I'd jumped in to help Isla, who did an excellent job defending herself by the way, I might not be on campus right now.

I slip past her into the room, and the first thing I notice is a few textbooks and notebooks scattered on her bed. I move the things out of the way and flop down onto the mattress, pretending I'm one hundred percent relaxed when I'm anything but.

Isla grabs a binder and leans over to place it on her desk so she can sit beside me. She folds her legs underneath herself and gives me a once-over. "How've you been holding up?"

"Me? Oh, I'm fantastic," I say with a grin that I hope looks genuine. "Just living my best life, starring in a new sitcom called *My Emotions Are a Hot Mess*—the ratings are through the roof."

She snorts out a laugh, and I gotta say, it's one of my better jokes. "I can imagine. Anything from Knox?"

"Nope and I'm not expecting anything. He can kiss my big ass for all I care."

Isla rolls her eyes at me. "Your ass isn't big, but I understand the sentiment."

I shrug, but I don't believe her. A lifetime of shrugging off compliments about my body has left me with Olympic-level shoulder strength. Isla means well, but she doesn't understand what it's like to walk around in a body that makes me feel as if I'll never be good enough.

I glance at her slender frame and quickly look away, feeling the familiar twinge of jealousy mixed with guilt.

It's not Isla's fault she's naturally petite, just as it's not my fault I'm mid-size. I constantly feel as if I'm literally caught in the middle. Still, it's hard not to compare, especially when every magazine cover and social media feed is filled with girls who look more like her than me.

"So," Isla says, drawing out the word like she's stretching dough, "I wanted to talk to you about something."

Here it comes. The intervention. The moment where she tells me that I've been too angsty, too dramatic, too much of a burden as a friend. I brace myself for the blow.

"Don't freak out," she adds, which, of course, makes me freak out more.

"Just spit it out," I say with a small laugh to soften my tone. "Whatever it is, I can take it."

"Maybe you need to find someone else to date? Or, hell, just have sex with?"

I pause for a moment, shocked that my best friend of over a decade would say something like that. She's serious. Maybe I am rubbing off on her in more ways than I thought. "You're suggesting a rebound?"

She nods, her ponytail bobbing with enthusiasm. "Or even just a distraction."

The idea is sounding better the more I think about it. I sit up straighter, the mattress springs complaining beneath me. "I mean, sometimes the best way to get over someone is to get under someone else," I say.

"The point is, you shouldn't let Knox have this much power over you. You deserve to be happy, Selene."

Happy. What a loaded word. I think about the last time I was truly happy and come up frustratingly blank. Life has been a series of manageable but persistent grinds —school, work, family—and most recently, the unexpected emotional rollercoaster with Knox. But I'd be lying to myself if I said the conversations we had with each other didn't make me happy.

At least, at the time they did. Now I kind of regretted them. But maybe Isla is right. Maybe I've been putting too much stock in one person, letting him dictate how I feel when I shouldn't.

"I don't even know where to start," I admit. "It's not like there's a queue of eligible bachelors worth a damn lining up for their turn."

Isla smirks and gives me a playful shove. "Please, you're gorgeous and you know it. We can start compiling a list."

I roll my eyes, but there is excitement brewing inside of me. A list. It sounds ridiculous yet kind of fun. Like we're in high school again, writing down our crushes during physics class.

"Fine, let's hear it," I say, crossing my arms but leaning in closer. "Who's number one?"

Isla taps her chin thoughtfully. "Well, there's Ryan from the soccer team. He's had a thing for you since freshman year."

"Ryan is cute, but he's also like a little puppy. I don't think I could break his heart and still sleep at night."

"Noted," Isla says, pretending to jot something down in an invisible notebook. "What about Derek from lab?"

"Derek?" I scrunch my nose. "He's got a girlfriend. Next."

Isla laughs. "You're so picky! Okay, let me think... Ah! What about Lucas? He's tall, smart, and single."

"Lucas the math tutor? He tried to mansplain calculus to me. Hard pass."

We go back and forth like this for a while, Isla suggesting names and me shooting them down with increasingly absurd excuses. Despite my refusal to take any of her suggestions seriously, I'm actually having fun. It feels good to be thinking about something other than Knox and the mess I've made of my life.

"And there's always dating apps," Isla says, throwing her hands up in a gesture of surrender. "Swipe right, swipe left. It's like online shopping for boys."

I make a face. "You know how I feel about dating apps. They're filled with creeps."

"Come on, it's the twenty-first century! How else are you going to meet new people? You don't have to marry the guy. Just have some fun."

I open my mouth to protest, but before I can say anything, the door swings open and Tessa walks in.

She's wearing one of those oversized flannel shirts and leggings. Her hair is in a messy bun on the top of her head, and she's carrying a stack of books so high I wonder how she even opened the door.

"Oh great, you guys are here," Tessa says, dumping the books onto her desk. The stack wobbles but miraculously doesn't topple over. "Having a gossip session? Some of us have actual work to do, you know."

"We were just finishing up," I say quickly, trying to defuse the situation.

"Good," Tessa says, already half turned toward her side of the room, ready to ignore both of us. "I'm ready to have some peace and quiet."

"Actually, Tessa," Isla interjects, her voice deceptively sweet, "we could use your expert opinion on something."

I wince. This isn't going to end well. It's obvious to me that Isla is full of shit, but I'm curious to see how all of this unfolds.

Tessa turns slowly with one eyebrow arched. "Oh? Since when do you value my opinion?"

I clear my throat, trying to cut in before Isla can escalate things further. "We're making a list," I say. "Of potential rebounds for me."

Tessa's eyes flicker with interest. "A rebound? For you?" She crosses her arms and leans against her desk, studying me. I can almost see the gears turning in her head. "That's ambitious."

"It was Isla's idea," I say, throwing my best friend under the bus but also hoping it will shift some of the growing tension away from me.

Isla shrugs nonchalantly. "Selene deserves to move on and be happy. We're just brainstorming options."

"Oh, I have no doubt Selene will move on," Tessa says, a sly smile creeping onto her lips. "So, who's on the list so far?"

I hesitate, but Isla jumps in with fake enthusiasm. "Ryan from the soccer team, Derek from her lab class—"

"He has a girlfriend," I interject.

"—and Lucas the math tutor."

Tessa snorts. "That's the best you can come up with? No offense, but it sounds like you're scraping the bottom of the barrel."

"Do you have a better suggestion?" Isla challenges.

Tessa looks directly at me, her eyes piercing through me. "No, but make sure it's not Knox. I assume you're connected to him since she's already dating Asher."

My eyes nearly pop out of my skull, but I do my best to control my expression. I spare a glance at Isla, and she looks as taken aback as I do. For a moment, the room is completely silent.

"Knox?" I say, my voice coming out higher and more strangled than I intended. "You're joking, right?"

Tessa shrugs, the sly smile never leaving her face. "He's off limits."

This almost feels like an outer body experience, but I need to ask. "Why is he off limits?"

Tessa shrugs. "He's my ex-boyfriend. We dated in high school."

This revelation hits me like a ton of bricks. I don't even know how to process this new information.

"Wow," Isla says, her voice more subdued now.

"I know. Normally, I wouldn't care if he was on your stupid list, but I have plans for him. That's why he's a no go," Tessa says, turning back to her desk and pulling out her chair. She throws her body into her seat before she looks at Isla and then me over her shoulder. "We're going to get back together."

Have I been transported to a parallel universe? That's the only explanation that makes sense. But it's all a bit too much. "Ah...okay," I say before turning to my best friend. "Isla, I'm going to head out, but I'll text you when I get back to my room."

"I'll come with you. We could do our homework...or drink. Either one."

I nod quickly. "Deal."

For a second, I just stand there, looking as if I'm watching Isla get ready, but in reality, my mind has actually been blown. I'm still reeling from Tessa's smug declaration about her and Knox. And what it could potentially mean when she finds out he and I slept together.

Going to my room and drinking sounds more and more like the likely outcome of all of this.

6

KNOX

Clank. The weights rattle as I rack them, my muscles screaming in protest. One more set. Push harder. Be better. Can't stop now.

I take a moment to catch my breath. By looking at me, you would think I just sprinted a mile or two. I wipe my face with my shirt, which is soaked through, then glance at the clock. I've been at this for two hours now, which is longer than my usual routine. But today isn't a usual day. Today, I need the distraction. I need the pain to drown out everything else.

I grab the bar again, knuckles white. Inhale. Brace. Lift. The burn rips through me, but I don't flinch. Pain is nothing new.

Eight. Nine. Ten. Eleven. Twelve.

With a grunt, I drop the weights, the crash echoing in the nearly empty gym. Bent over, I suck in air, lungs heaving, heart hammering against my ribs. When I finally straighten up, I catch my reflection in the mirror.

Sweat pours down my face, dripping off my chin and onto the mat under me. My short brown hair is plastered to my forehead. I look like hell, but there's nothing quite like working out late in the evening just before the gym closes. There's hardly anyone here, which means no one can bother me.

I stare at myself for a long moment. A bruise colors my jaw from practice yesterday. The scar under my jaw stands out, pale against my skin—a permanent reminder of the hit that nearly ended my career freshman year.

I touch it lightly, the skin still numb. That was the first time I realized how fragile all of this is. One moment you're on top, the next you're in an ambulance wondering if you'll ever play again.

A buzz from my phone pulls me out of my head. I wipe my hands on my towel and check the screen.

Tessa: Can we talk?

I clench my jaw involuntarily. Tessa. Why now? It's been years since we broke up, and she's never once tried to contact me even though we've been at the same college.

Ignoring the text, I make my way to the locker room. The tiled floor is cool against my burning skin as I strip off my soaked-through shirt and throw it in my duffel. I stand under a showerhead, but don't turn on the water yet. The silence hums in my ears.

I don't want to deal with whatever mess Tessa is trying to bring to my front door. But I do want to know why she's suddenly reaching out. The cautious part of my brain reminds me that dealing with her helped turn me into the asshole I am today. Yet, I hate leaving things unresolved.

Like I did with Selene.

That thought shocks me out of whatever paralysis my thoughts put me under. I turn the shower on, determined not only to wash away the grime from my workout, but thoughts of Tessa too.

The warm water washes away everything, including the images that are threatening to race through my mind. I finish up and dry myself off, the cold air biting into my skin. My body feels like jelly as I slip into a fresh t-shirt and sweatpants. I check my phone again; no new messages. I'm relieved that Tessa hasn't followed up because I don't want to open that can of worms again.

I toss my bag over my shoulder and head out into the night. The air is crisp, a sharp contrast to the stifling heat of the gym. My car is one of the few left in the parking lot and as I slide into the driver's seat, my phone vibrates again. For a moment, I consider not looking just in case it's Tessa. However, it could be my parents or one of my siblings reaching out as well.

I start my car and then unlock my phone.

Asher: Where r u?

Shit. I forgot Asher and Blaise were hanging out tonight and asked if I wanted to join. I can't blow them off like I did Wilder the other night because it's not like we were going out to a party and they are both more than likely sitting in our living room, watching a recap of all the latest sports news.

I put my car in drive and then tap on Asher's name.

"I'm on my way," I say when he picks up. "Just finished at the gym."

"Dude, you need to stop killing yourself," Asher says. I can hear Blaise in the background but can't make out what he is saying. "Come home. We got wings."

"I'll be there in ten," I say, then hang up before he can lecture me more about overtraining.

The drive through campus is quiet. Most students are either holed up in their dorms or out at the various bars nearby. As I pull onto our street, I think about Tessa again. What could she possibly want? An apology? Closure?

I slammed the door on all that years ago. Probably should have blocked her phone number then as well.

I find a parking spot a couple of houses away and turn my car off. I exit my vehicle and grab my duffel before I head to the house. The front door is unlocked, and I can hear the low murmur of the TV mixed with Asher and Blaise's voices. The smell of hot wings hits me, and my stomach growls. I realize I haven't eaten in a few hours and that needs to come to an end.

I stand in the doorway leading into the living room and find Asher and Blaise sitting on opposite ends of the couch. Blaise is holding a game controller while Asher is staring at him.

"I'm telling you, man, there's no way that move was legal," Asher insists, gesturing to the tv screen.

Blaise smirks, shaking his head as he continues chewing. "Don't hate the player, hate the game. Not my fault you suck at—" He glances up, noticing me hovering in the doorway. "Well, look what the cat dragged in."

I roll my eyes, dropping my bag by the door. "Didn't your mother ever teach you not to speak with your mouth full?"

Asher snorts and throws his head back. "She tried, but it didn't stick. Kind of like his last date."

"Hey, that's rude!" Blaise sputters, indignant.

I collapse into the armchair, propping my feet up on the coffee table. Asher shoots me a look, but I ignore it, reaching for the plate of wings. There has to be more food somewhere because this isn't going to fill me up.

"So what'd I miss?" I ask before taking a bite of the chicken.

Blaise shrugs, grabbing the controller. "Not much. Just Ash getting his ass handed to him. Again."

"Screw you, man. I was distracted." Asher chucks a pillow at him, which Blaise easily dodges.

"Yeah, yeah. Excuses, excuses." Blaise grins, unpausing the game. "Ready for round two?"

The game starts again, and I find myself drawn into the drama unfolding on the screen. At least it can distract me from the shit that is going on in my life right now.

"Why were you at the gym so late anyway?" Asher asks. It's then I realize that my hanging up on him on the way home wasn't enough to stop his line of questioning. And knowing Blaise, he'll double down on the inquisition.

I wipe my hands on a napkin that was left under the plate of wings, stalling for a moment. "Just trying to stay in shape. You know how it is."

Asher leans back, crossing his arms over his chest. His gaze is more piercing than usual, like he's trying to see straight through me. "Yeah, but there's staying in shape and there's working out to avoid shit."

"I'm fine," I say, perhaps a bit too sharply. The room goes quiet; even the hum of the television seems to dim. I sigh, trying to soften my tone. "Working out keeps my mind and body in check so I do it."

Blaise pauses the game, and I can feel both of their eyes on me. Even when things got rough with Asher for a while, they were my boys and always will be. They're supposed to understand this. Then again, how could they when I barely do?

"Knox," Asher starts, but I cut him off.

"Seriously, I'm fine." I lean back in the chair and stretch, trying to play it cool. "Just tired is all."

Blaise shrugs and unpauses the game. The sounds of virtual carnage fill the room, but the sound of unanswered questions lingers. However, they both seem comfortable with giving me the space I crave.

My phone buzzes in my pocket again and I close my eyes for several seconds. I take it out slowly, almost dreading what I'll see. The screen lights up and I confirm it's the person I would rather not hear from again.

"Knox?" Asher's voice pulls me from my thoughts.

I look up to see him staring at me. Blaise is focused on the game, but I can tell he's listening too.

I shove the phone back in my pocket. "What?"

"You sure you're okay?"

Fuck it. I can let them in on part of what is going on inside my brain. "Tessa, my ex from high school, texted me this evening."

Asher's eyebrows shoot up, and Blaise momentarily loses his focus on the game, his character taking a fatal blow. He doesn't even bat an eye, which is a first.

"What does she want?" Asher asks cautiously. He knows the history, knows how deep that wound went—or still goes.

I rub the back of my neck. "I don't even know. She just said, 'Can we talk?' and I've been ignoring her."

Blaise sets the controller down, turning his full attention to me. "Are you going to respond?"

After a moment I say, "I don't think I should. There's nothing but trouble there."

"Probably best if you don't," Asher agrees. "You don't need to go through all of that bull shit again. Wait... her name is Tessa?"

I know he's right and I know that means I've made the right choice. However the last part of his sentence made me do a double take. "Yes, why?"

Asher places the game controller down. "I saw her recently. Well, assuming that there aren't a lot of women named Tessa around here."

Wait what? I mean Crestwood's campus isn't enormous, but also...what? Blaise's gaze is jumping between the two of us as if he can't believe what he's seeing or hearing.

I turn to Asher, confused. "Where?"

Asher hesitates for a moment, then shrugs. "At Isla's place. I went over there a few weeks ago to see her."

And that's when it clicks. Isla is Tessa's roommate. How had I not put that together before? Isla is Selene's best friend, and Selene...

Fuck.

7

SELENE

I take a deep breath before I walk through the automatic doors. I can't remember the last time I walked into Crestwood's gym, but there is no time like the present.

The slight smell of chlorine from the indoor pool hits me, unlocking a memory. Has it been over a year since I've been in here? Wow. I pause, adjusting my tote bag on my shoulder, and survey the front lobby. I didn't know they renovated the reception area. It's sleek now, with modern touches like brushed steel fixtures and a minimalist, white marble counter. Everything looks so different that for a second I think I might be in the wrong place. The large, green potted plants behind the front desk add a touch of nature to the otherwise sterile environment.

"Can I help you?"

I jump slightly when I see a guy with a man bun

staring at me from behind the reception desk. I force a smile and walk over.

"Hi, yeah. Do I just swipe my ID here to be let in?"

"Yeah, that's right."

It takes me a couple of tries before the computer registers my ID.

"You haven't been here in a while," he says as he looks at the computer and then back at me.

"Yep. I definitely knew that," I say as I slowly nod. Thanks, Captain Obvious.

He shrugs. "Well, welcome back."

As I make my way past the desk, I can feel his gaze linger on me. That wasn't weird or anything.

I walk until I'm greeted by a bunch of machines and free weights. I'm a little bit nervous given that there are a bunch of people here right now, but I chose to come during prime time. This is something I need to do in order to get used to working out with a crowd. Or so I tell myself. If I go at odd hours, I'll just psych myself out when it's busy. And this works with my class and work schedule.

I survey the area like a general planning an attack. The weight section is packed with dudes in cutoff shirts and gym shorts, so I decide to start with some cardio. Maybe by the time I'm done, there will be fewer people over there.

I make my way into the locker room and drop my coat and bag off while making sure to grab my phone, headphones, water bottle, and hair tie.

I take another deep breath as I walk out to the main floor and put my red hair back into a ponytail. I swipe open my phone and find a playlist I made specifically for this: "Gym Torture." The first track is "Eye of the Tiger".

A line of treadmills stretches across the far wall near the windows. Most are taken, but I spot an open one at the end and quickly walk over. I step onto the treadmill and examine the control panel. It's been long enough that I have to reacquaint myself with all the buttons and settings.

I hit Quick Start before I lose my nerve. The belt jolts to life under my feet. My stomach lurches. God, I hate running. But I'm determined to make a change, to take control of at least one aspect of my chaotic life.

As I settle into an awkward jog, my mind starts to race, berating me with cruel jabs.

You're too slow. Too big. You don't belong here with all the gym rats. Everyone's probably staring at you jiggling with each labored step.

No. I shake my head, blinking back hot tears. I won't let the negativity win. Not today. One foot in front of the other. That's it. Just keep going...

Focusing on my breath, the music helps drown out the noise in my head. Slowly, I find a rhythm and realize this isn't so bad. I can do this. I AM doing this.

When I'm a couple of songs in, I steal a glance at the time display on the treadmill. Six minutes. It feels like an eternity, but I'm kind of proud I've lasted this long. My legs are starting to warm up and my breathing, while still heavy, isn't completely out of control. It's going to take me some time to get used to this sort of activity again, but I'll get there.

Because I AM doing this.

I let my eyes wander to the free weight section again. Still packed. A guy in a neon green tank top is grunting loudly as he does bicep curls, his veins popping out. Another dude in a backward cap high-fives his buddy after finishing a set on the bench press. The thought of walking over there makes me want to run right out the door.

But that doesn't matter right now. I'm here, and that's something.

I turn my focus back to the treadmill and up the speed just a tad, pushing myself into a faster jog. The burst of energy surprises me; a small spark of hope. Maybe all those fitness articles I've skimmed aren't complete lies—maybe there is such a thing as a runner's high.

However, that quickly changes a few minutes later. My legs start to feel like Jell-o and my lungs are on fire. Time to slow it down before I collapse in a puddle of my own sweat. I gradually decrease the speed until I'm at a brisk walk, then finally a leisurely stroll.

As I catch my breath, I can't help but notice how effortless everyone else makes it look. This girl several feet in front of me on the elliptical looks like she is barely breaking a sweat. Meanwhile, I'm over here panting like a dog in the middle of summer.

I half expect to see judgy looks or hear snickers as I wipe the sweat from my brow with the bottom of my t-shirt. But when I muster up the courage to actually take in my surroundings, I realize that no one is paying me any attention. They're all too focused on their own workouts, their own goals, their own journeys.

Huh. Imagine that. The world doesn't actually revolve around me and my insecurities. Who would've thought?

I can't help but chuckle at my own ridiculous assumptions. Here I was, convinced that everyone was silently mocking me, when in reality, they couldn't care less. It's oddly freeing, in a way, and I'll take a win where I can get it.

As I step off the treadmill on wobbly legs, I feel a sense of accomplishment wash over me. I did it. I survived my first workout. And you know what? It wasn't nearly as horrific as I had built it up to be in my head.

After I wipe off the treadmill, I grab my water bottle, headphones, and phone. The free weights area is still packed, and the weight machines might as well have flashing neon signs that say *Intimidating as Hell*, so I head to a quieter corner of the gym where a row of yoga mats is neatly stacked.

I drop my things beside one, unroll the mat, and sit down, stretching out my legs. My calves still feel tight from the treadmill, but the slow pull of the stretch feels good. After I'm done, I take a second to swipe open my phone to switch my playlist to something more mellow. I find myself nodding along to the soft beat that plays through my earbuds as I take a long sip from my water bottle.

Okay, so maybe cardio won't kill me after all. That's a relief. I still need to work on toning up and eating better if I want to see real changes, but... maybe this won't be so bad.

That thought alone should motivate me to continue. Instead, I find myself checking my social media accounts.

Procrastination at its finest.

I scroll mindlessly through my feed until without really thinking about it until I end up on Knox's profile.

I know it's a bad idea, but I do it anyway.

Most of his posts are hockey-related like action shots from games, team photos, a couple of candids with his teammates. I smile when I see that some of the photos have Isla credited. His follower count is ridiculous, which makes sense, at least to me. Hot guy + hockey + social media? Sounds like the recipe for a thirst trap if I've ever heard of one.

I scroll past a shot of him in his Red Wolves jersey, with his hair damp from what I assume is sweat and his gaze locked on something off-camera. The post has thousands of likes, plus enough comments to make my thumb cramp just from scrolling through them.

I know I shouldn't look.

But I can't help myself. Especially when one comment in particular catches my attention:

TESSAM9352: LOOKING GOOD AS ALWAYS.
SOME THINGS NEVER CHANGE ☻

My stomach tightens, heat rising up the back of my neck before I can stop it.

Seriously?

Then I catch myself. It's not like Knox and I are anything anyway, so why do I care? I shake my head, lock my screen and toss it beside my water bottle with a little more force than necessary.

I shove the thoughts from my mind and focus on doing two sets of crunches and feel the burn in my core. It's a familiar pain as I wince and let out a deep breath as I take a break between sets. It's amazing how quickly your body can start to remember what it's forgotten.

By the time I finish the second set, my abs are screaming, but there's a strange sense of satisfaction that comes with it. I take a moment to just lie back and breathe, staring up at the ceiling. I sit up slowly, not wanting to rush and make myself dizzy. I look over in the mirror across from me just to see how much a mess I look.

My face is bright red, my ponytail is a mess, and my t-shirt has sweat stains on it. I look like a drowned rat, but I'm at least I'm being productive, and it is time to wrap this up.

Stretching has always been my favorite part of any

workout. It's the one thing that doesn't make me feel like I'm dying. I sink into a runner's stretch, and the tension in my calves and hamstrings eases a bit. I probably should have done this before I got on the treadmill, but here we are. I move through familiar poses: downward dog, child's pose, seated forward bend.

When I'm done going through the motions, I wipe everything down, stand, and roll up the mat. After I'm done cleaning up, I stretch my arms over my head as if I'm reaching for the sky.

As I'm putting my arms down, I glance out the gym's large windows. The sun has dipped closer to the horizon, painting the sky with strokes of orange and pink. There's something romantic about the sunset that makes me pause and take a mental snapshot. I feel... hopeful. Like maybe this is the start of something better.

I head toward the locker room, my legs still a little wobbly, but I should be able to shake it off before I have to walk back to my room. Inside my locker, I find my gym bag and pull out a fresh t-shirt. I think about it for a second before stuffing it back in my bag. I'm just going to go back to my dorm and shower anyway.

Instead, I throw my coat on and take out my ponytail, allowing my hair to flow freely on my shoulders. As I walk out of the gym into the evening air, it cools me instantly, cutting through the warmth still radiating from my body due to the workout.

My phone suddenly vibrates in my pocket. I pull it out and look at the screen. It's a text from Isla.

Isla: How'd it go?

Me: I survived. I'll see another day.

Isla: Proud of you! See, it wasn't so bad. Next time I'll join you. But there's something I wanted to ask.

Me: Shoot.

Isla: Do you want to attend a campus event with me and Hailey tonight? I can send you details in a bit, but I know free food is promised.

I think about my lack of plans for the night and find myself typing a reply back before I've processed exactly what was happening.

Me: You're speaking my language. I'll definitely be there.

As I put my phone back into my pocket, I realize I haven't thought about Knox the entire time I was at the gym.

And that's freeing.

8

SELENE

I'm laughing so hard I nearly snort as Hailey, Isla, and I push our way through the people that are hanging around outside even though it's chilly. It's much more crowded than it usually is, but that doesn't matter because I have only one thing on my mind.

"Free pizza, here we come!" I say as I glance over at Isla. "I'm starving."

Healthy diet be damned, for tonight at least. Good thing I worked out today.

Hailey rolls her eyes, but I can see her smirk. "You know this means we have to stay for the whole presentation, right? They aren't just giving it away."

I shrug. "How bad could it be? Sustainable living or something, right? We'll learn some important things like how to compost our quinoa and save the whales." She glares at me because this is totally her thing and Isla and I are just along for the ride. "I'm kidding. I'm excited to see what this is all about."

"Same, I just tend to express my feelings better than Selene over here," Isla chimes in.

"Girl, whatever," I say waving her off.

We reach the doors to the building, and I make an exaggerated show of holding one open for Hailey and Isla. As soon as I cross the threshold, the smell of melted cheese and garlic hits me and my stomach growls so loudly that even Isla and Hailey hear it.

"Jeez, you weren't kidding." Isla shakes her head as she tries not to laugh.

All I can do is shrug and say, "Told ya so."

We walk toward the auditorium and find some seats that are in the middle but near an aisle. Hopefully, that will make it easier for us to escape if the presentation isn't what we have in mind.

Someone at the front of the room fiddles with a microphone, causing a burst of feedback that makes the whole crowd wince and grab their ears. I take this moment to scan the audience and notice a few familiar faces from classes and around campus. Looks like a decent turnout for a freebie event on a Saturday night. My eyes land on a tall figure at the back of the room, standing against the wall with his arms folded across his chest. My heart skips a beat when I recognize him—Knox. His dark hair is tousled in that effortless way guys like him always seem to pull off, and he's wearing a faded green jacket over a plain white tee. He looks almost bored, but there's an intensity in his gaze that makes it impossible to look away.

Isla follows my line of sight and raises an eyebrow. "Holy shit..."

That causes Hailey to look in the same direction we are. Her mouth drops open briefly before she catches herself.

I tear my gaze away from Knox and look at her with wide eyes. "Did you guys know he was going to be here?" My whisper-shout almost sounds comical and borderline hysterical.

Isla shakes her head slowly, clearly as surprised as I am. "We didn't have a game today, but I can't figure out why he would be here. I did tell Asher I would be going to this with you, but I'm not sure why he would mention it to Knox...."

Hailey reaches up to adjust her messy bun. "Levi is having dinner with his parents tonight so unless he texted Knox and told him, this might be just random."

"Maybe he's into the whole sustainable living thing?" Isla adds.

I haven't the slightest idea because it wasn't something we talked about via text message or while we fucked so... "Could just be here for the free pizza, like us."

But inside, my mind is racing. Knox and I aren't anything and I've been doing my best not to think about him. I'm convinced this is a test the universe is throwing my way because why in the hell would he be here? Yep, fate is playing some kind of trick on me.

The lights in the auditorium dim and someone steps up to the podium. I steal one more glance at Knox. He shifts his weight from one leg to the other and scans the room. For a moment, I think his eyes meet mine, but it's too dark to tell and I look away too quickly to be sure.

"Thank you all for coming out tonight," says the woman at the podium. She has short, cropped hair, and wears an oversized knit sweater and jeans. "I'm Maggie, and I'm excited to talk to you all about sustainable living in the modern world."

I shift in my seat, trying to get comfortable, but my mind is anywhere but on the presentation. What if Knox sees me here? What will he think? Would he come over and say hi? Do I even want him to?

Maggie talks about reducing waste and making eco-friendly choices. I try to pay attention, really I do, because I am interested. Plus, the promise of pizza at the end is a strong motivator. But every few minutes, I can't help but sneak a look back at Knox. He hasn't moved, still standing with that casual arrogance that only someone like him can pull off.

Isla nudges me and I snap back to reality.

"What?" I whisper, annoyed at being caught daydreaming.

"You're going to get whiplash from all that turning

around," she says smugly. "Just go talk to him if you're so desperate."

"I'm not desperate," I protest, maybe a little too loudly. Some heads turn in our direction, and I sink lower in my seat. "I'm just curious why he's here."

"You'll never know unless you ask."

I glare at her, then steal one last look at Knox. Part of me knows she's right. If I want answers, I have to be brave enough to seek them out. But another part of me—probably the smarter part—remembers that getting involved with Knox in any way is playing with fire.

And I already learned my lesson in that regard.

I hope.

The presentation continues, and I find myself fidgeting more and more. Hailey is actually taking notes on her phone, which makes sense given she's an environmental studies major. Isla looks as if she's paying attention to Maggie even though I know she came for the pizza just as much as I did. My mind keeps wandering back to Knox and I hate myself for it.

When Maggie mentions something about renewable energy sources, I force myself to focus on the slideshow she is presenting. Bright images of solar panels and wind turbines flash on the screen. My stomach growls again, and I start counting down the minutes until we can make a dash for the pizza.

Finally, Maggie wraps up her talk with a heartfelt plea to make small changes in our daily lives. The room fills with polite applause, and I can almost taste the pizza now. People start to shuffle out of their seats and move toward the back of the room where a table laden with stacks of pizza boxes awaits.

"See, that wasn't so bad," Hailey says, putting her phone away. "And now we're all a little more informed."

"Definitely, and once my belly is full, I can think about everything that was said," I say. "Can we eat now?"

We stand and merge into the crowd moving toward the food. I can't help but scan for Knox again, wondering if he's going to make a move for the pizza or if he's just going to bolt. Part of me hopes he'll leave so I don't have to deal with sharing the same air as him.

The line crawls forward, and Hailey grabs an extra plate before I even ask. She hands it over without a word, her attention locked on the pizza like it's the prize at the end of a marathon.

"You good?" Isla asks, already reaching for a slice dripping with cheese and pepperoni.

"Yeah, I'll catch up. Still deciding," I mumble, though I'm not really thinking about pizza. My thoughts are revolving around the one person they shouldn't be.

They don't wait. Isla and Hailey head toward an open spot near the windows, already biting into their slices like they haven't eaten in days.

I jump slightly when Lucas slides in next to me, a grin plastered on his face. We've seen each other on campus after he tutored me once. He tried to correct my math homework even though I was already right. Not exactly a highlight of that day.

"Selene, right?" Lucas says. "What did you think of the presentation? That Q&A went longer than expected, but it meant people were interested in the topic, I guess."

I force a polite nod. "Yeah, it was informative," I say, trying not to let my eyes wander around the room. But then I spot Knox heading over, and my stomach does a little flip.

He's wearing a half-smirk, that signature cocky set to his jaw. The second he sees me talking to Lucas, the smirk slips into something way more serious. What the hell is that all about?

Knox doesn't hesitate. He walks right up to us, like he owns the damn place, and puts himself between me and Lucas.

"Didn't know you were into environmental stuff," he says, his voice low as his eyes flicker from me to Lucas and back again. "Thought this kind of thing would bore you."

I narrow my eyes at him. "I'm full of surprises," I shoot back, trying to keep my tone light even though my pulse is suddenly racing.

Lucas chuckles awkwardly beside me. "It's cool to see people from different circles showing up to these things," he says, completely missing the tension that is now at level one thousand. "You here for extra credit or just the free pizza?"

Knox's gaze locks onto Lucas, and I swear I see his jaw

tighten. "What do you think?" he fires back, the edge in his voice impossible to miss. "I don't need extra credit."

Lucas blinks, thrown off by the sudden fire in Knox's voice. "Right. Well, the pizza's good, at least."

Knox doesn't even acknowledge that. "You're a math tutor, right?" he asks. "I heard you love correcting people even when they're not wrong."

Damn it. I knew I shouldn't have mentioned that to him.

Lucas's eyebrows shoot up. "Uh, I just try to help people understand the material," he says, his smile faltering a bit.

"Yeah, I'm sure you do," Knox mutters, grabbing a plate with a little more force than necessary. He flips open the pizza box and snatches a slice.

"Knox," I hiss under my breath. He has some freaking nerve. "Seriously?"

He shrugs, biting into his pizza. "Just making conversation."

Lucas clears his throat, obviously picking up on the vibe now. "Anyway, Selene, if you need any more help with math, please let me know."

Before I can even open my mouth, Knox cuts in. "Yeah, well, Selene's got a lot on her plate right now," he says, leaning just slightly toward Lucas, like he's daring him to push back. "Pretty sure she doesn't have time for that."

Lucas blinks, glancing between us. "Oh, I didn't realize—"

"That's because there's nothing to realize," I snap, turning on Knox, my cheeks burning. "I can speak for myself, thanks."

Knox just takes another bite, looking way too satisfied with himself. "Sure you can."

Lucas gives me an awkward smile, clearly deciding this isn't his scene anymore. "Well... guess I'll see you later, Selene." He backs off quickly, disappearing into the crowd.

The second he's out of sight, I spin around to face Knox. "What the hell was that?"

Knox lifts a shoulder, like he didn't just chase someone off with his attitude. "What? I'm saving you from a lecture about calculus. You don't really wanna hang out with that guy, do you?"

"That's not the point!" I hiss, frustration bubbling over. "You can't treat me the way you've treated me and then act like some jealous asshole. Hell, you can't do that anyway."

His smirk falters, and for a second, I think I've actually stunned him into silence. But then he steps in closer, lowering his voice so only I can hear.

"Jealous?" he repeats, his eyes darkening like I've just flashed him or something. "You think that's what this is?"

I glare up at him, refusing to back down. "Yeah, Knox. That's exactly what this is. You don't get to be hot and cold with me and then scare off anyone who talks to me. You can promptly fuck off."

I hate that we're having this showdown in public, but

there's no time like the present. I can see the war going on behind his eyes. The cocky exterior slips, just for a moment, before his smug expression is back in place.

"I'm not trying to have it both ways," he mutters, voice low and tense. "I just don't like seeing guys like him think they've got a shot."

My chest tightens, and I hate the way his words sends fire through my body. I'm not supposed to be feeling anything but hatred toward him given what we've been through at this point. "That's not your decision to make."

He leans in even closer, his breath warm against my ear. "Maybe not. But that doesn't mean I have to pretend I'm cool with it."

For a second, I can't breathe. The space between us is suffocating me, like one false move and I'll be taking my last breath. My heart's pounding so hard it's a wonder he can't hear it.

But then I pull back, shaking my head. "You're unbelievable," I toss over my shoulder, pushing past him before I do something even more ridiculous—like stay.

I don't look back as I make my way through the crowd, but I can feel his eyes on me, burning into my skin with every step. As much as I want to be furious, some stupid part of me knows this isn't over. Not even close.

I'm almost to the other side of the room when I hear it. "Knox!"

The voice cuts through the chatter, sharp enough to make me freeze mid-step. I don't turn around. I keep moving, pretending like I'm unaffected, but every part of me is humming with leftover adrenaline.

Thankfully, there's another table where pizza is being given out and once I reach it. I let my curiosity win for a second. I glance sideways, catching a glimpse of a tall guy with a scruffy beard waving at Knox from across the room, a half-eaten slice of pizza in his other hand.

I don't wait to see what Knox does. I don't need to. Instead, I grab a slice of pizza, and make my way toward Isla and Hailey, who look way too pleased with themselves.

"Close call," Isla says, taking a huge bite of her pizza as I walk over to them. "I thought for sure you were going to melt into a puddle."

I scowl at her. "Thanks for the rescue. Both of you."

"What are friends for?" Hailey responds with her mouth full. Isla just shakes her head and takes a more dainty bite of her own slice.

We move to the side of the room, away from the rush of people still trying to get a slice or two. I keep my back to Knox, hoping that out of sight will mean out of mind, but it's not working. Every nerve in my body is still on high alert from that short interaction.

And I hate myself for it.

9

KNOX

It feels as if I'm skating harder than normal as I push myself through drills. Each stroke that I take is more aggressive than the last. Focus, dammit. But my mind won't cooperate. I curse under my breath as another pass slips past me, clattering uselessly against the boards.

This is supposed to be my escape, the one place where everything else fades away. But today, even the ice isn't enough to clear my head. Selene's face flashes through my mind for the hundredth time, and I grit my teeth, trying to remove the image.

I shouldn't be thinking about her. Not now, not ever. But I can't seem to help myself. There's just something about her that gets under my skin, no matter how hard I try to ignore it.

Not to mention seeing her during an environmental

presentation this weekend hadn't been a part of the plan, yet here we are. Now I can't stop thinking about her, and I'm annoyed about it.

The scrimmage starts, and I throw myself into it with a vengeance. Maybe if I skate hard enough, hit hard enough, I can finally shake this restlessness that's been plaguing me for the last couple of days.

But my frustration only builds as the minutes tick by. My teammates are moving too slow, too sloppy. Don't they realize we have to keep our shit together in order to get into the Frozen Four? I grit my teeth and push harder, my muscles burning with the effort.

And then it happens. One of the rookies thinks he's hot stuff and tries to maneuver past me with a fancy move. Instinct takes over and I lash out, slamming him into the boards with a satisfying crunch.

"What the hell, Sanchez?" he yelps, struggling to his feet.

I don't answer, just skate away without looking back. I can feel the tension rippling through the rest of the team, see the wary looks they exchange when they think I'm not looking.

But I don't care. They don't get it. They don't know what it's like to have your head so screwed up that you can't think straight. I take a deep breath, trying to calm the anger that is dancing in my veins.

Get it together. You're better than this.

But am I? Sometimes I wonder. Hockey used to be

the one thing I could count on, the one place where I knew exactly who I was and what I was doing at all times.

Now, with Selene lurking in my mind at all times, I'm not so sure anymore.

And that is what scares the hell out of me.

Coach blows the whistle and signals for me to come over to him. I'm not surprised and do as he asks.

"Sanchez," Coach Johnson says. "A word."

Great. I tug off my helmet and run a hand through my sweat-soaked hair, breathing heavily as I glide over to him.

"What the hell was that?" he asks, and I can see the anger bubbling under the surface of his usually calm exterior.

I shrug, though I know it won't do me any favors. "Just playing hard, Coach."

"Playing hard?" He tightens his grip on his clipboard, white-knuckled. "You're playing like a damn wrecking ball. We're a team, Knox. You don't take your problems out on your teammates."

"I know," I say, but he cuts me off with a sharp glare.

"Do you? Because from where I'm standing, it looks like you've got a death wish or something. You think scouts are going to be impressed by this kind of bullshit? By you injuring your own guys?"

My jaw clenches at his words. The scouts have been a sore spot for me all season. I've put everything into this year, my last shot at making an impression before the draft. The idea that I could be sabotaging myself is almost too much to take.

"Look," Coach says, his tone softening slightly. "I know you've got a lot on your plate right now, but so does everyone else. You need to find a way to deal with it that's not going to tear this team apart. We need you, Knox. But we need you in control."

He's right, of course. He's always right. That's what makes him such a damn good coach, and why I've respected him even when he's talking to me like this.

"I'll get it together," I say.

"You better," he says, then pauses. "Take the rest of practice off. Cool down."

I open my mouth to argue but think better of it. He's giving me an out, a chance to reset before I do any more damage.

"Thanks, Coach," I say, though the words taste bitter. I slip my helmet back on and skate toward the locker room. There's a bit of pain in my chest as I listen to the sounds of my team fading behind me. A part of me wants to turn around, apologize to the rookie, and jump back into the scrimmage. I know I can prove that I'm still the player they need me to be. But I know it would be useless right now. My head's too fucked.

In the locker room, I peel off my gear slowly, deliberately, trying to stretch the time. The cold air stings my sweat-drenched skin as I sit on the bench. I take out my phone to scroll through messages. There's one from Mom asking how practice went. I put the phone down without answering.

I sit back and close my eyes, enjoying the silence of the empty locker room. This used to be where I could put my head on straight before and after practice and games. Now it just feels like everything else.

I sigh and look at my phone again. Mom's message stares back at me, and guilt gnaws at my gut. I swipe to open it, because I shouldn't have ignored it to begin with.

> Mom: Knox, hope you're doing okay.
> How was practice? Don't forget to check
> in on your sister and let me know when
> you're coming home for the birthday
> party in a few weeks. Love, Mom.

I smile at my mom signing off her text message. It's something she does on purpose to annoy me.

> Me: Practice was fine and I'll text Willow
> later. Will also let you know about when
> I'll be home when I know for sure.

Only the former is a lie.

I should check in on Willow, but she's doing her own thing, as always. Not to mention, she's made it clear that she doesn't want my interference in her life at Crestwood, and I've respected that. Mostly. But just because she doesn't want me hovering doesn't mean I shouldn't check on her.

I stand and head to the showers, letting the hot water

pound against my sore muscles. I will say, it feels good not having to compete with the other guys for the shower, although the reason for this is something I don't prefer.

The heat seeps into my bones, and for a moment, I let myself relax. I think about the party Mom's planning for my abuela, affectionately known as Mamita. She'll be ninety and is still as feisty as ever. The thought of being around family makes me feel a little better, and the change of scenery might do me some good.

I finish up and get dressed before stuffing my gear into my duffel. I sling it over my shoulder and make my way out to the parking lot without saying a word to another soul.

That was probably for the best.

I toss my hockey gear into the back of my car and slide into the driver's seat. I sit for a moment, staring at the steering wheel, unsure of where to go. Home is close, but the thought of sitting alone in my house, with nothing but my thoughts to keep me company, is suffocating.

However, it's not like at least someone wouldn't be home soon anyway. Practice is almost over, and as far as I know, Coach had no plans of going over the allotted time.

Shoot, maybe I should just go home and take a nap. That would fix everything right?

With that in mind, I start my car and pull out of my parking spot. The ride home is quick and easy as usual, and as I'm stepping out of my car, my phone rings. A quick glance down at the screen shows it's my little sister, Willow.

She's calling me? What the—?

"Hey," I say as I'm locking my car door behind me. "I didn't think you still had my number."

"Very funny," Willow shoots back, but I can hear the smirk in her voice. "I called because Mom asked me too."

"Well that makes me feel all warm and fuzzy on the inside."

"You could have also called me too, bro."

I sigh. "I was planning on sending you a text later."

"Cause Mom told you to."

I open the front door and quickly close it behind me. "Yep."

"Well, why don't we make Mom happy and grab lunch sometime this week? Take a photo and send it to her so she has proof that we can actually stand each other."

That makes me chuckle. "Are you cool with being seen with me? I know how much you don't like being around me because of my status symbol as a hockey all-star and—"

"Shut up and I'll make an exception this one time. Stop being annoying."

"But that's my job," I say. "Look, I just got home so I'll shoot you a text and we can figure out lunch."

"Perfect, I'll talk to you later then."

"Later."

I put my phone in my pocket, drop my gear near the

door, and walk into the kitchen. The fridge hums softly as I open it and look inside. A couple of leftover takeout containers, some beer, and a sad-looking lettuce head are all that greet me. We need to go shopping at some point soon, I guess. I grab a beer, twist off the cap, and take a long pull. I shouldn't be drinking this early, but here we are.

And then Selene enters my brain once more.

I wonder how she's doing right now. Is she still angry? Of course she is; she looked rightfully pissed when I walked up to her this weekend. I fucked this up royally. The thing is, I didn't mean to push her away like that. It all happened so fast—us getting together, the incredible high of it, and then the crushing fear that followed. Fear of feeling something more than just physical attraction.

I take another swig of beer and pull out my phone again, staring at the screen like it's a crystal ball that can show me the future. Should I text her and apologize? Would it even make a difference at this point?

But the truth is, it has gotten to the point where I can't stop thinking about her and no one else holds my interest. No one else holds a candle to her.

Maybe it is time to try to fix what I've so irrevocably broken.

10

SELENE

This is exactly what I needed.

The bass thumps through my body as I move to the beat, my red hair whipping around me. Isla and I are in the thick of it, laughing and dancing like there's no tomorrow. Deciding to go out and party tonight was the best decision I made in a long time. I'm considering it a reward for myself because I managed to make it to the gym three times this week and I'm already feeling stronger.

Not sure that I'm looking any stronger, but that's a discussion for another time.

"This is our song!" I shout over the music. It's "After Hours" by Kehlani, and as I'm singing the lyrics, I grab Isla's hand and twirl her around.

She throws back her head and lets out a carefree laugh. "Hell yeah it is!"

We lose ourselves in the music and it's almost the perfect cure. Tonight isn't about worrying or overthinking; it's about living in the moment.

Isla pulls me closer and yells, "I'm getting another drink! You want something?"

My body is buzzing from the two vodka cranberries I've already downed. "Just water!" I shout back.

She nods and starts to weave through the crowd toward the bar at this house party. I keep dancing, letting the music take over, closing my eyes and imagining that I'm the only one on the dance floor.

My mind drifts, and for a moment I let myself think about Knox. It's been over a week since I saw him and distance really makes the heart grow fonder and because the number of times I think about him has increased tenfold. But then the beat drops and I'm pulled back into the present.

"Selene!"

I turn to see Isla waving a bottle of water in the air, her other hand clutching a neon-green drink that looks toxic but delicious. She makes her way back to me, half dancing, half stumbling as someone bumps into her.

"Drink up," she commands, thrusting the water into my hand. "You're turning into a lightweight."

I unscrew the cap and take a long swig. The cool liquid is a relief on my throat, which is already starting to feel raw from singing and shouting over the music. "That sounds like something I would say to you," I tease her.

She smirks, taking a large gulp of her own drink. "Roles can reverse, you know. And if you want some of this, let me know." She gestures to the cup in her hand.

"Ah fuck it," I say as I take the drink from her and hand her my water bottle.

She raises an eyebrow and gives me a mocking yet approving nod. "That's the Selene I know."

I take a tentative sip, bracing for the burn of alcohol, but instead I'm met with a surprisingly smooth, fruity taste. "What is this? It tastes like... candy."

Isla shrugs. "Some concoction the guy at the bar threw together. Said it was the 'house special.' Probably all the leftover mixers and a splash of every bottle."

I take another swig, this one longer. "It's dangerous. I could drink a gallon of this and not even realize how drunk I am."

"That's the point," Isla says with a wicked grin. "If you want the rest of it, it's yours."

"You're such an asshole. You know that, right?" I find myself finishing the drink in one go and then I wipe my mouth with the back of my hand.

And it's then I realize I've probably ruined the lip gloss I'd put on tonight. Who am I fooling? I'm sure it was screwed up years ago at this point.

"You're welcome," Isla says, her smile widening as she watches me.

"Yeah, yeah, yeah," I reply as she hands me back my water bottle. I can already feel the warmth spreading through my chest and I know that's a sign of hell potentially breaking loose. But trouble is exactly what I'm looking for tonight.

I stumble toward a garbage can and thankfully manage not to throw up as I do so. I toss the plastic cup in before I make my way back to Isla on the dance floor. "Let's get back to dancing," I say.

She hesitates, studying me with a look in her eye that screams she's known me for way too long. "You sure? I don't want you passing out on me."

I wave her concern away. "I'm fine! Just need to burn off some of this energy."

"Alright." She waves me off, but her eyes still linger on me. We dive back into the mass of bodies, the music now switching to a more electronic beat that's almost hypnotic in its repetition. My limbs feel loose, and the world isn't spinning yet so that's a plus.

For a moment, I forget about the little voice in my head that's always pointing out my flaws. Right now, I'm just Selene—the life of the party, the girl everyone wants to be around.

And that's fine by me.

The next hour blurs together in a haze of laughter, sweat, and moments of us singing at the top of our lungs. Isla and I meet up with old friends and make new ones, the kind you only ever see at parties like this. My phone vibrates in my pocket, but I ignore it. Whoever it is can wait because I'm having the time of life, and I don't care.

"Selene, I need to use the bathroom!" Isla shouts into my ear.

I look around for a clock but find none. That proves that time is irrelevant here, at least in my mind. "Want me to come with you?" I ask, knowing the answer.

"Duh!"

We link arms and start to navigate through the sweaty bodies. The house is a maze of bodies, every room packed with people partying their asses off. We pass by the kitchen, and I see a pyramid of red Solo cups stacked high on the counter, with someone attempting to knock it over using a football. The ball flies out of his hand just as we turn a corner, and I hear the crash along with a chorus of drunken "ooooohs" as we make our way up the stairs.

I would have had the same reaction.

The line for the bathroom snakes down the hall, and Isla groans. "Are you fucking kidding me? I'm going to burst."

I shrug. "You could always use the yard like old times."

She glares at me but there's a playful twinkle in her eye. "Those were desperate measures! You were seventeen and stupid."

"Me?" I laugh. "I distinctly remember you being there too."

She sticks her tongue out at me and then crosses her legs dramatically. "I'm gonna die."

"You'll survive," I say, leaning against the wall. My head is starting to feel light, like it's filled with helium, and I welcome the floaty sensation. The alcohol has done its job; all my anxieties have taken a backseat for now.

I glance at the line and then back to Isla. "Remember when we thought sneaking into college parties would be more exciting than this?"

She sighs, leaning against the wall next to me. "That was just you being a bad influence."

"Once again, you were there too. Don't make this about me. Remember how freaked out we were as we ran from that house party when the cops came? Not to mention we ran into Grace there."

"Yeah, that was the night I met Asher."

I'm blaming it on the alcohol, but I forgot about that part. The night she met the love of her life, who broke her heart. Now by some weird twist of fate, they are back together and happier than ever.

His only flaw is that he's teammates with Knox.

"Asher's a good guy," I say, trying to steer the conversation into safer waters. "I'm glad you two worked things out."

Isla gives me a small, grateful smile. "Yeah, me too. It was rough for a while, but sometimes you just need to grow up a bit to see things clearly, you know?"

I nod, though I'm not sure I do know. Growing up has only made things more complicated for me. But I'm happy for her. For them.

The line inches forward quicker than I thought, to be honest. Isla shifts from foot to foot impatiently. "So how's... everything?" she asks, and I know she's really asking about Knox without wanting to come out and say it.

"Everything's fine," I lie. "I'm operating on just vibes and alcohol at the moment."

"That's a whole mood. Oh thank fuck."

I look up and notice that we are at the front of the line and the bathroom door just opened. Isla almost sprints inside, and I quickly follow behind her, making sure to close and lock the door behind us so no one walks in on her.

"You know," she hiccups, and I try my best to contain my giggle. "This reminds me of Asher going down on me in my parents' bathroom the evening of the team bonding event."

It takes everything in my drunken brain to not turn around and stare at her because of her bizarre statement. It came so far out of left field that I feel as if I missed the last thirty minutes of our lives and only just recently tuned back in.

I busy myself by looking in the mirror, pretending to fix my hair. "Isla, that was so random, and that's saying something coming from me. Too much information," I say, though a part of me is curious about why she's bringing this up now.

"Oops, just drunken thoughts said out loud. My bad." I hear the toilet flush and turn to see Isla washing her hands, swaying slightly from side to side. She catches my eye in the mirror and gives me a smile. I decide I should probably empty my bladder too since I'm already in here.

"I'm starting to get a headache," Isla says. "It's probably a good idea that I head out."

"You mean we head out. You're staying with me tonight to get away from Tessa, remember?"

"You're right," she hiccups again. "I forgot. Let me text Asher to let him know we're fine and that we are headed back to your room."

I finish up in the bathroom and Asher ends up calling Isla as we are headed out of the party. He almost came down to walk us back to my dorm, but Isla managed to convince him that just talking to us was more than enough. I'm glad she was able to because the alcohol is wearing down my initial burst of energy, and a wave of tiredness is starting to creep in. I close my eyes for just a second as we are walking and silently pray I don't trip over anything.

When we get to my dorm, Isla collapses onto my bed and I chuckle because it looks anything but graceful. I shut the door quietly and slip off my shoes, happy to finally be back in my sanctuary. By the time I turn on the lamp near my bed, Isla is already half asleep, her phone still in her hand.

I tiptoe over and gently take the phone from her, setting it on the nightstand. "You need water," I whisper, but she just mumbles something incoherent and rolls onto her side.

I figure she's good for right now, but water would do us both a bit of good. As I grab my ID to head to the vending machine on the main floor, I notice a white envelope on the floor near the door.

What the hell?

I bend down and pick it up, thinking it must be something about an event Crestwood is hosting. I turn the envelope over in my hands and find my name on it. Our school would be going way out of their way to personalize each envelope that I'm sure everyone in my dorm got.

Then it dawns on me. Most of the mail we get from the school ends up in our mailboxes at the campus center. So who is this from?

I slide my finger under the flap and tear it open, half expecting a glitter bomb or some ridiculous prank. Instead, there's a single sheet of paper inside, folded neatly. I pull it out and smooth it open, squinting to read the words on the page due the activities I just partook in.

Selene,

I'm sorry.

I know that doesn't make up for anything, but I needed to say it. I messed up big time when I treated you like you were nothing. You have every right to be mad at me, to hate me even. But I hope you can give me a chance to apologize in person. Maybe a chance to make things right with you.

\- Knox

I find myself staring at the paper and then looking around my room to see if there are any video cameras set up because there's no way this is real. I make my way over to my bed and sit down on the edge, confused beyond belief. An apology from Knox? This can't be happening. I take a moment to analyze the letter and realize that he didn't apologize about the incident with Lucas. Looks like he isn't sorry about that.

"What's that?" Isla mumbles, her eyes still closed but her senses apparently sharper than I gave her credit for in her current state.

"Nothing," I say quickly, folding the paper and slipping it back into the envelope. "We can talk about it in the morning."

That's when I remember I received a notification while I was at the party that I ignored. I snatch my phone and find a text from Knox.

> Knox: Hey, I slid something under your door and just want to make sure you receive it.

Nope. It's then I decide that I'm way too drunk for this and that I'll deal with everything tomorrow.

Maybe.

11

KNOX

I feel the tension building in my chest from the second I step onto the ice. No matter how hard I try to push it out, the crowd's roar rattles my skull. Even though the scoreboard says we're tied with the Windhaven Saints 2-2 with just minutes left in the third period, I know my frustration has nothing to do with the score. It's got everything to do with Selene, even if I refuse to admit it out loud.

I haven't heard from her since I saw her at that environmental science presentation, which is surprising since I left that apology letter for her. Not to mention that I texted her to make sure she received it.

Yet I haven't heard a word. Not that I'm owed anything, but that doesn't soothe the irritation I'm feeling.

But none of that matters right now because I have a game to win.

One of the Saints' forwards takes a slapshot from the blue line, and I'm relieved when I see it ricochet off Blaise's shin guard instead of whizzing into the net. Although his demeanor is usually on the quieter end, I know Blaise is tough as nails. He skates it off like it's nothing, but I can see from his wince that it stung like hell. Blaise stays in position near the crease, ready to block another shot or clear the puck if needed.

The puck bounces into the corner and I'm on it in a flash, digging it out from the boards with a backhanded swipe. The Saints' center is right on top of me, jabbing at my ribs with the blade of his stick, but I shrug him off and wheel around our net, building speed as I go. Blaise has already recovered and is supporting from the right side, while Wilder keeps an eye on the play, directing traffic with shouts and sharp glances.

"Knox!" someone yells—I think it's Asher—but I don't look up to see. My eyes are locked forward, my focus razor sharp. I'm in the zone now, every muscle and nerve ending in my body synced up.

I thread a pass through two Saints sticks to Levi, who drives through the middle lane, cutting through the neutral zone with precision. He gives it right back to me as I cross center ice. The crowd is on its feet now, the roar rising to a fever pitch, but it's all background noise to me. White static. My mind is finally a quiet void where only the game exists.

We enter the offensive zone three-on-two—me, Levi,

and Asher—with the Saints defenders backpedaling furiously. I make a move left, then cut hard to my right, slicing through with ease. One of the defenders takes a desperate swipe at the puck, but I sidestep it with a tight, controlled pirouette.

For a split second, time slows. I see their goalie square up, his eyes laser-focused on me. I see Asher peel off to the left side of the net, his stick cocked and ready. I see Levi trailing just enough to clean up any rebounds or chaos we can create.

I fake a wrist shot high, the goalie biting hard and rising to meet it. At the last possible moment, I flick my wrists and dish the puck softly to Asher, who buries it.

The red light behind the net flares up and the sound of the horn mixes with the crowd's explosion. Asher is instantly swarmed by our guys, but I hang back a moment, taking it all in. We've broken the tie, and with so little time left on the clock, it feels like the game winner.

Maybe this will pull me out of my funk.

I glide over to join the celebration, tapping Asher's helmet with my stick. He's grinning ear to ear, and why shouldn't he be? That was a beauty.

As we skate back to our bench, I steal a glance at the Saints. Their coach has called a timeout, and they're huddled up. One face stands out—Beck, their new winger. He's been a menace all game and I'm ready to send his ass packing in particular.

As soon as the puck drops again, Beck charges at me,

catching me off guard with a brutal body check that slams me into the boards. Pain explodes through my shoulder and ribs as I crumble to the ice. The world tilts for a moment, adrenaline surging to mask the worst of it. My vision clears just in time to see Beck standing over me, smirking.

Rage ignites in my chest. I shove myself to my feet, my muscles fueled by pain and fury. Without thinking, I plant my gloves on Beck's chest and shove him hard. He stumbles back a step, but the look in his eyes tells me he's ready for this.

The first punch comes from him, glancing off my helmet. I don't wait for a second. My fist connects with his jaw, and then it's chaos. We're grappling, trading punches, the roar of the crowd and the shrill blast of whistles fading into the background. Out of the corner of my eye, I see other players piling in, scuffling as the refs rush to break it all up.

Beck manages to grab the front of my jersey, yanking me forward as he swings again. I duck, throwing an uppercut that clips his chin. The refs finally grab hold of us, pulling us apart as we're both breathing heavily, jerseys twisted and fists still clenched.

The crowd is deafening, half cheering, half booing. I spit out the blood pooling in my mouth and glare at Beck as the ref ushers me toward the penalty box. He's smirking again, his lip split but his expression smug. My chest heaves as I drop onto the bench in the penalty box, adrenaline still coursing through me, but the pain in my shoulder is harder to ignore now.

The refs confer briefly before signaling major penalties but not ejecting either of us, a surprising leniency given the strict rules. Coach Johnson throws his hands up in frustration but doesn't argue. "Blaise, you're double shifting now! Levi, you're covering Knox's spot until further notice," he barks, already strategizing to keep the team on track.

I shift uncomfortably in the box, the ache in my shoulder a constant reminder of Beck's cheap shot. I rotate it gingerly, testing the range of motion. It's stiff and painful, but I know I can play through it when my penalty is up. I glance at the ice, watching Wilder make a sprawling save, his glove snapping up just in time to rob the Saints of a tying goal. The crowd erupts, and I grip the edge of the boards, leaning forward.

I fucking love this team.

Beck sits opposite me, glaring from his own penalty box. His laughter from earlier has twisted into a glare. The game might be ending shortly, but I know this fight isn't over. Not by a long shot.

The final whistle blows, and we hold on for the win. My team pours onto the ice in celebration, their sticks raised high as the crowd erupts into cheers. I step out of the box slowly, dragging my stick along the boards, the sound of it faint against the noise of the arena. My shoulder throbs with each slide, but I refuse to not celebrate this.

Beck doesn't move immediately, staying in his box for a beat longer. His glare burns into my back as I finally turn away, leaving everything behind on the ice.

"Good game, boys!" I hear Coach yell and his eyes stare at me for a moment as if to say that we'll need to have another talk later.

That's fine. I'm willing to deal with it when the time comes.

As I make my way through the tunnel, the ache in my shoulder grows, but I push forward. I pause for a moment near the locker room, leaning against the wall to catch my breath. The physical pain is manageable, but the emotional turmoil feels insurmountable. I press a hand to my shoulder, testing the range of motion, and wince at the sharp jolt it sends through me. I shake my head, trying to focus, but thoughts about fighting Beck out back and fighting for Selene's attention are all that's up there.

I push off the wall and continue walking with a bigger sense of determination. With every step, I try to convince myself that the fight with Beck was worth it. That standing up for myself, for the team, was the right thing to do. But doubt begins to grow with in me. What if I've just made things worse? Not to mention I know Coach Johnson is already questioning my judgment.

I reach the locker room, my hand still pressed to my shoulder and let out the biggest sigh.

Because I know that none of this is over.

12

SELENE

I take a deep breath as I try to push away the urge to run in the opposite direction. The last thing I want to do is be here, but I came here for moral support. And look what that got me.

"Stop looking like you would rather be any place but here," Isla says as she steps in front of me and gives me a look.

"But that's the truth. I would rather be *any* place but the mall right now," I throw back at her.

She cocks her head to the side, studying me like I'm a fashion misfire. "Selene, we've been to the mall before, and you've had no issues with it. What's wrong?"

"It's just... really crowded today. You know I'm not great with crowds."

Isla raises an eyebrow. "But you have no issues with

going to college parties where we are jam packed in a room like sardines."

"That's different," I protest, though I know she's right. College parties have a kind of chaotic, familiar energy that I can handle. The crowds here actually have nothing to do with why I don't want to be here.

Isla gives me a sad smile and hooks her arm through mine. "Selene, if you don't want to be here, just tell me. I can come back another time."

I meet her gaze, and for a moment, I'm tempted to tell her the real reason why I'm doing my best not to freak out, but I swallow the urge. No, I can handle this. I need to handle this.

"I'm already here," I say, forcing a smile. "You need some new clothes, and I'm here for moral support."

"Okay, but if you get too overwhelmed, we can bail. Promise."

"Promise," I say, hoping I won't have to break it.

Isla stares at me for a split second and then pulls me forward. "Fine. But you owe me a giant pretzel for this stress."

I laugh, feeling some of the tension ease from my shoulders. "Deal. A giant pretzel is a small price to pay for your expert fashion advice."

Isla grins. "Flattery will get you everywhere, my dear." She tugs me, and soon I'm following her toward this trendy boutique. "Now come on, I saw the cutest top in here last week that I think would look amazing on you."

My stomach twists at the thought of trying on clothes, but I paste on a smile and let Isla pull me inside. The store is filled with bright colors and bold patterns, racks packed with the latest styles. Isla makes a beeline for a display of flowy blouses, and I'm left trailing behind her.

"What about this one?" She holds up a blue top with delicate embroidery along the neckline. "It would pop because of your hair."

I barely glance at it before shaking my head. "Not really my style."

Isla frowns but doesn't push, moving on to another rack. I follow behind her, trying to pretend to be interested as she gives her opinion on the clothes. But with each passing minute, the knot in my stomach grows tighter.

It's not that I don't like shopping. I do, usually. But lately, every time I step into a dressing room, all I can see are the ways my body doesn't measure up. The way the fabric is tight across my stomach, the way my thighs look huge in skinny jeans.

Isla pulls out a floral sundress and holds it up to me. "This would look so cute on you! You have to try it on."

I take the dress from her, running my fingers over the soft fabric. It's beautiful, but I can already imagine how it will cling to all the wrong places. "I don't know. It's not really my style either."

She puts her hands on her hips. "Selene, what's going

on? You love sundresses. And you've vetoed everything I've suggested so far."

I sigh and do everything I can to avoid looking her in the eyes. "I'm just not feeling it today, okay? Maybe we should just go get that pretzel."

Isla's expression softens and she takes my hand, giving it a gentle squeeze. "Hey, talk to me. What's really bothering you?"

I blink back the sudden tears that spring to my eyes. I fucking hate how emotional and vulnerable I feel. "It's stupid. I just... I don't feel good about myself right now. Nothing fits right and I feel like everyone is staring at me, judging me for not being as thin as you or the other girls here."

Isla's eyes widen with surprise just before she pulls me into a tight hug. "Oh, Selene. I'm so sorry. I had no idea you were feeling this way. You are beautiful, inside and out. Your worth is not defined by your dress size or what anyone else thinks. You are strong, confident, and amazing just as you are."

I sniff, trying to keep the tears at bay. "I know; logically I know that. But sometimes it's hard to really believe it, you know? I need to get a handle on all of this again," I say, gesturing to my body.

"I do know," Isla says softly. "Body image stuff is no joke. It can mess with your head. But I'm here for you, always. And I think you're a total goddess, for the record."

Her words make me smile even as a few stubborn tears escape down my cheeks. I break our hug and then say, "Thanks and this is obviously why we are best friends."

She pulls out a tissue from her purse and hands it to me. "It's one of many reasons. I'm not sure I would have gotten through living in NYC or my PCOS diagnosis without you."

"Okay, now you're going to make me start sobbing in public. Thanks a lot."

I can see tears starting to well up in Isla's eyes now. "Look at us, getting all emotional in the middle of a store. People are going to think we're crazy."

I smile at her through my tears. "Let them. We're allowed to have a moment."

We both take a few seconds to collect ourselves, dabbing at our eyes with tissues. When we've composed ourselves, I tell her, "Okay, enough of the pity party. Let's just grab that pretzel and call it a day."

Isla pauses, but then says, "I have another idea if you're okay with it."

"What is it?"

"I think I might have a store in mind that you might feel more comfortable in if you want to check it out. If not, I'm down to go get pretzels."

She takes my hand and leads me out of the shop and after five minutes, we finally stop in front of a store I've never been in before. The window display features mannequins of all shapes and sizes, dressed in trendy but comfortable looking clothes.

"This place just opened last month," Isla explains. "They specialize in clothes for all body types. And look, they even have a sign about body positivity right in the window."

I look at the sign she's pointing to. In bold letters, it reads "Love Your Body. Every Body is Welcome Here."

Something about the message makes my throat tighten with emotion. Isla gives my hand a squeeze. "Let's go in, just to look around. No pressure, okay?"

I nod and let her pull me inside. The store has a warm, inviting atmosphere, with soft lighting and upbeat music playing. A saleswoman with the name 'Kate' written on her nametag greets us with a friendly smile.

"Hi there! Welcome in. Let me know if you need any help finding your size or trying things on."

I manage a small smile back at Kate. "Thanks, we're just browsing for now."

Isla leads me further into the store, her eyes already scanning the racks. "Ooh, look at these jeans! They have so many different fits."

She holds up a pair of dark wash skinny jeans with a high waist. "These would look amazing on you, Selene. And they go up to size 18!"

I hesitate, running my hand over the soft denim. "I don't know, Iz. Jeans and I haven't exactly been on speaking terms lately, which is why I wear the same ones I've always worn or leggings."

"Just try them on," she encourages. "No commitment required. And look, they have stretch!"

I take a deep breath and accept the jeans from her. "Okay, fine. But if they don't fit, we never speak of this again."

Isla mimes zipping her lips. "Deal. Now go. I'll grab a few tops that would look cute with them."

With the jeans and an armful of blouses and sweaters Isla picked out, I make my way to the fitting room. Kate unlocks a door for me with a reassuring smile.

"Take your time! And remember, if you need anything I'm right here, gorgeous."

Her unprompted kindness catches me off guard. "Oh, um, thank you," I stammer before ducking inside.

In the privacy of the dressing room, I strip down to my underwear and avoid looking at myself in the mirror. With a deep breath, I slip on the first pair of jeans Isla picked out. I'm surprised when they glide over my curves without resistance. Slowly, I turn to face the mirror.

The girl looking back at me looks...good. Really good. The jeans hug my hips and thighs in all the right places, smoothing and shaping rather than squeezing and pinching like I'm used to. For the first time in a long time, I actually feel sexy in a pair of jeans.

Fighting back a smile, I try on one of the tops. It's a flowy, off-the-shoulder burgundy blouse. The color is stunning against my red hair and the drape of the fabric skims over my stomach in a way that makes me look effortlessly chic rather than self-conscious about my midsection.

I can't help but do a little twirl in front of the mirror, watching the way the outfit moves with me. I feel confident, beautiful, like I could take on the world. Tears rise again at the corners of my eyes. When was the last time I felt this good about myself?

A soft knock at the door startles me out of my reverie. "Selene? How's it going in there?" Isla's voice filters through.

"I'm...I'm good, actually." My voice shakes slightly. "Really good. I think you need to see this."

I open the door and step out. Isla's hands fly to her mouth as she squeals in delight. "That outfit was made for you. Seriously, you're a total bombshell."

I can't help but grin. "You really think so? I don't know, it's been a while since I felt this good in clothes..."

"Oh this makes me so happy! I did ask Kate to grab a couple of other things for you to try on. And if I'm doing too much, please tell me."

My gaze narrows at her. "Isla, what did you do?"

At that moment, Kate appears with some more clothes, but not too many thank goodness. However, when I notice that several of them have lace, I know this is actually what Isla was referring to. "I found a few more pieces

I thought would be perfect for you and a few pieces of lingerie if you're interested."

I feel my cheeks grow red as I take in the lacy lingerie Kate is holding up. "Oh, um, I don't know about all that," I barely get out, but I manage to shoot Isla a look.

She just grins at me. "Come on, Selene. You deserve to feel sexy, inside and out. At least try a couple pieces on?"

Kate chimes in, "The material is so soft, you'll forget you're even wearing it."

My eyes dart between the two women in front of me before I give in.

"Okay, fine," I relent, taking the garments from Kate. "But if I hate them, I'm never speaking to you again!"

"Yeah, yeah whatever. If you need me, just holler. I'll be trying on my own clothes."

Back in the fitting room, I slip a matching bra and panty set in a rich plum color over my own underwear. The bra has a plunging neckline that showcases my cleavage in a way that manages to be both tasteful and sexy. The panties are a cheeky boyshort style that highlights the curve of my ass.

I take a deep breath before turning to face the mirror. The reflection staring back at me takes my breath away. The lingerie hugs my curves in all the right places, accentuating my figure rather than trying to hide it. I feel powerful just wearing this for myself. For the first time in a long time, I don't immediately zero in on my perceived flaws. Instead, I see a confident, sexy woman looking back at me. Not to mention I notice the gains I've been making at the gym as well. All of this is a reminder that I am more than just my doubts and insecurities.

I hear Kate's muffled voice from outside the fitting room. "Are you okay in there? Do you need help with anything?"

A smile plays on my lips as I call back, "I'm fine, thank you for this. I'll be out in a minute."

Taking one last look at myself in the mirror, I straighten my posture, feeling a newfound sense of confidence that is anything but fake. With a deep breath, I push open the door and allow Kate to see me.

"Wow," Kate says as she checks that the items fit properly. "Told you the lingerie would make you feel amazing."

"You're right. I'll definitely take these and maybe another set if you have them in a different color?"

Kate gives me a big smile with that announcement. "I'll see what I can find."

Once she leaves, I close and lock the dressing room door behind her and take another look at myself in the mirror. I can't help but smile at myself because, for once, my anxiety has decided to let me just be. And I'm okay with that.

13

SELENE

A big sigh leaves my lips as I walk into the library to begin my shift. Finally, a moment to breathe, to escape the never-ending whirlwind of my freaking life.

I slide behind the front desk, where a stack of returned books teeters like a miniature city skyline. Of course the staff that was here before me left this mess for me to clean up.

Typical. I grab the nearest book and scan the barcode, watching the computer screen flicker to life. This won't take me any time to get through, but I can't say that I'm not annoyed by it.

Still, the mundane task is almost a comfort. I need something brainless right now, something that doesn't require me to think too hard. Because when I think, I remember. And when I remember, it hurts.

Because all I can think about is the apology from Knox that is currently in my bag. It's been a couple of days, and I haven't bothered responding to it or his text. I'm not sure what to say, if I'm being honest, and while I enjoyed the conversations we've had, I'm still rerunning how he treated me after we had sex in my head. It's something I'm not sure I'll ever move past.

I finish scanning the last book and set it on a cart with more force than necessary. The apology letter weighs on me like an anchor, pulling my thoughts and me down constantly. Why does he even think an apology can fix things? Why do I care so much if it does?

I swear nothing matters in this chaotic, messed up world.

With another sigh, I sit down at the front desk. I dig into my bag to grab my laptop, figuring that I can find something to do that will burn time. Doing homework would be wise, but I can't even begin to get my brain in the frame of mind where anything I'm reading will make any sense, let alone be absorbed.

So streaming a couple of episodes of a sitcom it is. I put one earbud in my ear, giving me the ability to still pay attention to my surroundings in case I need to help anyone, but other than that, I'm ready to zone out.

Just as I'm about to click play, I catch sight of something that makes me stop all movement. In the far corner of the library, almost hidden behind a tall shelf of encyclopedias, sits Blaise Dalton with a pair of glasses resting on his face.

I shift myself so I can get a better look at him, and I notice all of the books spread out before him. He's hunched over, scribbling furiously onto a piece of loose-leaf in his binder. I don't think I've ever seen him here before, so this is interesting.

I take out my earbud and set it down gently, watching him for a few more seconds. Everything is warning me to leave him alone, but for some reason, I'm fascinated that he's here tonight.

A dedicated student? Who would have thought? That's rude of me to say, but what else is new?

A part of me wants to walk over and say hi, maybe tease him about being such a studious nerd. Another part of me just wants to sit back and observe, which might quickly get awkward if he finds me staring at him.

Before I can talk myself out of it, I'm already up and walking toward him. Is this the wrong move? Probably, but I seem to keep making them, so why stop now?

"Hey, Blaise," I say, keeping my voice low so as not to disturb anyone else. "I've never seen you here before."

Blaise looks up, his blue eyes magnified comically large behind his glasses. For a split second, he looks like a startled owl. Then he smiles, and it's warm enough to melt the permafrost around my mood.

His eyes widen when they land on me. They dart to the front door before they return to me. "Selene, hey," he says, taking off the glasses and rubbing his eyes. "Yeah, I usually do this stuff at home, but I wanted to get out of the house, so here I am."

"Nice glasses," I say, leaning against the bookshelf. "I didn't know you had bad eyesight."

He chuckles, a soft, easy sound. "They're just reading glasses. I'm getting old, you know."

"Right. Ancient at, what, twenty-one?"

"Twenty-two next month, thank you very much," he says as he gives me a little bow while sitting down. "Time flies when you're about to have a quarter-life crisis."

That makes me laugh. Blaise and I have chatted before when I've seen him at a couple of hockey parties, but never anything really in depth. That's probably because I was too wrapped up in Knox. Still, I always thought he was nice. Maybe even the nicest out of all of the hockey guys.

"So what class has you in a bind?" I nod toward the pile of books, which look like a mix of history and political science texts.

"It's for my poli-sci capstone," he says, running a hand through his already disheveled hair. "I'm trying to tie everything together, but it's like herding cats."

I raise an eyebrow. "A poli-sci major? I would have pegged you for something more... athletic."

He smirks. "Because I'm a dumb jock, right?"

"I didn't say that."

"You didn't have to," he says, but there's no edge to his

voice. If anything, he sounds amused. "We can have brains and brawn, you know. It's allowed."

"Touché," I say, crossing my arms. "So what's the topic?"

He hesitates for a moment, as if he's not sure whether to dive into it. As he's about to open his mouth, another voice comes out.

"There you are, man."

I turn to see Knox standing a few feet away. The sight of him sends a jolt through me—part excitement, part dread. I'm convinced everyone in the room is holding their breath.

Or maybe it's just me.

Knox's eyes lock onto mine, and for a moment, I forget where I am. Then I remember Blaise, who is now looking between Knox and me with an expression I can't quite read.

"So much for a quiet night," Blaise mutters under his breath, but loud enough that I can hear. He folds his arms across his chest and leans back in his chair as if he's about to watch a show.

"Selene," Knox says, taking a few steps closer. "Can we talk?"

Every fiber of my being is torn in different directions. Part of me wants to hear him out, to see if he can say something that will make it all better. Another part of me wants to tell him to get lost, that I'm done with his roller-coaster. And then there's the part of me that's just plain scared—scared of what he'll say, scared of what I'll feel, scared of making yet another wrong move.

"Maybe later," I say to Knox, though I'm not sure I mean it. "I'm working right now."

Knox looks around the nearly empty library and then back at me. "It doesn't seem too busy."

"Still," I say, standing a little straighter. "I need to be available."

Knox's jaw tightens, and I can see that he wants to call me out on my obvious lie. "Fine," he says, his voice low and controlled. "I'll wait."

He walks around me to grab a seat at the table Blaise is sitting at. When I turn back to Blaise, he's already put his glasses back on and is flipping through a book, though it's clear he's not reading.

"I'm going to go, but...if you need anything I'll be at the circulation desk."

I turn on my heel and walk away quickly before either of them can say another word. My mind is racing as I make my way back to where I'm supposed to be. Why is Knox here? What does he think he's going to accomplish by ambushing me like this? Heck, was all of this just by chance? And why do I still care?

I sit down and put my head in my hands, trying to block out the swirl of thoughts and emotions. I need to get myself together and fast.

I glance over at Blaise and Knox. Blaise is pretending to work, but it's obvious he's just waiting for something to happen. Knox is staring at me, his hands clasped in front of him as if he's doing the same.

I force myself to look away and take a deep breath. All I have to do is put my headphones back in my ears and ignore them both. Great idea.

I set up the episode I was preparing to watch again and put my earbud in. After taking a second to close my eyes and refocus my energy, I press play. If this doesn't take my mind off Knox, nothing will.

The show bursts to life on my screen, and for a moment, it is a welcome distraction. I zero in on the storyline, the characters, the setting, because anything is better than focusing on the mess my life currently is.

Five minutes in, I'm almost relaxed. Almost.

I sense someone come up to the desk and I look up to see Knox standing there. "What?" I say, probably louder than I need to, but that's what I get for having one earbud in.

"I just want to talk," he says, his voice softer than I expect. "Please."

I glance over at Blaise, who is still at his table, now tapping a pen against his book in a rhythm that's almost musical. He catches my eye and gives a small shrug.

I turn back to Knox. His face is pleading, but there's also that stubborn set to his jaw that I've come to know so well. He won't leave until he gets what he wants.

"Fine," I say, not making any effort to come closer to

him. "But keep your voice low because this is still a library."

For a moment, neither of us says anything. I cross my arms, more out of self-defense than defiance. Knox stuffs his hands in his pockets and winces. His hand comes up and reaches for his left shoulder as he shifts his weight from one foot to the other. Is he nervous? Never would I have thought to see the bad boy hockey player apologizing and nervous, let alone in the same week.

"Are you hurt?" I ask before I can stop myself.

"Hockey injury. I'm fine. But Selene," he begins, and I brace myself. "I'm really sorry about everything. About how I handled things after... you know. I shouldn't have been a dick."

"I know," I say finally. "You already apologized."

"Yeah in the letter," he says, leaning in just a bit. "I guess that means you read it?"

I stay quiet for a bit, letting the silence stretch just long enough to make Knox uncomfortable. "Yes, I read it." I uncross my arms and lean on the desk, closer to him. "It was very... heartfelt."

Knox's eyes search mine, looking for something—maybe forgiveness, maybe understanding. "I meant every word."

"I know you did," I say. "But words are easy, Knox. Actions are harder. And what you did hurt. I knew the score. You told me you weren't interested in anything more than a casual hookup and you still treated me like shit."

Knox looks down, and for a moment, I think he might actually walk away. Part of me hopes he does, because this is hard—harder than I thought it would be. But then he looks up, and there's a determination in his eyes that makes my heart do that stupid flutter thing it's been doing since the first time we met.

"You're right," he says. "I was wrong and I'm sorry. I'm not going to lie; I got a little scared."

That admission takes me by surprise. Knox Sanchez scared? Of what?

"Scared?" I echo, raising an eyebrow.

"Yeah," he says, running a hand through his hair. "Look, I'm not good at this stuff. At feelings. At... relationships."

"We weren't in a relationship," I say, though hearing him even imply it sends a confusing rush through me.

"I know," he says, quickly. "That's what I'm trying to say. We weren't in a relationship, but it started to feel like something more. Between the text messages we were sending and then the fun we had...that freaked me out. So I pushed you away because it was easier than dealing with... whatever this is."

I process his words slowly. He's opening up in a way that I never expected him to, and it's throwing me off balance.

"So you pushed me away to protect yourself?" I ask. "That makes it all better then."

"No," he says, shaking his head. "It doesn't make it better. I'm just trying to explain why I acted the way I did. It doesn't excuse it, but that's what happened."

I study his face, trying to figure out if he is being sincere or feeding me a line. This is the most honest I've ever seen him, and it's weird in a way. I want to believe him.

"Okay," I say slowly. "You've explained. Now what?"

Knox shifts again, and I can see he's weighing his next words carefully. "Now... now I want to make it right. To make amends."

"Make amends?" I almost laugh, but there's no humor in it. "How do you plan to do that?"

He hesitates, and for a moment, I think he might actually be at a loss. Then he takes a deep breath and says, "Let's hang out. Like go grab lunch or something."

Wait, what? My mind reels. This is not what I expected him to say. Is this his way of making amends, or is it something more? Is he just trying to get over his guilt, or does he actually...

I don't let myself finish that thought. It's too dangerous.

"And if I say no?" I ask, testing him.

"Then I'll respect that," he says without missing a beat. "But I'll still hope you'll say yes."

I look over at Blaise again. He's abandoned his book

entirely and is now just watching us openly. When he sees me looking, he doesn't even try to hide his curiosity.

"I'll think about it," I say, turning back to Knox.

A flicker of relief crosses his face, but he quickly masks it with a nod. "That's all I can ask. And now I'll let you get back to work."

He starts to turn away, but I stop him with a soft, "Knox."

He turns back around with an eyebrow raised.

"Thank you," I say. "For explaining. It does help."

He gives me a small, almost tentative smile. "I'm glad. See you around, Selene."

As he walks back to where Blaise is, I sink back into my chair, exhausted by the emotional rollercoaster of the last ten minutes. My mind is a whirlpool of conflicting thoughts and feelings. I look at my laptop and I'm convinced my life would make an excellent storyline on the show that is still playing on the screen. With a sigh, I close the lid and take out my earbud. There's no way I'll be able to focus on anything now.

The rest of my shift drags on because I'm hyperaware of Knox. With seven minutes left in my shift, I start to pack up my things. The library is almost completely empty now. and I start the lockup procedures. I take one last look at Knox's table. Blaise is gone, but Knox remains, flipping through a textbook with the kind of disinterest you'd expect from someone sentenced to read.

I walk over to the loudspeaker to announce, "Last call

for anyone who wants to check out books. The library will be closing in five minutes." The intercom crackles as I set it back in its cradle. Knox doesn't even flinch, just continues to turn pages like he's killing time.

Strange.

I head back to the front desk and make sure everything is exactly where I left it. Then I double check that the back room is locked up tight, and once that is confirmed, I walk back to where my things are, surprised to see Knox standing there for the second time tonight.

"You're closing up alone?" he asks.

"Yeah," I say cautiously. "Why?"

"It's late," he says, and I can see him trying to play it cool. "Just thought maybe you'd want someone to walk you to your car."

"I can take care of myself," I say, though the offer is tempting. The campus isn't exactly dangerous, but walking alone at night never feels entirely safe.

"I know you can," he says, shoving his hands into his pockets. "But still."

I take a moment to study him. This whole evening has been one surprise after another, and I'm not sure how many more I can handle. "Okay," I say finally. "If you're going that way anyway."

He nods, and I gather my things and throw on my coat. Once I'm bundled up tight, we walk to the library's entrance. I double check that the doors are locked before we leave the building.

As we are walking across the street to the parking lot, Knox walks beside me. He's not too close but not distant either. I appreciate that he's not trying to force a conversation on me because at this point, I'm all talked out.

When we reach the parking lot, I fish my keys out of my bag and let them dangle from my finger. "This is me," I say, pointing to my silver sedan. "Thanks for walking with me."

"Anytime," he says, stopping a few steps away. There's an awkward silence where it feels like he wants to say something more, but he's holding back.

I unlock my car and open the door, setting my bag on the passenger seat. The cold air bites at my cheeks, and I pull my scarf tighter around my neck. I turn back to him, expecting him to have already started walking away, but he's still there, watching me.

"Get home safe, Selene," he says finally.

"I will," I reply, not sure what else to say. "You too."

Knox gives me a small wave, but stays until I get into my car and lock the doors behind me. He starts to walk away as I pull out of the parking lot, and I notice he's walking to the only vehicle left in the lot. And on my drive back to my dorm room, I'm left wondering what are the chances that this evening was truly a coincidence or perfectly planned out by the man I can't get out of my head.

14

KNOX

"Think Coach is going to let you play in our next game?"

I want to roll my eyes at Blaise to show him just how much he's annoyed me, but I refrain. I know he's talking about my shoulder and the fact that I've been out the last two games because of an injury I sustained due to one of the assholes on the Saints.

"He better. I'm over sitting on the sidelines," I say as I check my phone to see the time. My sister should be here in a few minutes.

I take a swig from my water bottle and glance at Blaise, who is now busy flipping through the channels. He finally settles on a rerun of one of last week's NHL games. After watching two of the players slam into the boards, my shoulder aches in sympathy.

Blaise looks over at me, a hint of concern hidden

behind his generally carefree expression. "You sure you're ready, man? I mean, we don't want you coming back before you're ready because we need you in top form."

I shrug with my good shoulder. "I'll be fine."

The doorbell rings, and I feel a wave of relief. Not that I don't appreciate Blaise's concern, but I don't want to talk about it anymore. I get up and open the door to see my sister, Willow, standing there.

"Hey," Willow says and gives me a small smile. She steps inside and I close the door behind her.

Blaise stands there with a wide grin on his face. "Willow, good to see you again."

It's then that I remember that they briefly met once, maybe a year ago, when she stopped by the room Blaise and I shared on campus to drop something off. I wasn't there, so he grabbed it for me.

She removes her knit cap, shaking out a cascade of dark hair, and gives Blaise a once-over. "Yeah, you too," she says, but I can see that she really wants to say, 'And why are you here?'

"We were just talking about my shoulder," I tell Willow, hoping to shift her focus from Blaise. "Blaise thinks I should sit out longer."

"What happened?" She tilts her head as her eyes shift between my shoulders.

Oh. I forgot I didn't tell her. "I got injured a couple of games ago because of some cheap shot by the other team. I'm fine."

"Well, I think you should listen to your body," Willow says, looking at me intently. "You only get one shoulder."

"I mean, technically I have two," I add.

She rolls her eyes at me, but she's right, of course. And that's not something I'm going to admit in front of them.

Blaise chuckles, probably the only one in the room feeling comfortable at this point. "He's got a point. Balance is key in our line of work." He winks at Willow, who remains stoic.

I can almost see the tension lines forming around Willow's mouth. She's never liked jocks, not since high school when she dated a football player who broke her heart and then laughed about it with his buddies. Let's just say he quickly learned his lesson.

I clear my throat, trying to stop the awkwardness that is quickly growing. "Blaise, don't you have class or something to study for?"

He raises an eyebrow, knowing a dismissal when he hears one, but shrugs it off. "Yeah, I should get going." He picks up his backpack and slings it over his shoulder. "Knox, take care of that shoulder and I'll see you later. And Willow," he pauses, giving her a genuine smile, "nice seeing you."

As soon as the door closes behind him, Willow turns to me. "Does he always hang around this much?"

"He's my teammate and he lives here," I say, as if that explains everything.

"I guess that's true. Anyway, are you ready to head out?"

"Yeah, and I'll drive."

"Are you sure you can drive with that shoulder injury?"

I sigh. "I'm fine, Wills," I say as I grab my coat from the back of the couch and slide it on carefully. Willow eyes me, probably noting how gingerly I treat my injured side. She doesn't say anything else though.

As we step outside, Willow puts her cap back on, and I notice how tired she looks. Her eyes have the faintest of shadows beneath them, like bruises that are just starting to form.

We reach my sedan, and I manage to open the driver's side door without too much struggle. Willow slides into the passenger seat and rubs her hands together to warm them up.

I start the engine, and it roars to life with a familiar growl. Turning on the heater, I glance over at Willow. "You doing okay?"

She shrugs. "Just a lot going on with school right now."

I know she's lying, or at least not telling the full truth. Willow has always been able to juggle schoolwork like a pro, even when she was taking twice the course load of a normal student. Something else is eating at her, but I don't push. If there's one thing I've learned about my sister, it's that she'll talk when she's ready.

The drive to downtown is short and thankfully not painful. We park near the new restaurant I suggested we try out. It's called Bean & Leaf, and one of its highlights is that its interior is all reclaimed wood. The warm, rustic ambiance reminds me a bit of Brewed Beginnings yet it's still different. And thankfully it's warmer in here than it is outside. A hostess greets us and seats us immediately, handing us menus that are more like wooden tablets. The place is semi-packed, the kind of busy that makes you think a restaurant must be doing something right.

Willow and I take off our coats, and I notice she's wearing one of the flannels Dad gave her for Christmas last year. It's too big on her, but it looks comfortable.

I glance at the menu and see a list of artisan sand-wiches and salads, along with a variety of teas and specialty coffees. "This place looks legit," I say. "What are you thinking?"

Willow scans the menu with the intensity of someone studying for an exam. "Maybe the avocado and brie pani-ni...and a chai latte."

"I'm going for the roast beef melt," I say, setting my menu down. "And probably just water."

A server comes by to take our order, and we settle back into our chairs. There's a moment of silence where we just watch the activity around us, but soon we turn our atten-tion back to each other.

"So, how's Dad?" I ask, breaking the silence. "I haven't talked to him in a bit." I probably should call him instead of waiting on an update from Willow and Mom, but here we are.

Willow leans back in her chair, crossing her arms loosely. "He's good. Busy with some things at work, but you know how he thrives on that stuff." She pauses, then adds, "He's been talking about taking Mom on vacation sometime soon. He also mentioned that he misses you."

Guilt tugs at me. It's not that I don't miss my family, but between practices, games, and now this injury, I just haven't made the time. "I need to call him. Maybe this weekend."

"You should," Willow says, and for a moment I think she's going to leave it at that. "At least we'll be going home for Mamita's birthday party soon."

I nod, relieved that we've shifted to safer territory. "Yeah, that'll be fun. I can't wait for her famous tamales. You would think that because it's her birthday celebration, she wouldn't be cooking."

"But it's one of the many ways she expresses her love." Willow smiles softly, and I can see her remembering the same scenes I am: Mamita in the kitchen, humming to herself as she kneads dough, the whole house filling with the smell of slow-cooked meat and spices.

Our food arrives, and the warmth from the plates creates little pockets of steam that mix with the restaurant's cozy atmosphere. We dig in, the first bites always a test, and from Willow's expression, I can tell she's pleased. I take a bite of my sandwich; the roast beef is tender, the cheese perfectly melted. It's solid comfort food, the kind that temporarily makes everything in life seem manageable.

Willow sips her chai latte and then sets it down gently. "So, what's going on with you, really? Outside of hockey and school?"

I chew slowly, buying time. How much do I want to tell her? "Not much. It's just the season kicking my ass," I say finally. "And now this shoulder thing."

She looks at me, her green eyes—so much like Mom's—studying me as if she doesn't believe a word I'm saying. "Knox, come on. I'm your sister and I know when you're bullshitting me. You can talk to me."

I set my sandwich down and wipe my hands on a napkin. "It's just... I'm worried about the draft, Wills. Scouts are at every game now, and I feel like I'm under a magnifying glass with this injury. One bad play could screw everything up."

Her expression softens. "You've always done well under pressure. This is just another challenge."

"Yeah, but it's different now. It's my future." I run a hand through my hair, wincing as the movement pulls at my shoulder. "And if this injury takes me out for a few weeks..."

"You'll recover. It's not the end of the world."

Maybe not for her. For me, it feels like a ticking time bomb. Every game I miss is one less opportunity to impress the scouts. Every practice I sit out puts me further behind.

I look at Willow, wanting her to understand the weight of it all. But how could she? She's always been into creating things while I was the athletic one. It's all I've ever known.

"I know you think sports are ridiculous," I say slowly, "but this is everything to me."

She doesn't respond right away. Instead, she takes another sip of her latte, then looks out the window. "I don't think they're ridiculous," she says finally, turning back to me. "I just have different priorities. But that doesn't mean I don't get why it's important to you."

I want to believe her, and deep down I do. It's just that I didn't think I would be spilling out my deep, dark worries to my little sister, when it's me who has been there to help her pick up the pieces of her life when they've fallen apart.

But you haven't been around recently.

I take another bite, the sandwich now tasteless in my mouth. Willow's words linger, and I know she's right. She's always been more perceptive than I gave her credit for.

The thing is, I don't doubt that she understands. It's just easier to believe that she doesn't—because if she truly gets it, then I can't dismiss her opinions as easily.

"I'm sorry," I say, surprising myself. "I didn't mean to make it sound like you don't care."

Willow uncrosses her arms and leans forward, resting her elbows on the table. "It's okay, Knox. I know you're stressed. But remember, it's not just you who has stuff going on."

A spark of irritation flares up in me. Of course I know that. "Like what?" I ask, perhaps more sharply than intended. "What's going on with you?"

She hesitates, and in that brief pause, I realize how little I actually know about her life right now. We've always been close enough to keep up with each other, but lately it seems like we're both playing catch-up.

"Remember that internship I applied for months ago?" she says.

"I know you've been applying to internships all over, hopping between journalism and creative writing," I pause for a second. "Wait, you mentioned one with a newspaper. Did you hear back?"

She nods. "They offered it to me."

A smile appears on my face because I'm genuinely excited for her. This is huge; an internship like that could set her future career up.

"Willow, that's amazing! Why didn't you tell me sooner? We need to celebrate!"

She shrugs, but I can see the pride and also the conflict playing out on her face. "I wasn't sure how to break it to you. The internship is in New York."

"So?" I say. The summer is months away and she

deserves to get out of Crestwood if that's what she wants to do. "Asher's girlfriend, Isla, went to college in New York for years, so I'm sure she could help you plan your summer there."

"Wait, you said her name is Isla? Isla Johnson?"

"That's her. Why?"

Willow sits back in her chair with a small smile on her face. "She's in my creative writing seminar class and we recently ran into her while hiking. She was with three other girls. We exchanged numbers and I keep forgetting that I said I would follow up with her about photography."

The tune to "It's A Small World" plays in my mind, but I don't mention it. Instead, a question pops up that I can't help but ask. "Do you know who the other three girls were?"

Willow stares at me for a second before she replied. "Um, I think their names were Hailey, Jade and...shoot. Her name started with a S."

"Selene?"

Willow snaps her fingers. "That's it. How did you know?"

This time it's my turn to lean back in my chair, knowing I should have kept my mouth shut. "Lucky guess," I say, though it's anything but.

Willow narrows her eyes at me. "Knox, are you dating her? Is that what this is all about?"

"No," I say quickly, too quickly. "You know that I don't date."

"So then you're fucking her."

I shake my head at my younger sibling. "I don't want to ever hear you say that phrase again."

"Knox, I'm not a kid anymore," she says, clearly annoyed. "Just tell me what's going on. It'll be less painful than me guessing."

I sigh, knowing that if I don't tell her now, she'll just keep digging until she figures it out. "It's complicated, Wills. Yes, we slept together. I got freaked out after and iced her out. I've now apologized and offered to make amends, but I haven't heard anything back yet."

"It's taking everything in me to not tease you about how the Sanchez charm doesn't seem to be working. In fact, I'd say its backfiring on you." She chuckles and then speaks again. "But seriously, if you like her, why not just tell her?"

"I don't know if I like her," I lie. "It was supposed to just be casual."

"Casual," Willow repeats, as if testing the word on her tongue. "And where is casual getting you with this? You need to go all in."

I open my mouth to argue, but she's right again. Casual has gotten me nowhere except more confused and frustrated. I close my mouth and run a hand through my hair, thinking of Selene and the way she laughed the first night we met. It was so carefree and beautiful. I thought I could keep my distance, that I could separate the physical from the emotional. But I was wrong.

"Look," I say, trying to change the subject. "The point is that you have some awesome news. We should focus on that."

Willow studies me for a moment longer, as if deciding whether to let me off the hook. "Yes, it's great news," she says, though her tone is more subdued now. "But it's also scary. New York is huge and expensive, and what if I'm terrible at it?"

"You'll crush it," I say with the confidence she should have in herself. "Remember when you thought you couldn't handle the high school newspaper? You were editor-in-chief by your junior year."

"That was here, with people I know," she says, biting her lip. "This is different."

"Different, but not impossible. You have talent, Willow. And passion. Those are things you can't teach."

She smiles then, a real one this time. "Thanks, Knox. That means a lot." She checks her phone and then says, "We should head back soon. I still have a story I need to write."

I finish the rest of my sandwich and use a napkin to wipe my mouth. "But not before we take a photo to send to Mom."

Willow rolls her eyes but smiles. "Yes, let's do that."

Once our server has come back and handed us our

bill, I give him my credit card and ask if he can take a picture of us when he comes back. Willow and I slide out of the booth and stand near the entrance, where a large mural of Crestwood's skyline serves as a backdrop. We cross our arms so that they are slung over each other's shoulders because we can't give our mother everything she wants. However, we both decide to give genuine smiles to the camera. The server holds up her phone and counts to three; on the last count, Willow uncrosses her arms and makes a peace sign.

"Got it," the server says, handing the phone back to her. I look over and watch Willow quickly swipe to find the photo and send it to Mom with the caption, "Sibling lunch! 🤍"

"Ugh, I look terrible in that, but it'll make her happy."

"Oh be quiet. You look fine. Now let's get out of here," I say as I walk toward the door to hold it open for her.

We walk back to my car and silence fills up most of the ride back to campus. I steal a glance at Willow. She's staring out the window, lost in her own thoughts. Probably thinking about New York and the big, scary future that awaits her. She's grown up so much, yet in moments like these, I can still see the little girl who used to follow me around with a notebook, trying to interview me or write stories.

We pull up to her dorm and she hesitates before getting out. "Thanks for lunch, bro, and remember what I said about Selene."

I shake my head. "Get out of my car."

That makes her laugh as she slams the door behind her. I wait until she's swiped her ID against the card reader before driving away.

And once again, I hate to admit that she's right.

15

SELENE

I step into the main area of Crestwood's gym, happy to be back after taking a couple of days off to rest. The familiar sounds of weights clinking and treadmills humming create a rhythm that feels oddly comforting now. I never thought I would say this in a million years. Working out used to feel like a chore—a punishment, even—but now, a few weeks into my "new life," it's become something I actually look forward to doing.

The treadmill is calling my name. It's safe, predictable, my go-to when I just need to move. But today, I'm trying something different. I force myself to ignore it and walk over to grab a mat instead. I've been reading about the importance of stretching and how warm-ups and cool-downs can make a big difference. So, here I am, determined to do this right.

Hell, I should get a high five just for being here even though I forgot my headphones.

As I unroll the mat, I settle into some stretches. They're basic—nothing fancy—but even as I reach for my toes and hold a lunge, I feel a subtle sense of accomplishment. My body feels stiff but alive, like it's waking up. I try a few halfhearted yoga poses, my balance wobbly, and can't help but laugh at myself. It's not perfect, but it's something.

I let my mind wander as I stretch. Thoughts of my to-do list, random snippets of conversations from the last couple of days, and flashes of self-doubt all swirl in my head. But then I catch sight of the free weights area out of the corner of my eye. My movements slow. The people over there look so confident, like they belong in a world I've always been too afraid to step into. My gaze lingers over there, and I know it's because I'm both curious and intimidated. The thought of trying it myself feels both exhilarating and impossible.

For a moment, I sit back on the mat and watch. I shake my head, trying to brush off the feeling, but the idea stays with me. Maybe, just maybe, it's time to stop staying in my comfort zone.

I roll up the mat slowly, buying myself time. The treadmill is still there, and I could just do a quick jog, tell myself I'll tackle the weights another day. No one would blame me; it's not like I have a personal trainer breathing down my neck. This is all on me.

I take a deep breath and stuff the mat back into the rack. The free weights area is still a steady fixture in my mind. But right now I feel comfortable on the treadmill, so that's where I go. It's like my body is on autopilot, choosing the path of least resistance. I swipe my finger across the screen of my favorite machine, setting it to a walking pace, and step on.

As the belt starts to move, I let out a sigh of relief. Maybe I'm not as ready as I thought. The view from the treadmills is perfect for people-watching, and my eyes drift back to the free weights area. I'll make it there eventually. I crank up the speed on the treadmill, transitioning into a light jog. Sweat starts to bead on my forehead, and my ponytail swishes in time with my steps. Running has become a sort of meditation for me, a way to clear out the mental cobwebs. Today, though, it's just adding fuel to my anxiety.

Why am I so scared? It's just a bunch of dumbbells and benches. Maybe it's the thought of doing something wrong or looking stupid in front of people who know what they're doing. The image of me dropping a weight on my foot or fumbling through an exercise I don't understand flashes through my mind, and I wince.

My speed slows as I consider my options. There's a part of me that knows the fear is irrational, that everyone has to start somewhere. But then there's the louder part, the one that remembers every failed attempt at getting fit in the past. It's not just the free weights I'm afraid of; it's failing again.

I wipe my forehead with the back of my hand and slow to a walk. My heart is pounding, but it's not just from the running. I need a plan. Something to make the idea of venturing into uncharted territory less terrifying.

What if I just go over there and look around? No commitment, no pressure. I could see what equipment they have, maybe watch how other people do it. After all, knowledge is power, right?

I step off the treadmill, my legs slightly rubbery from the sudden stop. The logical thing would be to stretch again, to cool down properly like I'd planned. However, something else at the free weights area gets my attention.

Or should I say someone?

I'm starting to become convinced that Knox is following me around campus. First the library and now the gym? Well him being at the gym makes more sense given that he's a hockey player and probably has to do strength training and cardio related to that. However, I didn't expect to see him. Plus, I haven't answered him about his apology and going out on what I assume is a... non-date?

It's not like I'm avoiding him—I just need time to figure out what I want. At least, that's what I keep telling myself.

Knox is deep in conversation with another guy, someone even taller and bulkier than him. It takes me a second to realize it's Wilder, his teammate and roommate. They're laughing about something, and I take the moment to observe Knox in his element. There's an ease to him that I find intriguing, a confidence that's not overbearing but quietly assured. He catches me looking, and for a split second, I consider bolting. Instead, I give a small, tentative wave.

Knox's face lights up with a smile that could melt the polar ice caps. He says something to Wilder, who glances over at me and gives me a goofy smile before he walks off toward the locker rooms. My heart does this weird little flip-flop in my chest as Knox starts making his way over.

"Selene," he says, his voice cutting through all of the noise that surrounds us. "How's it going?"

I wipe my hands on my leggings, suddenly aware of how sweaty I am. "Good. Just finished a run."

He looks at the treadmill and raises an eyebrow. "Excellent. Are you thinking about coming over to the free weights?"

Shit. How does he—Oh right, he probably saw me eyeing them earlier.

"I was," I say, trying to sound nonchalant. "Just checking them out for now."

He laughs, but not in a mean way. More like he's amused by my cautiousness. "They're not as scary as they look, you know."

"Easy for you to say."

"Everyone starts somewhere," he says, shrugging. "I can show you some basics if you want."

I hesitate. It's one thing to fumble through on my own; it's another to have someone like him watching me. But having someone who knows what they're doing could make all the difference. It's a chance to learn without diving in completely blind. And if I say no, then what? Back to the treadmill for another mindless jog? Leave the gym all together?

"I don't want to interrupt your workout," I say, testing the waters.

Knox waves a hand dismissively. "I just finished my sets. Besides, helping you out sounds more fun."

Fun. I didn't know he knew what that words was. "Okay," I say, and it feels like I'm leaping off a cliff.

"Cool," he says, and there's something warm in his eyes that makes me think he really does want to help.

We walk over to the free weights area together. The closer we get, the more my stomach tightens. People are grunting and sweating, their faces scrunched up as they hit their sets. It's a far cry from the stretches and running I'm used to.

Knox picks up a light dumbbell and hands it to me. "Let's start with something easy. Ever done a bicep curl?"

I take the weight and shrug. "Once or twice."

"Stand with your feet shoulder-width apart," he says, demonstrating. "Keep your elbows close to your sides and slowly lift the weight up toward your shoulder."

I mimic his motions and notice he winces slightly. "Everything okay with your shoulder?"

"Yeah, it's much better. Thanks for asking...you have good form."

I glance at him, half expecting sarcasm, but it seems as if he's being genuine. The compliment makes me straighten up more, and I feel a tiny spark of pride. Maybe this won't be so bad.

We go through a few more exercises: shoulder presses, triceps extensions, and some variations of lunges with weights. During one of the lunges, Knox steps behind me, gently placing his hand on my lower back. "Keep your spine straight," he says, his voice low but clear. The warmth of his hand lingers, and I do my best to keep my balance without overthinking it. "Engage your core too," he adds, moving to my side to demonstrate. "This will help you stay steady."

I try to follow his instructions, adjusting my posture slightly. His presence is grounding, even as it leaves me hyperaware of every movement I make. "That's it," he says, and I can hear the smile in his voice. "You're getting it." Knox is patient, correcting my form with gentle suggestions rather than taking over. At one point, he steps closer, lightly placing his hand on my elbow to adjust the angle. "Here, just a little lower," he says, his tone calm and steady.

I'm convinced the brief touches he's giving me are about to set me off like a rocket. My brain is transported back to the way he touched my body, bringing me pleasure in ways I could never imagine. I refuse to think about what happened after that for fear of ruining this moment.

After finishing the set, I set the weights down and take a deep breath, feeling a mixture of accomplishment and exhaustion. "I'm starting to think you missed your calling as a personal trainer," I say, half teasing.

Knox chuckles. "Maybe. But I don't know if I'd have the patience for everyone." He leans back against the nearby wall, his towel slung over his shoulder. "You did great today. Seriously."

The sincerity in his voice catches me off guard. "Thanks," I say softly, glancing down as I wipe my face with a towel. "I didn't think I'd actually enjoy this."

"Told you," he says with that easy smile. "So, are you going to make it a regular thing?"

I think about it. The idea of coming here on my own still intimidates me, but now it feels a little more doable. "Maybe. We'll see."

Knox takes a step closer, and my heart starts its flip-flop routine again. "If you ever need a workout buddy, I can be around as much as my schedule allows," he says. "No pressure."

I nod, not trusting myself to speak. His proximity is doing strange things to my thoughts, muddling them in ways I'm not prepared for. Aren't I supposed to be mad at him?

"So," he continues, rubbing the back of his neck.

"Have you thought any more about... what we talked about? The apology and the—"

"Outing?" I add for him because I'm not sure how else to describe it. "Yeah, I've thought about it."

More often than I care to admit.

Knox looks at me with an intensity that makes goosebumps appear on my skin.

"I appreciate the apology, Knox. Really, I do. It means a lot that you're sorry for how things ended. But I'm not sure what us going out will accomplish."

Knox's eyes narrow slightly, as if he's trying to read something deeper in my expression. "It's not just about accomplishing something. It's about giving us a chance to... I don't know, clear the air?"

A part of me wants to believe him, to let go of the hurt and dive back into whatever confusing thing this is between us. But another part—perhaps the more sensible, self-preserving part—reminds me how deep that hurt runs.

I take a deep breath and let it out slowly, trying to expel some of the tension that's built up in my shoulders. "It's not that simple, Knox."

"I know it's not," he says quickly, almost too quickly, like he's afraid I'll walk away before he can finish. "But maybe it could be. Simple, I mean. Like, we go out, we talk, and we see where things stand."

I adjust my stance as I repeat what he said in my head. "And if things stand in the same place they are now?"

He runs a hand through his hair. "Then at least we tried."

I study Knox's face, searching for any hint of disingenuousness, but all I see is the earnestness of a guy who believes what he's saying. The problem is that I believed him once before, but my emotions got the best of me and look where that got me.

"Trying takes a lot of energy," I say, stalling. "Energy I might not have after all these workouts."

He laughs, a short burst that sounds like relief. "You'll build up your stamina."

I want to laugh with him, to let this tension dissolve in the easy banter we used to share. Instead, I just nod, still weighing my options.

"Okay," I say finally. "One outing or whatever."

His face lights up briefly before he catches himself. "Great. When are you free?"

I think about my schedule, about the safest distance I can put between now and this potential minefield of a conversation. "Next week. Maybe Monday."

"Monday works," he says. "I'll text you the details. Are you done working out for the day?"

I nod quickly. There's no way I could go back now even if I wanted to. "I am."

"Do you need a ride home?"

This time I shake my head. "I drove here right after class."

"Well how about we grab our things, and I'll walk you to your car?" he asks.

I hesitate, but finally say, "Sure, that'd be nice."

We head to the locker rooms, and I'm grateful for the break from Knox and for bringing an extra set of clothes with me. As I change into my street clothes, I replay our conversation in my head. Can we really clear the air? Is it even possible to start fresh after everything?

I take an extra moment to tie my shoes. The truth is, a part of me is terrified to let go of the anger I've held onto. It's been easier to blame him for everything than to face the fact that I might have been just as foolish because I was warned about him.

When I step out, Knox is waiting with his gym bag slung over one shoulder. He's changed into jeans and a t-shirt, looking every bit the guy I met that fateful night at a party. My heart does its traitorous flip-flop again.

"Ready?" he asks.

"Yeah," I say, though I'm not sure what I'm ready for. But here goes nothing, I guess.

16

SELENE

W hy do I have a sense of déjà vu?

Oh it's probably because the last time I was staring in the mirror, blasting music, and trying to calm my nerves, I was headed over to Knox's place and I know how that ended up.

Pleasure. And then misery.

And what's the saying about people who do the same thing but expect a different result? However, this time, we'd be in public with none of the naughty things we did behind closed doors.

But being in public increases the risk of us being seen, and I still have Tessa's warning sitting in the back of my mind. It is easy to take this "outing" the wrong way depending on who might see us and report back to her.

Or, heck, if we run into her ourselves. And that would be just my luck.

I switch off the music and find something I can medi-
tate to instead. I quickly find a guided meditation that will
hopefully soothe every nerve in my body because I swear
I can hear my own pulse in my ears right now. The soft
voice in the meditation app urges me to take deep breaths,
but my lungs feel like they're on strike. I close my eyes and
try to follow along, imagining myself in a serene forest,
but all I can see is Knox's stupidly handsome face and
think about how this "outing" is going to go.

Damnit.

The meditation isn't working. I kill the app and stare
at my phone, at the message he sent an hour ago.

Knox: Still on for this evening?

I quickly answered yes before I could talk myself out
of it.

I check my makeup one last time. My lipstick is too
bold for a "friendly chat," but wiping it off now would just
smear it across my face, and I don't have the time or the
energy to start over. Besides, this red looks great on me
and will give me the confidence I need to get through
tonight. Not to mention, I purposely chose to dress down
a bit to not give the impression that this was a date date.
My sweater, jeans, and boots look great, as do I.

And that's the story I'm sticking to.

When my phone vibrates on my desk, I nearly jump
fifteen feet in the air. I assume it's a message from Knox.

Knox: I'm downstairs. Make sure you're
dressed warmly.

He's here with five minutes to spare and thankfully, I am dressed what I assume is appropriately.

I don't bother to answer, instead choosing to hurry up and put on my coat and grab the bag I'd be using for the night. After giving myself one more look and concluding that I do actual look put together, I make sure I have everything I need before locking my dorm room behind me.

The evening breeze swipes at my hair as I walk out of my dorm, expecting to see Knox leaning against his car like he always does. But instead, I stop dead in my tracks.

He's not by a car.

He's straddling a black and white motorcycle, helmet tucked under one arm, the other casually resting on the handlebar like he's posing for some kind of magazine cover. I'm not sure if I'm annoyed or... intrigued.

He looks up as I approach, that familiar cocky grin spreading across his face. "What's the matter? Never seen a bike before?"

I blink, trying to hide the way my heart just flipped in my chest. "I just wasn't expecting... this," I say, waving a hand toward the bike. "Isn't this a bit much for an 'outing'?" I add, using my fingers to throw up air quotes.

Knox swings his leg over the seat and steps closer,

holding out the extra helmet like it's no big deal. "I thought we could have a little bit of fun."

I take the helmet hesitantly, my fingers brushing against his as I do. He doesn't let go right away.

"Ever been on one before?" he asks, tilting his head slightly, like he's trying to read my reaction.

I huff, gripping the helmet tighter. "Would it make a difference if I said no?"

His smirk deepens. "Yeah. It would." He flips the helmet around in his hands, then carefully settles it onto my head like he doesn't entirely trust me to do it right. His fingers brush along my jaw as he secures the strap under my chin.

I swallow. Fantastic. Now I have to deal with him being hot and helpful.

"There," he murmurs, stepping back. "Fits."

I roll my eyes. "What, no matching leather jacket to complete the look?"

Knox chuckles, before putting his own helmet on. He taps the side of it before reaching over to tap mine. "These have built-in comms," he says. "Mic's already on. Just talk."

My eyebrows lift. "So you did think ahead."

He grins. "Maybe. Or maybe I just like the sound of your voice."

Before I can respond—not that I have a good comeback for that—he swings onto the bike and nods for me to get on.

"All right, let's go over a couple things before you get on," he says. "Step up from the left side, and when you sit, keep your feet on the pegs. Stay close, but don't lean too much, or we'll tip."

I raise an eyebrow. "Oh, so you do care if we crash?"

"I like my bike in one piece."

I scowl, but I step up carefully, gripping his shoulder for balance as I swing my leg over the seat. Knox steadies me with a hand on my waist, not letting go until I'm settled.

Once I'm on, I hesitate, my hands hovering awkwardly before I finally give in and wrap them around his waist.

Knox snorts through the mic. "Selene, I'm not made of glass. You're gonna want to hold on tighter."

I grit my teeth, but do as he says, my arms tightening around him. The second I do, he revs the engine, the sound is like a deep growl beneath us that makes my stomach flip.

Then his voice slides into my ears. "Welcome to a very exciting evening."

And just like that, we take off. My heart pounds in time with the hum of the engine, and I can't decide if it's from the thrill of the ride or the man I'm holding onto.

It could be both. Damn, what the hell have I gotten myself into?

My thoughts come to a halt when Knox's voice crackles through the helmet mic, breaking the silence between us. "So, how have you been since I saw you at the gym?"

I adjust my grip around his waist, trying not to think about how hard and strong he feels beneath my hands. Focus.

"Busy. Classes, work, trying to keep up with everything. I assume you've been doing the same—plus hockey?"

"Yeah, I'm just happy to be playing again. Having to sit out with a shoulder injury was rough. Thankfully, it was mild."

Knox takes a smooth turn onto Main Street, the main strip in town where all the best restaurants and stores are. The streets are strung with white faerie lights, even though we still have a few weeks until the holidays really kick off. The glow reflects off the glossy black and white of the bike, making everything feel a little more surreal.

"I'm glad you're back in action," I say, meaning it.

For a second, he doesn't respond. Then his voice comes through the mic, slightly softer.

"Thanks. It means a lot."

A beat of silence, just the low rumble of the engine beneath us. Then he speaks again. "You should come to a game sometime."

Dangerous territory. Because it could be even more public than tonight depending on what we are doing and where we are going.

"We'll see," I say, deliberately noncommittal.

Knox doesn't push it. Instead, I feel his body shift slightly as he leans into the next turn. My gaze drops, catching the way his hands flex against the handlebars. Is it weird to like someone's hands? Because suddenly, I do.

In high school, I dated this guy Jason for a hot minute, and I thought he had the nicest hands in existence. Until now. Knox's hands are strong yet precise, gripping the throttle with a casual confidence that makes something in my chest tighten. Hands that could—and have—ruined me for anyone else.

I shake my head slightly, trying to dislodge that train of thought. This is exactly what got me into trouble last time—letting my mind wander to places it shouldn't go when it comes to Knox.

The bike slows as he pulls into a small parking lot tucked behind one of the buildings on Main Street. The sudden silence as he kills the engine makes everything feel sharper—the distant murmur of traffic, the faint sound of music drifting from a nearby bar.

"We're here," Knox says, resting both feet on the ground.

I blink, glancing around. The back entrances of a few different shops and food spots are visible, but nothing stands out as particularly special.

I unclip my helmet, running a hand through my hair. The time I spent making sure it looked good was probably a waste now. "Where's 'here,' exactly?"

Knox twists slightly, that familiar smirk playing at his lips. "You'll see."

He swings off the bike first, steadying it before turning back to me. "Need help?"

I roll my eyes. "I think I can handle it."

Still, he stays close as I climb off, one hand casually gripping the handlebar like he's ready to catch me if I mess up. I don't, but the way his gaze lingers for a second on me as I move sets my nerves buzzing.

I hand my helmet to him, and he locks both his and mine onto the bike.

Then, with a tilt of his head, he motions for me to follow. We end up walking down a small alleyway that opens up onto Main Street. As we turn the corner, I see a storefront that makes my heart do a weird little flutter. It's a combination bookstore and wine bar called "Prosecco & Prose." I've walked by it numerous times but have never gone in, mostly because I feared I'd never leave once I set foot inside.

"No way," I say as I stare up in amazement.

"Yes way," Knox responds.

"This place is adorable." I'm unable to hide the smile creeping onto my face.

Knox stuffs his hands into his coat pockets and shrugs. "Thought it might be your kind of place. Come on."

He opens the door for me, and a small bell tinkles as we step inside. The warmth is immediate and soothing, like stepping into a hot bath after a long day in the cold.

The interior is even more charming than I imagined, with white wooden shelves lined with books and a small bar in the corner that serves wine and cheese plates. Soft jazz music plays in the background, just loud enough to create an ambiance without overpowering conversation.

A woman in her mid-forties with dark, curly hair and glasses perched on the end of her nose greets us from behind the bar. "Welcome to Prosecco & Prose! Can I get you two a table?"

Knox looks at me, raising an eyebrow in question. When I nod, he says, "Yes, please," and the woman grabs two menus before leading us to a small table near the back of the store.

I take off my coat and drape it over the back of my chair, then sit down and look around the room like a kid in a candy store. Knox watches me, and for once, I don't mind.

"So," he says as he takes his seat and starts to remove his coat. "Is this acceptable for an outing?"

"It's perfect," I say, although every thought in my mind is shouting there's no way in hell this isn't a date. Instead, I quickly add, "I mean, it's clever. Not what I expected."

Knox leans back in his chair, a hint of a smug grin playing on his lips. "I'm glad you think so. I figured you'd enjoy a place where you can feed both your book and wine addictions."

My head jerks back slightly. "How did you even know I

loved to read? The wine part I can kind of see given the...
ya know, partying."

He points to his phone but never takes his eyes off me.
"You mentioned it in one of your text messages a while
ago. Plus, you work in the library so I assumed this
wouldn't be too big of a stretch."

Touché. "How did you even know about this place?" I
ask, genuinely curious. This doesn't strike me as the sort
of venue he would go to.

Knox shrugs, his confidence ever present. "I did some
research about places near Crestwood and found it. I used
what I thought you might be interested in."

This new information sits oddly with me. It's easier to
categorize Knox when he fits neatly into the box I've put
him in: arrogant, bad boy athlete with a one-track mind.
Every time he shows another layer, it throws me off
balance.

The woman from behind the bar returns and says,
"Can I start you with anything to drink?"

Knox looks to me, and I bite my lip, hesitating. If this
were truly just two friends hanging out, there'd be no
harm in a glass of wine. But if it's something more...

"Sangria for me," I say, breaking my internal tug-of-
war.

"Just water for now. Since I'm driving," Knox responds
a second later.

The woman nods and walks back to the bar. Knox

studies me for a moment, and I can tell he's weighing whether to say something.

"So," he finally begins, "why the hesitation?"

I fiddle with the corner of the menu, not really reading it. "Hesitation about what?"

"About tonight." He pauses, and I feel his eyes boring into me. "About spending time with me so that I can clear the air."

I look up, meeting his gaze head on. This is the moment where I could either lie and make things easier in the short term or tell the truth and potentially complicate everything.

"Knox," I start slowly, choosing my words wisely, "it's not that I don't appreciate you making an effort. It's just... last time things moved too fast and—"

"I freaked out and took it out on you," he finishes for me.

I slowly nod. "Yeah. You did."

And that's something he could never take back.

17

KNOX

This underlying tension between Selene and I has been simmering for a while, but it has now hit an all-time high. Not that I didn't expect this when I asked her to come out with me this evening in order to 'clear the air'.

"That's why I wanted to talk," I say, leaning forward. "To make things right."

Selene's eyes drift back to the menu, but I know it's because she doesn't want to look at me. "And once again, I appreciate it but—"

"But you're scared it'll happen again," I interject, trying to soften my tone. "That I'll freak out and hurt you. Selene, I get it. I really do."

She sighs, closing the menu and setting it aside. "It's not just that I'm scared, Knox," she says. "It's that I don't know if I can go through it again. The whiplash was...

hard. I know we were casual, but for that to happen was insane."

Silence follows her statement. I can almost see her calculating an escape route, weighing the cost of staying versus the cost of running now while she still has the chance. This is uncharted territory for me because, usually, I'm the one bailing before things get too real. The irony isn't lost on me.

"I was an idiot," I say, breaking the silence that had started to stretch uncomfortably long. "A complete and utter idiot. You have every right to be pissed."

"Pissed?" She snorts, a bitter twist of a smile playing at her lips. "Knox, this isn't about being angry. If I were just pissed, it would be so much simpler."

"Then what is it?" I ask, though I already know. Or at least, I think I do, but I'm not ready to voice my opinion. This is her time, her opportunity to tell me everything she's been feeling.

She doesn't answer right away, and during that time, we're served our glasses of water and her sangria. Instead, she takes a sip of water and studies our surroundings before her eyes land back on me.

"I was hurt. Part of it was your words, but...the other part of it is how I view myself."

I expected her to say something along the lines of how much I hurt her, but I wasn't expecting the rest of that sentence. "How you view yourself?"

"Yeah," she says, swirling her sangria, watching the

fruit spin in a lazy orbit. "Knox, I've heard about your type. They're... different from me."

I let the weight of her words sink in. I never thought Selene was the type to care about labels or what other people said. She always seemed so sure of herself, so confident. But now, seeing this vulnerable side of her, I realize just how deep my actions have cut.

"Selene," I start, but she holds up a hand to stop me.

"I'm not saying that to fish for compliments or reassurance," she says firmly. "I just need you to understand where I'm coming from. When you pulled away like that, it wasn't just confusing. It made me question everything. Why did you entertain these conversations with me? Or why did you want to have sex with me in the first place, if I was just some kind of... experiment for you?"

"An experiment?" The word tastes like bile in my mouth. "You think that little of me?"

"I don't know what to think," she admits. "That's the problem."

I run a hand through my hair, frustrated, but more at myself than at her. This whole thing is a mess, and it's a mess I created. How do I even begin to untangle it?

"We had something good," I say slowly, choosing each word carefully. "Something easy and fun between our text messages and conversations at parties. When it started to shift into something more, I panicked because I didn't expect it. Because I didn't expect things to feel so... intense."

She raises an eyebrow, skepticism clear on her face. "Feel so intense? Knox, you were the one who said you don't do feelings."

"I don't," I say quickly, then catch myself. "I mean, I didn't think I did. Fuck."

I pause, taking a deep breath. This is harder than I thought it would be, and every second that ticks by feels like a countdown to an explosion I can't defuse.

"Look, I'm not good at this," I confess. "At talking about what's going on in my head. But I'm trying, Selene. I'm really trying."

She takes another sip of her sangria, her eyes never leaving mine. She's waiting for something, and I hope like hell I have whatever it is she needs to hear.

"When we started talking and hanging out, I liked you. A lot more than I planned to," I continue. "But liking someone isn't the same as being with them. I thought I could keep it casual, keep it cool, but then, when we had sex... everything just rushed in all at once."

"Rushed in?" she echoes, her tone softer but still guarded.

"Yeah," I say, as I run a hand over my face. "The way you laughed at my stupid jokes, the way you looked at me when you thought I wasn't paying attention. The way you kissed me. It was all so much more than I bargained for."

She sets her glass down gently, and for a moment I think she might reach across the table, but her hands rest in her lap instead.

"So you freaked out because you started to care," she says, more as a statement than a question.

I nod slowly. "Yeah. And because caring means risking something. Means putting myself out there in a way I'm not used to. And the last time I did that, I got hurt."

"By Tessa."

I'm taken aback by her matter-of-fact statement. "How do you know about her?"

This time Selene rolls her eyes. "Long story short, she warned me about sleeping with you because she wants to get back together."

Tessa wants to get back together? And she's been talking to Selene?

"She what? That's probably why she was texting me a few weeks ago..." My voice trails off.

Selene waves me off. "I don't want to know about your conversation."

"There wasn't one. I didn't reply to her because I'm not interested."

"Fascinating," she says as she turns to look at the woman who was standing behind the bar who has now brought over a selection of cheeses, fruits, and crackers.

"Is there anything else I can get for you?"

I wonder if she can sense the tension between Selene and me. Selene looks at me, then at the bartender. "Can we have one more minute?" she asks, and the woman nods, walking away with a curious glance over her shoulder.

We sit in a silent standoff, each of us deciding what we want to eat. Once we place our orders, Selene folds her hands on the table, and the way she's looking at me, I swear she's staring through my soul.

"So," she says slowly, "you didn't reply to her because you're not interested. But if you had replied, what would you have said?"

I lean back in my chair, crossing my arms. "I would've told her exactly that. That I'm not interested, that it's over and has been over for years now."

She studies me, her eyes narrowing as if she's trying to read the fine print of a contract. "You could've just blocked her number."

"Maybe I should have," I admit. "But I didn't because... I don't know. Maybe because some part of me wanted closure? Or maybe because I'm an idiot who likes to keep his options open, even when he knows he's not going to take them."

Her expression shifts subtly, a flicker of something I can't quite place. "At least you're honest about being an idiot."

"I'm trying to be honest about everything."

For a moment, it seems like we might have reached an understanding, but that only lasts long enough for Selene to finish the cheese and fruit she was eating. But just as quickly, that thought flees my mind when she tilts her head.

"So what does all of this mean? Are you 'trying to

come clean' because you want me to be some option you're keeping open?"

"Selene, it's not like that."

"Then what is it like?" she demands. "Because from where I'm sitting, it looks a lot like you're playing the same game with me that you did with Tessa. Keeping me in some kind of holding pattern until you figure your shit out."

"I'm not playing a game," I say, more forcefully than I intend. "I'm just trying to be real with you."

"Real?" She lets out a bitter laugh. "The reality is, Knox, I don't think you even know what you want."

She's right, of course. That's the shitty part. I thought I had everything figured out: my life, my friends, the girls I hooked up with. It was all simple and straightforward. Predictable. Now, with Selene, everything is murky and complicated, and I'm floundering.

I unclench my fists and take another deep breath. "You're right," I say, the words heavy on my tongue. "I don't know what I want. But I do know that I want to figure it out. That I want to figure *us* out."

She crosses her arms as she regards me. "But there isn't an *us*. Why should I wait around while you 'figure it out'? Why not just cut your losses and leave me alone?"

"Because I think we could have something real," I say. "Something more than just easy and fun. Something worth the risk."

Selene's eyes soften, but only for a fraction of a

second. She's built a wall around herself, one that I'm all too familiar with because it's the same kind of wall I've spent years hiding behind.

"I liked you, Knox," she says, and the past tense stings more than I want to admit. "I liked you a lot and respected the fact that you wanted to keep things casual. But you hurt me. You can't just come in here and expect to say a few nice things and make it all better."

"I don't expect that," I say quickly. "I know it's not that simple. I just... I just want a chance to show you that I know what I did was wrong, and hopefully you'll give me another chance."

"I don't know, Knox," she says. "A chance is asking a lot."

"I know. But it's all I'm asking for. Just a chance."

She closes her eyes and sighs. "Fine, but I'm not giving you a chance in the way you think I am."

"I'm listening," I say cautiously.

Selene crosses her arms but keeps her hands on the table. "You said you want to figure us out. That you think we could have something real. If that's true, then you need to understand who I am and what I want."

"I'm willing to—"

"Knox," she interrupts, "this isn't about you just sitting here and nodding along. This is about you actually getting it."

"Okay. Please continue."

"Here's the thing," she continues. "I'm not looking for

some grand love affair that's going to sweep me off my feet and change my life overnight. I'm not even looking for a relationship right now. What I want is stability. Consistency. Something that I can count on, whether it's with a friend or—"

"A lover," I finish for her.

She nods. "Yeah. Someone who isn't going to freak out and disappear when things get too real or too complicated."

"I can be that person," I say without a second thought.

"You say that now," Selene replies, her voice tinged with skepticism. "But can you really? Can you be steady and constant when everything about you screams volatility?"

I pause, considering her words. The bad boy persona I've cultivated over the years has become a second skin, but underneath it, I'm just as uncertain and vulnerable as anyone else. Maybe more so.

"I can try," I say finally. "And if trying isn't enough, then I'll keep trying until it is."

"Fine. Let's see how this goes."

It feels like I won the battle, but the war is far from over. Our meals arrive along with the receipt, and for a moment, the tension is gone. Selene picks at her salad, and I cut into my steak with more force than necessary, but things feel peaceful. Hopefully, this is the start of something better between the two of us.

"How's your food?" I ask.

"It's great," she says, then takes a sip of water. "Yours?"

"Great. I didn't realize how hungry I was until the food arrived."

Silence takes over again until I can't take it anymore. "I miss when you used to send me those random recipes," I say suddenly, unable to stand the quiet any longer.

Selene looks up from her salad. "You miss them?"

"Yeah," I say, shrugging. "I never actually tried cooking any of them, but it was nice to see what you were into."

"I thought you deleted them."

"I archived them," I admit. "Figured I might need some culinary inspiration someday."

She smirks, but it's not the playful kind I'm used to. "Cooking is like therapy for me. It's consistent. Predictable. You follow a recipe, and if you do everything right, you get the result you were aiming for. Too bad it's harder to cook on campus."

"I'm sure the guys wouldn't mind if you used our kitchen. Let's be honest, none of us are Michelin star chefs."

"I'm not sure your teammates would be thrilled with me hanging around."

"Selene, come on. You're always welcome." When she doesn't respond, I continue talking to fill the silence. "So... would you say, I'm unpredictable?" I ask, smirking slightly as I cut another piece of steak.

Selene tilts her head. "I mean, yeah. You're...complicated."

"Complicated, huh?" I lean back in my chair. "Maybe I'm just full of surprises. Like...did you know I'm a biology major?"

Her eyebrows lift slightly. "Wait—you? Seriously?"

"What? Jocks can't be into science?" I ask with a smirk.

She laughs softly, the tension between us easing by degrees. "I just didn't expect that. What made you pick biology?"

I pause for a second, unsure if I want to dive into this part of myself. But something about Selene makes me want to let her in.

"My mom's a biologist by trade and became a stay at home mom when she had me. She moved here from Mexico for college, met my dad, and...well, here I am," I say with a shrug. "He took her last name, actually. Thought it was important that we carried on her family name."

Selene's eyes soften. "That's...really sweet."

"Yeah. Growing up, science was always there. Plus, it was one of the few constants I had since we moved around so much. Well, that and hockey."

Her brows furrow slightly. "Moved around?"

"Yeah. My dad was in the military. Every couple of years, it was a new base, a new city. New school, new friends... or trying to make them, anyway." I let out a low chuckle, though it doesn't quite reach my eyes. "Guess I got used to not staying in one place for too long."

Her expression shifts into something softer, more thoughtful. "I didn't know that."

"Didn't exactly put it on my profile on Crestwood's website," I say with a shrug.

She offers a small smile. "So...this whole hockey thing. Is it about finally putting down roots somewhere?"

I blink, surprised at how easily she cuts through to the truth. "Maybe. Hockey's the first thing that ever made me feel grounded. Biology's the backup plan... but hockey? That's the dream."

"And if the dream comes true?" she asks, tilting her head slightly.

"Then I get to have my cake and eat it too," I say with a grin. "Or, you know...cake and pumpkin pie. Perks of having a November birthday."

Selene blinks. "Wait—your birthday's in November?"

"Yeah, a few days before Thanksgiving," I reply as I watch her reaction carefully.

She taps her fingers lightly against her glass as she processes what I said. "That's right around the corner."

"Yup. Cake, pie, and food comas. The holy trinity of November birthdays."

Selene's smile turns mischievous. "So, should I start brainstorming gift ideas now, or are you one of those 'no presents, just vibes' people?"

I chuckle. "Let's just say I'm open to surprises."

"Good to know," she says, her gaze lingering on mine for a moment too long. She polishes off her sangria and then says, "I'm done eating and ready to go check out some books when you're ready."

I look at my plate that's completely empty and then at Selene. She's already standing, brushing invisible crumbs from her sweater. I grab the receipt and walk up to the front before she can protest. After I'm done paying for our meal, we make our way to the bookstore section of the restaurant.

Selene's eyes light up as we enter the cozy space filled with towering bookshelves. She runs a finger along the spines of various titles, her earlier tension seeming to melt away. This is her element and I'm glad to be sharing this with her.

She picks up a book and flips through the pages, then sets it back down with a sigh. "It's dangerous for me to come here, especially after having a drink. I already have a stack of unread books at home."

"Get whatever you want. It's on me."

She glances back at me, skeptical. "Why are you being so nice all of a sudden?"

"I'm always nice," I say, feigning hurt.

"Right," she says, rolling her eyes but with a hint of a smile. "Nice is the first word that comes to mind when I think of you."

She has a point. "I'm trying to turn over a new leaf," I say. "You know, be more consistent and predictable."

Selene raises an eyebrow but doesn't comment. Instead, she picks up another book, examines the cover, and puts it back. I can see her mind turning, calculating whether she should let me buy her anything or tell me to shove it.

She finally speaks. "You know, buying me things isn't going to make me forgive you faster."

"I know," I say. "But it can't hurt, right?"

She laughs, a genuine sound that momentarily warms the cold front between us. "Fine. If you're so insistent, I'll take you up on it. But remember, this doesn't mean anything."

"Noted," I say, feeling a small victory.

Selene takes her time browsing, moving from one shelf to another. I grab a basket and trail behind her, not wanting to intrude but also not wanting to be left out. She grabs a few titles, considers them, then puts them back. This cycle repeats several times until she has a small stack cradled in her arms.

"I'll take them. Put them in here."

She looks over at me as if she's just now noticing me for the first time. "When did you grab a basket?"

"A while ago. I didn't know how many books you were thinking of getting."

"Ah, okay," she says as she delicately places the stack of books into the basket. "These are just maybes. I haven't committed yet."

I glance down at the covers: a mix of fantasy, romance, and a cookbook. "Interesting selection."

"I'm a woman of varied tastes," she says, then pauses. "You know, you could pick out a book for yourself."

I shrug noncommittally. "I don't have much time to read these days. Practice, classes, and other stuff keep me pretty busy."

"Other stuff," she echoes, and I can hear the unspoken accusations in those two words.

"Yeah," I say, not rising to the bait. "But maybe I'll make time. What do you suggest? Or how about we both buy the same book, and we can read it together and talk about it or something?"

"You're serious?"

"Yeah."

Selene tilts her head, studying me like I'm an alien who just landed in her bookstore. "You mean like a book club for two?"

"Sure," I say, trying to sound casual. "Why not? It could be fun."

She gives me a big smile and says, "Okay. Let me find something we'll both enjoy."

And that's when I knew I would do anything to get her to give me that smile for as long as she'd have me.

18

SELENE

The door clicks shut behind me as I step into my dorm room. My hair is still damp from my shower, the scent of my vanilla body wash lingers in the air as I walk across the room.

Finally.

It's been a long day—too many classes, too much noise, too much time spent pretending I wasn't exhausted. But now? Now it's just me, a bed, and the book I've been dying to get lost in.

I throw my towel over the back of my desk chair just before putting on my oversized sweatshirt and leggings. I quickly climb into my bed and sigh as my body starts to relax. This is the kind of comfort I need after a day of pretending I have my life together.

I toss my wet hair up into a ponytail and then I grab the book I've been dying to read for months. This is the first evening in a long time I've had absolutely nothing to do and the thought of that makes me giddy. There are no pressing assignments, no shifts at the library, no impromptu study or group project work sessions. Just me and my bed and a whole night of uninterrupted reading. Not to mention, it's the book that Knox and are supposed to be reading as a part of our very small "book club".

Once my headphones are in and I have a playlist that contains soft, relaxing music, I find myself transported into another world. I'm so engrossed in the story that when my phone vibrates next to my thigh, I jump, nearly dropping my book in the process. I hesitate for a moment before pulling off my headphones and reaching for it.

A text from Knox greets me. Of course. I sigh, pushing my book aside, and open the message.

> Knox: Hey. You bored?

> Me: No. I'm in the middle of the book you and I are supposed to be reading. You?

> Knox: Interesting. Have you gotten to the part where the heroine arrived on the island to help locate her missing best friend?

Wow. He's actually reading the book.

> Me: Yes, I have and I'm glad you didn't just spoil a major part of the book for me.

Knox: I was pretty confident you made it
up to that point.

Me: Okay fine. What are you up to?

Knox: Made a big ass mess when I tried
to make a protein smoothie so I'm trying
to clean it up. Turns out it's not as easy
as it looks.

I bite my lip, trying not to smile as I start typing a response. Then I start, then stop, and then start again. This shouldn't be so hard. They're just texts. It's not like I'm committing to anything by answering him. Still, a part of me knows that where this path is leading down.

I put the phone down for a second, pick my book back up, then immediately set it back down. My gaze shifts to the screen, and I grab it. I type quickly, then erase it. Ugh. Why am I overthinking this so much?

He's just being friendly. I can be friendly, too. That's all this is. And with that, I manage to come up with something else to say to him.

Me: That sucks. Need some help?

The moment I hit send, I regret it. This is exactly what I've been trying to avoid. Ever since our "outing" at Prosecco and Pose, we've been falling back into old patterns. Or at least I have.

But before I can overthink it, my phone buzzes again.

Knox: Nah, I got it. Wouldn't want to
interrupt your reading time.

Me: How thoughtful of you.

Knox: I try.

There's a pause, and I can see the little three dots appear, disappear, and appear again. It looks as if I'm not the only one who is having issues figuring out what to say to the other person. I can almost picture him hesitating as he debates his next words.

Knox: But seriously, thanks for the offer.
Rain check?

Me: You're planning on making another
mess?

Knox: You never know. There might be
other messes I'd like you to help me
clean up.

I stare at his last message like I can't believe what I'm seeing. Is he... flirting with me? Nope. There's no way. I chew on my bottom lip, fingers hovering over the keyboard as I think about what I should say back. Do I flirt back? Shut it down? Ignore it altogether?

After a long moment, I find something to say.

Me: I think you're perfectly capable of
cleaning up your own messes.

There. Friendly but firm. Establishing boundaries without completely icing him out. I set my phone down, determined to get back to my book and not let myself get sucked further into this...whatever this is.

But seconds later, my phone buzzes again. I groan, grabbing it against my better judgment. I might be better off turning my phone off at this point.

> Knox: Ouch. And here I thought we had
> something special.

He ends the message with a winking emoji, letting me know that he actually meant what he said, but he wants me to think he's being chill about all of this.

> Me: In your dreams, Sanchez.

> Knox: Every night, Davis. Every night.

I roll my eyes but can't suppress the grin that appears on my face. This back-and-forth banter feels so natural, so effortless. It reminds me of how things used to be between us before everything got so complicated.

I set my phone down, still smiling to myself. As much as I hate to admit it, I've missed this, but now it's time to shift gears. I pick my book back up, determined to get lost in its pages once more. I manage to read a few sentences before my mind starts to wander as Knox's words echo in my head.

Every night, Davis. Every night.

I know he meant it as a joke, but I can't help but wonder...does he really think about me that often? The idea sends a little thrill through me, even as I try to squash it down.

I'm just getting to an exciting part of my book when my phone vibrates again. I already know who it is.

> Knox: What are you wearing?

I nearly drop my phone. He did not just ask me that. What. The. Hell?!

> Me: Excuse me??

> Knox: I meant to read! What are you reading? Damn autocorrect.

I stare at his response for a second and raise an eyebrow. Autocorrect my ass. He knew exactly what he was saying.

> Me: Just something short and lacy. You know, my typical bedtime attire.

I hit send before I can change my mind. I can't believe I just sent that. I stare at my phone, waiting for his response. The three dots appear, disappear, then reappear.

> Knox: Damn. Warn a guy before you go putting images like that in his head.

I smirk, feeling a rush of satisfaction. It's nice to know I can still keep him on his toes.

Me: You asked. 🙊

Knox: Touché. But seriously, what are you actually reading?

I pause, debating whether to tell him the truth or not. It's a romance novel, one with a particularly steamy scene I just finished. The idea of him knowing that seems like a blessing or a curse.

Me: Just some light bedtime reading. Nothing too scandalous. ☺

Knox: I don't believe that for a second, but I'll let it slide. For now.

Me: How generous of you.

Knox: I'm a giver, what can I say?

I roll my eyes, but I know that to be true in more ways than one. This is dangerous territory, and I know it, but I can't seem to make myself stop. It just feels too damn good to talk to him like this.

Me: A giver, huh? I'll believe that when I see it.

Knox: Careful what you wish for. I might just have to prove it to you. Again.

His response sends a shiver down my spine. Is it wrong that I want him to prove it? I want to see just how much of a giver he can be? I shake my head because I need to clear my thoughts. We're just friends. Barely even that.

> Me: I think I'll take my chances. Besides, don't you have a smoothie mess to clean up?

> Knox: Way to change the subject. But you're right, I should probably get on that. It'll probably eventually smell like shit if I don't.

I wrinkle my nose at the image, but a laugh escapes from my lips anyway. He clearly has a way with words.

> Me: Gross. On that lovely note, I think I'll get back to my book. Good luck with your mess.

> Knox: Thanks. Enjoy your "light bedtime reading." 😏 Goodnight.

> Me: Night.

As I settle back down into my book, I can't quite shake the warm feeling that talking to him put in my chest. After reading the same paragraph three times without absorbing a single word, I sigh and set the book aside. It's clear my focus is shot for the night. I glance at my phone because I'm tempted to grab it and text him again, but I resist the urge. Instead, I lay my head down on my pillows and stare at the ceiling.

Where is all of this even going?

I roll over and bury my face in my pillow with a groan. Why does this have to be so complicated? Why can't I just enjoy whatever this is without over analyzing everything? But I know the answer to that without having to waste an ounce of brain power on it.

Because it's Knox.

19

KNOX

The bus rumbles beneath me as I lean against the window, scrolling through my phone. The guys are loud tonight, laughing and shoving each other in the cramped seats, but my mind is somewhere else. Well, not somewhere else—with someone else. I glance up from my phone, taking in the controlled chaos of the team bus driving down the highway. It's nothing but another travel day for an away game in the life of the Crestwood Red Wolves.

My phone buzzes in my hand and I can't help but grin when I see who it's from.

> Selene: I hope you didn't forget to pack your teddy bear. I hear the Sparks are super intimidating.

I chuckle, imagining Selene's smirk as she types out her text.

> Me: You mean the one you gave me for Christmas? Never leave home without it.

I hit send and picture her rolling her eyes, the way she does when she's pretending to be annoyed but is actually amused. Since our "outing" at Prosecco & Prose last week, things are getting back to the way they were. Our text message conversations have resumed, and I think she's starting to realize that I meant every word I said.

Another buzz.

> Selene: Good. I'd hate for you to be scared and alone in your big bad hotel room.

"Yo, Sanchez!" someone yells from the back of the bus. I look up and see Wilder, who I swear hasn't shut up since we left Crestwood.

"We're hitting the pool when we get there!" he continues. "You in?"

"Maybe," I shout back, not really committing. The last thing I want is to be a buzzkill, but my head's just not in it tonight.

I turn back to my phone and think about what to say to Selene. Something flirty? Something serious? Is that pushing the line? I hate how indecisive I am when it comes to this type of thing because it's not the norm, but I'm trying to tread carefully with her this time around.

> Me: Don't worry about me. I've got
> plenty of company in Wilder.

The bus takes a sharp turn, and I brace myself against the window, eyes still glued to my phone as I wait for Selene's response. The guys are now arguing over something, but I can't tell exactly what it is. Frankly, I don't care, but I can already feel the beginnings of a headache forming.

> Selene: Wilder, huh? Should I be jealous?

I laugh out loud, earning a few curious glances from my teammates. They probably think I'm losing it because I've been quieter than usual this trip.

> Me: He wishes and that's not a joke.

I stare at the screen, wondering if I should add something more. Maybe tell her how much I'm looking forward to seeing her after we get back from this trip. Or how I think we should go back to Prosecco & Prose sometime soon. Before I can overthink it anymore, my phone vibrates in my hand again.

> Selene: Sounds like a real bromance.
> Maybe you should take him on an
> "outing" too, haha.

> Me: Nah, he's not my type. But I do
> happen to know he's a cheap date.

I don't even get a chance to lock my screen before she replies.

> Selene: Cheap dates can be fun. You'd
> know all about that, wouldn't you?

There's a tiny sting in her words, but I know she's just teasing. With anyone else, that last text might have pissed me off, but with her, it just makes me chuckle.

And think about how she might actually see me.

> Me: You make it sound like I'm some
> kind of playboy...

I hesitate before hitting send, not sure if I'm walking into a trap with this one. But if we're going to be real with each other, we have to address stuff like this, don't we? I send it and lean back, stretching my arms over the seat. My eyes drift to the blur of streetlights outside as the bus rumbles on.

My phone buzzes again with a message from her.

> Selene: Aren't you?

> Me: Used to be.

Selene: Changed your ways, have you?
That's good to know.

I stare at her last message, rolling it over in my mind. She's giving me an out—letting me claim I've changed and leaving it at that. But if she's going to believe me, really believe me, she needs to know the truth.

Me: People can change, at least I'm
trying to prove that.

The bus pulls into the hotel parking lot, and the guys erupt in a chorus of cheers. I slip my phone into my pocket and stand, stretching out the stiffness from the long ride. The headache has settled into a dull throb, and all I can think about is how good it will feel to crash in my room for a bit. The team starts filing out, and I hang back, not in any rush.

"Knox, you coming?" Wilder asks as he stands in the aisle, blocking traffic.

"Yeah, just need to grab something," I lie. He shrugs and makes his way toward the front of the bus.

I pull my phone out again, hoping for one last message from Selene. Nothing. I scroll back through our conversation, reading it over like an idiot. *Used to be. Changed your ways, have you? That's good to know. People can change.*

But nothing else from her.

I stuff my phone back in my pocket and make my way

off the bus. The guys are already unloading their gear from the storage compartments beneath the bus, joking and shoving each other. It's typical of them to act this way and I can't say I've never joined in.

"Sanchez!" Coach Johnson yells from near the front desk. "Come get your room key."

I walk over, dodging a duffel bag someone tosses across the lobby. Coach hands me a keycard and gives me a once-over. "You alright? How's the shoulder?"

"It's good, Coach," I say, rotating my arm to show I'm fine. There's still a little pain, but it's gotten better mostly on its own. I still want to beat the shit out of Beck, the Saints' player who caused this.

"Make sure you're icing it. We need you at full strength for tomorrow." He pauses, his expression softening just a bit. "And get some rest, Knox. You look beat."

"Will do," I say, though I'm already calculating how many hours of sleep I can get once my head hits the pillow.

I take the elevator up to the fourth floor, where the team has a block of rooms reserved. The hallways are lined with ugly, floral-patterned carpet, and gaudy sconce lighting. It's the kind of place that probably looked nice twenty years ago but now just comes off as dated. I find room 412 and swipe my keycard. The door clicks open, and I step into the suite. It's a decent setup with two queen beds, a small desk, and a TV.

Wilder bursts in behind me and I'm not sure why I'm

surprised. He flings his bag onto one of the beds and plops down, already scrolling through his phone. He looks up at me tilts his head and says, "Are you a zombie?"

I stop moving and stare at him. "What?"

"I mean usually you do have a stick up your ass, but it seems particularly wedged up there today."

"You know that you can just fuck all the way off, right?"

"Come off it, man," Wilder stays, sitting up and tossing his phone aside. "I'm just messing with you. But seriously, what's going on? You've been in la-la land this whole trip."

I sigh and rub my temples. The throb in my head is getting worse. "It's nothing. As I told Coach, I'm just tired. Need to rest up for our game tomorrow."

Wilder studies me for a moment, and I can see the wheels turning in his head. For all his goofing around, he's still very perceptive. He knows when something's up.

"You need to get laid."

That wasn't what I was expecting him to say, but I should have been.

"Wilder, seriously," I groan, collapsing onto the other bed. I don't want to deal with this.

"I'm just saying," he continues, undeterred. "Sex is a great stress reliever. And we're in a hotel, dude. It's practically tradition."

I prop myself up on an elbow and glare at him. "Tradition? You mean like how you hooked up with that cheerleader a while ago and her boyfriend tried to kill you?"

He grins, unfazed. "Worth it."

I flop back down and close my eyes, trying to will the headache away. Maybe Wilder's right; maybe I do need to get laid. But the only person I want to hook up with is Selene. I wonder what she's doing right now. I also wonder what is wrong with me.

Wilder must sense he's losing me because he changes tactics. "Look, all I'm saying is that you're wound tighter than usual. You used to be somewhat fun, man. What happened?"

"Nothing. Now drop it."

Wilder puts his hands up as if to show he means no harm. "Fine. What I really came up to tell you was that I checked out the pool and it looks sick. You sure you don't want to come? Might be relaxing."

I consider it for a moment. The cool water might do my shoulder some good, and who knows, maybe blowing off some steam with the guys would help clear my head. But then I think about Selene and how every spare minute I sink into this team takes away from time I could be spending with her.

"Rain check," I say, kicking off my sneakers. "I just need to lie down for a bit."

Wilder shrugs and stands, stretching like a cat. "Suit yourself. Don't die of boredom while I'm gone." He grabs a towel and swim trunks from his bag and heads for the door.

"Wilder," I call out just as he's about to leave.

He turns, one eyebrow raised. "Yeah?"

"I appreciate it," I say, not really sure what I'm thanking him for. His concern, maybe. His stupid jokes. The fact that we are sharing a room this weekend and he will have to put up with me sulking this trip.

He gives me a nod. "Don't mention it. Everything is good." With that, he slips out the door, leaving me alone in our suite.

I sit there in silence for a few minutes before my phone makes a light noise. I reach over to grab it and check the message.

> Selene: Yes, they can. And I'm interested to see how different this change will be.

Interested. That has to be a good sign, right? I start typing a response, delete it, then type something else, stare at it, and delete that too. I'm overthinking this way too much, but I don't want to screw it up.

Then an idea comes to mind.

I sit up quickly then debate with myself before making a decision. Hearing the sound of her voice would do me better than just trading text messages back and forth. My finger hovers over her name for a moment before I press down on the screen.

Now all I have to do is wait.

20

KNOX

"Hello?" The greeting sounds like a question, but I understand why. Selene is probably just as confused as I am about why I called her. Although I did think about it before I did it, it is impulsive in a way because I'm still left wondering exactly what it is I'm doing.

"Hey, picosita," is the only thing I can think of to say. I'm definitely not prepared to talk to her, yet I jumped off that cliff with a flying leap.

"This is a pleasant surprise. Why'd you call?"

Good question, I think. I know it's because I wanted to hear her voice, but I don't think she's ready to hear that.

"I just wanted to—" I start, then pause. "I thought it might be easier to talk on the phone." That reasoning sounds lame to my ears.

"But talk about what?" Selene asks. I can almost see

the way she's tilting her head, a half-smile playing on her lips.

"The book we're joint reading together? Sports? The weather?" Each suggestion I make sounds worse than the last.

Selene doesn't say a word at first but then she laughs, a bright and infectious sound that makes me grip the phone tighter.

"Knox, that might be the dorkiest thing I've ever heard," she says with a small giggle. Add a point to the tally for me. "But let's talk. What are you up to?"

"Nothing really. Just hanging in my hotel room by myself."

"So, what's a big, strong hockey player like you doing all alone in his room on a Thursday night?" Selene teases, her voice low and playful. "Don't you have hordes of girls beating down your door?"

"You think I'm big?"

"Of course that's the first thing you pick up on."

I snort, shaking my head even though she can't see me. "I'm just going to keep that in mind." I wait a beat before I continue. "I gave all the ladies a night off. Figured I'd grace you with my presence instead."

"Wow, I'm honored," she drawls. "And here I thought you only called me when you were bored or desperate."

I chuckle, even though her words sting a little because they're not entirely inaccurate. Still, I appreciate the banter. It's easier than diving into the real reason I called, which I'm not ready to admit to.

"Come on, picosita," I say, trying to regain some ground. "You know I value our... whatever this is."

"Friendship?" she offers, and for some reason, the way she says it makes me think she's testing the word out, seeing if it fits.

"Yeah, friendship," I agree, though my chest tightens. "So, have you finished the last chapter yet?"

Selene sighs dramatically. "Of course I have. Unlike some people, I take our joint reading very seriously."

"I'm just savoring it," I lie. The truth is, I've been swamped with training and games, and when I do have a moment to breathe, my mind's been elsewhere. Mainly on Selene and how this thing between us is evolving. It's freaking me out more than I'm willing to admit.

"Savoring," she repeats, clearly skeptical. "Well, it's not like Tolstoy. You could finish it in an hour if you really tried."

"I'll get there. Maybe tonight before bed," I promise. "So what did you think of the twist?"

She launches into a passionate analysis, her voice animated and full of life. I let her words wash over me, half listening because what really fascinates me is how much she cares about this and the sound of her voice. It's one of the things I've come to admire about her, even if it sometimes intimidates me. As she dissects the plot and character motivations, I find myself smiling. This is why I called, I realize. Not just to hear her voice, but to feel connected to her in this way, to share something more than just text messages, which can feel impersonal.

"...but I won't spoil it for you," Selene finishes. "You better catch up soon."

"I will," I say. "I want to know what happens next."

"Do you?" she asks. The tone of her voice makes me think she's talking about more than just the book.

"Yeah," I say slowly. "I do."

There's a pause, and in the silence I can almost hear the gears in her mind turning.

"Well then," she finally says, her voice gentler now, "you'd better read fast."

"I will," I repeat, this time with more conviction. "Promise."

"So, are you ready for the game tomorrow?"

"I hope so. Are you going to watch? My invitation for you to come to one of my games still stands."

"Maybe I'll watch. I do have a bunch of homework to catch up on," she admits.

"I get it."

"Wait. Is Knox pouting? I didn't know it meant so much to you for me to watch or attend."

I didn't either. Until now.

"I'm just saying," I add, "it'd be cool to have a friend cheering me on."

"Ah, a friend," Selene repeats. I swear I can hear her

smirking through the phone. "Well, friend, I'll see what I can do."

Having her admit to being friends is a step up from where we were, but does this friendzone this whole situation? I'm not sure.

"So what are you up to?" I ask quickly before the conversation potentially comes to an end before I'm ready.

"Nothing really. I just got done taking a shower. Then I was doom scrolling and texting you."

That explains the gap between her texts. I don't even try to stop the image of her wrapped in a towel, water dripping down her body. Damn, I wish she was here right now. I'd be annoyed that the fabric is covering the parts of her that I want to see the most. I can almost feel the heat radiating from her body, smell the faint scent of her fruity shampoo. My hands itch to pull the towel away so that I can run my fingers over all of her curves.

In my mind, she steps closer, her breath warm against my chest as she looks up at me with those big, expressive eyes. I snatch the towel from her grasp, and I—

Fuck, why am I torturing myself like this?

"Knox? You still there?" Selene's voice pulls me back to reality, and I shake my head to clear the vivid daydream.

"Yeah, sorry. Just... thinking."

"About what?" she asks.

"About how nice it would be to have you here," I say before I can stop myself. The silence that follows is deafening, and I immediately regret the confession.

"Here?" she finally says, her voice smaller now. "In your hotel room?"

"Yeah. To hang out and do other things." Why can't I just say it?

"Like what?"

"You're really going to make me spell it out for you?"

That causes her to chuckle, but this one is low and breathy. "Yes, I am."

This conversation is shifting hard and fast into dangerous territory, but I can't seem to stop myself. It's like we're on a runaway train, speeding out of control. The smart thing would be to pull the emergency brake, to steer us back to safer ground since this chapter is so new for us, but a bigger part of me doesn't want to.

"If you were here, I'd want to kiss you," I say, my voice rough. "Everywhere. I'd want to taste your skin, feel your body against mine."

Selene inhales sharply. "Knox..."

"I'd lay you down on the bed," I continue, emboldened by her response. "Take my time exploring every inch of you. Spend hours making up for our first time together. Fuck the hockey game."

"If only I could teleport, I'd be there in a heartbeat, letting you do all those delicious things to me."

I groan, my free hand making its way toward my sweatpants. "Don't tease me like that, Selene. It's not fair."

"Who says I'm teasing?" she challenges. "Maybe I'm

touching myself right now, pretending it's your hands on me."

Fuck. The mental image is so vivid that I'm instantly rock hard. I can picture her sprawled out on her bed, one hand between her thighs as the other holding the phone to her ear. The thought of her getting herself off to the sound of my voice is almost too much to handle.

"Are you?" I ask hoarsely. "Touching yourself?"

There's a pause, and then, "Yes. Wishing it was you."

A strangled noise escapes my throat. "Fuck, Selene. What are you doing to me?"

"Exactly what you're doing to me," she whispers. "Making me so horny I can barely stand it."

I manage to release a shaky breath. "I want you so bad right now. You have no idea."

A soft moan drifts through the phone. "I think I have a pretty good idea," Selene says. "Because I want you just as much."

I want to question how we got to this point, but that would be foolish. My hand slips beneath the waistband of my sweatpants, fingers curling around my dick. I give myself a slow stroke, imagining it's her touch instead of mine. "Tell me what you're doing," I demand. "I want to hear every detail."

"I'm running my fingers over my...clit," she reveals, a small gasp punctuating her words. "Circling and rubbing, pretending it's your tongue."

"Fuck yes," I groan, pumping my hand faster. "I'd

devour you, lick and suck until you forget your name. The only thing you can do is beg me for more."

"I'm so close already," Selene whimpers. "Just from thinking about your mouth on me."

"I bet you taste amazing," I growl, my grip tightening as I imagine burying my face between her thighs. "I'd stay down there for hours, making you come over and over until you can't take it anymore."

"Please, Knox," she begs breathlessly. "I need you."

My hips jerk at her words, thrusting into my fist. "Just imagine I'm there with you. Pinning you down and driving into you deep and hard."

"Yes, just like that," Selene moans. "Don't stop. I'm going to...I'm..."

"That's it, come for me," I command roughly. "Let me hear you."

A sharp cry pierces the phone as Selene falls off the edge with my name on her lips. The only sound I can hear is the harshness of her breath as she tries to catch it.

"That was—"

"Amazing," I finish for her. "I don't mean to be an asshole, but I need to go because I have something I need to take care of."

"Wait, what? Do you...Oh."

I let out a quick laugh. "Yeah, oh. I'm going to take a nice cold shower, but I'll text you when I'm done, picosita. Deal?"

"Deal."

21

SELENE

I plop down onto Hailey and Jade's couch, sinking into the pile of plush pillows. Hailey walks into the room, and I immediately jump back up again. "Are you sure you don't need any help with the snacks?"

She waves me off with a grin. "Nah, I've got it covered. You just relax and get ready for the game." She disappears into the kitchen, leaving me to settle back onto the couch.

Jade emerges from her room, arms laden with Red Wolves merchandise. "I found the perfect gear for us to wear." She softly tosses a t-shirt at me.

"You have a lot of Red Wolves gear."

Jade snorts. "Wilder keeps finding a way to give me more shit. Don't ask me why because I don't know either."

I hold up the t-shirt, a white shirt with a dark red wolf logo. "Pretty sure this counts as a bribe at this point."

Jade shrugs, setting the rest of the gear on the coffee

table. "If it is, it's the lamest bribe ever. It's not like I need seven different foam fingers." She picks one up and waggles it in my direction with mock enthusiasm. "Go team!"

I laugh and slip the t-shirt over my head. It's a size too big, but the soft cotton feels comforting. "So you're not a fan?"

"I support them," Jade says diplomatically, sitting down next to me. "But I'm not about to paint my face and scream at the TV or anything."

"Yet," Hailey calls from the kitchen, and I can hear the smirk in her voice. "I think Wilder is determined to turn her into the biggest Red Wolves fan there is."

"Are you dating him?" I can't help but ask.

Jade's eyes widen for a second, before she relaxes. "Dating him? Who Wilder? No. Nooooo."

I raise an eyebrow at Jade's exaggerated denial. "You sure? I mean, he is pretty cute. And all this free merch..."

Jade crosses her arms, leaning back into the couch with a huff. "We're just best friends, girl." She gives me a pointed look, then softens. "Not that it would be a bad thing if we were, you know. He's a good guy. Well, for the most part."

"But?" I prod gently.

Jade shrugs one shoulder. "But nothing. It's just... complicated when feelings get involved. Easier to keep things simple."

I nod, understanding more than she knows. My own

situation with Knox is anything but simple, especially with us having phone sex last night.

Hailey returns from the kitchen carrying a tray loaded with chips, dip, and various finger foods. "Alright, feast your eyes on this spread." She sets it down on the coffee table and takes a step back, hands on her hips, as if admiring her own handiwork.

Jade wastes no time digging in, and I follow suit, though more cautiously. "This looks amazing, Hails."

"Thanks," she says, sitting down next to Jade. "So, are you excited for the game?"

I hesitate. "Yeah, totally," I say. "Not really. Isla is way more into this type of thing than I am. And it's too bad she's at the game taking photos instead of here with us now." Not to mention that her father is also the coach of the Red Wolves.

"She'll have amazing shots, I'm sure," Hailey says with a shrug. "And don't worry, Selene. We'll ease you into it. Watching with friends is way more fun than doing it alone. And I'm saying that from experience because I wasn't into this until Levi and I started dating."

"That's true. In fact, she didn't like him just because of his celebrity status on campus," Jade chimes in.

Hailey rolls her eyes, and I chuckle. I appreciate their optimism. It's not that I dislike sports; it's just that I don't have the same passion for them. Well, I've never tried so maybe there will be something there.

I settle back into the couch cushions as Hailey flips on

the TV, navigating to the sports channel broadcasting the game. The pre-game commentary drones on in the background as we chat and munch on snacks.

"So, Selene," Jade says. "What's going on with you and Knox?"

I nearly choke on a tortilla chip. "What? Nothing. Why would you think there's something going on?"

Jade and Hailey exchange a knowing look. "Please," Jade says. "The tension between you two is thicker than Hailey's seven-layer dip."

"Is that rude? That sounds rude," Hailey says. "She's not wrong though, Selene. You've never wanted to watch hockey with us before and with what Levi and Asher are saying about Knox..."

I feel my cheeks heat up. "It's... complicated," I mumble, echoing Jade's earlier words about Wilder. "Wait a minute. Did Knox say something about me?"

Hailey and Jade exchange high-fives, and I realize I've been had. This was obviously a test, and I failed.

"Ah, so there is something to tell! Levi didn't give me details, but he said Knox has been acting 'off' lately. More distracted, more quiet than he normally is in practice, which says a lot apparently. And your name came up."

My heart skips a beat. Knox has been thinking about me? Talking about me to his teammates? I try to play it cool. "That could mean anything," I say with a wave of my hand.

Jade snorts. "Mmhmm. Sure, and I'm Beyoncé. Come on, spill the tea! What's the deal with you two?"

I sigh, fiddling with the hem of the Red Wolves t-shirt. "Honestly, I don't even know. We've been trying to repair things after everything went sideways between us. Things were going great. Well until last night..." I trail off, running a hand through my hair.

Hailey and Jade lean stare at me with wide eyes. "Last night?" Hailey prompts.

I take a deep breath. "We kind of... had phone sex?"

"What?!" Jade shrieks, nearly knocking over the bowl of chips. "How do you 'kind of' have phone sex?"

I bury my face in my hands, feeling the heat of my blush. "Okay, fine, we definitely had phone sex. It just sort of... happened."

Jade rests a hand on my knee. "And how do you feel about it?"

I peek out from between my fingers. "Confused mostly. I mean, it was amazing. Like, mind-blowingly hot. But now I don't know what it means. For us, for our friendship, situationship, or whatever this is."

Jade nods. "The dreaded 'what are we' question. I've been there."

"With Wilder?" I ask, hoping to deflect some of the attention.

Jade narrows her eyes at me. "Nice try, but we're not talking about me right now. This is about you and Knox."

I groan, leaning back against the couch. "I don't know

what to do. I don't want to make things weird, but I also can't stop thinking about him. And now, knowing that he's been thinking about me too..."

"All you can do is talk to him, Selene. Figure out where you both stand. It's clear there's something between you two, but you'll never know what it could be if you don't communicate," Hailey adds on.

I nod slowly, knowing she's right. "Yeah, I guess so. But also, I don't want to even go down that road."

The conversation is interrupted by the roar of the crowd on the TV as the game begins. I'm grateful for the distraction, not quite ready to dive deeper into my feelings for Knox.

We watch as the players take their positions on the ice, the camera panning across the Red Wolves lineup. When it lands on Knox, I feel my breath catch. He looks focused, intense, his dark eyes narrowed in concentration.

The referee drops the puck and the game begins. I try to follow along, but my eyes keep drifting back to Knox when he's within the view of the camera.

"Damn, he's good," Jade comments, echoing my thoughts. "No wonder you're into him."

I elbow her lightly but can't suppress a smile. "Shut up and watch the game."

As the first period unfolds, the Red Wolves struggle against their opponents. The other team is aggressive, slamming our players into the boards at every opportunity. I wince as Knox takes a particularly hard hit, but he shakes it off. I'm glad it seems as if his shoulder is fine.

Jade and Hailey cheer as the Red Wolves manage to clear the puck out of their defensive zone. "Come on, boys!" Jade shouts, clapping her hands. "Let's go!"

I lean forward, my eyes glued to the screen as Knox races down the ice. He weaves past a defender, the puck seeming connected to his stick like a magnet. With a quick move, he slips the puck between the goalie's pads and into the net.

The room erupts in cheers as the Red Wolves celebrate the goal. Jade high-fives Hailey, then turns to me with a grin. "Did you see that? Your boy just scored!"

I can't help but smile, feeling a flicker of pride. "He's not my boy," I protest weakly.

Hailey rolls her eyes. "Sure. Just freaking admit it at this point, Selene. You're into him."

I open my mouth to deny it, but the words won't come. Because the truth is, I am into Knox. More than I want to admit, even to myself.

As the game continues, I find myself getting more and more invested. I cheer when the Red Wolves score again, and groan when the other team manages to tie the game up. By the time the third period starts, I'm on the edge of my seat, my heart pounding.

As the clock ticks down, the intensity on the ice increases tenfold. Both teams are desperate for the next goal that will more than likely mean they are the winner of the game. Knox seems to be everywhere at once, and I'm impressed even more by his athletic ability.

With less than two minutes left, Knox gains possession of the puck and he charges forward. Two players on the opposite team are on him, but he spins away from them, maintaining control of the puck.

I'm gripping the couch cushions so tightly my knuckles turn white. Jade is screaming at the TV, urging Knox on, while Hailey has a hand over her mouth.

Knox skates across the blue line, his movements confident and controlled. Even though I barely understand the rules, I'm freaking out internally. His stick is raised, his body angled toward the goal, and the camera zooms in like it's anticipating something big is about to happen.

I hold my breath because I'm afraid to move even slightly.

He looks like he's going to shoot, every muscle in his body coiled, but then, at the last possible second, he shifts. His shoulder dips and the goalie reacts instantly, dropping down to block the shot that never comes.

For a second, I think he's lost his chance, but then he's gliding around the goalie, faster than I can process. The puck slides into the net, and I leap off the couch. The cheers from the crowd on the screen are deafening, but I swear I'm louder.

"Oh my god, he did it!" I scream, my voice blending with Jade and Hailey's as we all jump up and down, hugging each other.

The buzzer sounds, signaling the end of the game. The Red Wolves have won, 3-2, thanks to Knox's last-second goal. On the screen, the team swarms him.

"That was amazing," Hailey says. "Holy hell."

I'm still staring at the screen, my heart racing as I watch Knox remove his helmet. His dark hair is plastered to his forehead with sweat, but he's grinning from ear to ear. The camera lingers on him as he accepts congratulations from his teammates.

Suddenly, his head turns, and he looks directly into the camera. For a moment, it feels like he's looking right at me. Like he knows I'm watching.

Then the moment passes, and I sink back onto the couch. I'm feeling dazed and slightly lightheaded.

Jade joins me again, nudging me with her elbow. "So, still think hockey's not your thing?"

I laugh, shaking my head. "Okay, fine. I admit it. That was... intense. And kind of thrilling."

"Mmhmm. And I'm sure it had nothing to do with a certain dark-haired, brooding winger," she teases, waggling her eyebrows at me.

I grab a pillow and hit her with it, but I'm smiling. "Shut up. I can appreciate a good game without it being about Knox."

"But it doesn't hurt that he's the one scoring the winning goal, right?" Hailey raises an eyebrow at me.

I give her a grin. "You're right. It doesn't."

22

SELENE

The bass from the speakers practically vibrates through the walls as I step into Knox's place. Sounds of laughter and celebration come together, filling every corner of this place with high vibrations. It's understandable because the Red Wolves just had an amazing win. I pause in the doorway, taking it all in, and I know it's time to turn my confidence on.

All eyes are fixed on the television in the guys' living room, which is now playing highlights from today's game, even though no one can hear the commentary over the music. The place is packed and there's a sea of red and white. Some of the faces I'm familiar with and there are several people I don't know. I spot Levi and Hailey standing close together. His arm is draped around her and when she looks up, she gives me a small wave. That causes Levi to turn and give me a nod before he goes back to whatever he was whispering in Hailey's ear. I think about walking over to say hi, but something in their body language tells me it can wait.

My gaze darts around, scanning the crowd for someone else I can talk to, and then I find a flash of blonde hair that I'd recognize anywhere. As soon as our eyes meet, Isla waves me over.

"Selene! You're here!"

Isla wraps me in a tight hug, almost causing her to spill the drink she's holding. "Congrats on the win," I say.

"Don't congratulate me. It's all the boys," she says, but I can tell she's basking in the afterglow of the victory just as much as any of the team. "Did you end up watching it? I know you said you might go watch the game with Hailey and Jade."

"We did. The game was very interesting and more intense than I thought it would be. I'm sure it was even wilder with you being there, close to the action."

"It was. I almost wish I didn't have to take photos. Think you'll come to a game?"

I think about the fact that Knox asked if I would only a day or so ago. "We'll see," I say with a noncommittal shrug. "I'm still learning the rules."

Isla laughs. "You don't need to know the rules to enjoy watching a bunch of hot guys skate around."

She has a point. "True."

"Speaking of hot guys that are not named Asher," she says, leaning in closer. "Where's Knox?"

"You haven't seen him? I assumed that he was around here somewhere. In that same vein, where is Asher?"

"He went to the kitchen..." She moves so she's about to look down the hall. "Ah. I've found both of our guys."

I want to remind my best friend that he's not my boyfriend, but I know it's no use. Instead, I follow Isla's gaze down the hallway. Sure enough, there's Asher, towering over the crowd with his usual easygoing grin. Next to him is Knox, casually leaning against the counter with a beer in his hand. He says something that makes Asher laugh.

"Come on," Isla says, nudging me lightly. "Let's go join them."

I hesitate for a moment, but Isla's already taking my hand and we're walking. As we near the kitchen, the music isn't as loud, allowing me to catch bits and pieces of what Asher is saying. Knox listens with a smirk.

"Asher!" Isla calls out, and he looks over, his eyes lighting up when he sees her. He reaches down to scoop her into a hug, lifting her off the ground briefly, causing the drink in her hand to slosh over the rim.

"Hey, sunshine," he says, planting a kiss on her forehead.

Knox's eyes meet mine, and for a split second, I see something like relief wash over his face. "Selene," he says, pushing off the counter and walking toward me. "You made it."

"Of course," I say, trying to sound as nonchalant as

possible. He leans in and I think he's going to kiss me, but he stops short, perhaps reading my uncertainty. Instead, he brushes a strand of hair from my face with a tenderness that catches me off guard.

"Do you want a drink?" he asks.

"Sure."

He turns to open a cooler filled with ice and assorted bottles. I take the moment to observe him; there's something different in the way he's carrying himself tonight. More relaxed, maybe even happier. He hands me a bottle of hard cider and clinks his lightly against mine.

"To the Red Wolves," he says, and we both take a sip. The cold fizziness of the cider is a welcome distraction from the knot of nerves in my stomach.

Asher and Isla are already deep in conversation about what might be something related to the game. Isla gets animated, waving her hands in the air as she makes her point. Asher just laughs and agrees, probably more interested in her than the actual topic.

"So, what did you think of the game? Really," Knox asks, drawing my attention back to him.

I take another sip, stalling. "It was exciting. A lot more than I expected honestly. You played well."

He raises an eyebrow. "You watched me?"

Busted. "I mean, we watched the whole game. It was hard not to notice."

A slow smile spreads across his face. "I'm glad you're starting to get into it."

Before I can respond, someone bumps into me, and I nearly drop my bottle. Knox steadies me with a hand on my waist, pulling me slightly closer. "You okay?"

"Yeah, I'm fine."

He doesn't let go immediately, and I can feel the warmth of his hand seeping through my shirt. This friendship, or situationship, or whatever it is, feels so messy, but also not at the same time.

"Asher," someone calls from behind us, and we all turn to see Wilder making his way over with a massive grin on his face. "Dude, you were on fire with that last assist!"

Asher beams. "Thanks, man. Team effort."

Wilder gives Asher a high five and then turns to Isla. "Stole your man for a second, hope you don't mind."

Isla rolls her eyes but smiles. "As if I could stop you."

I look down at Knox's hand that has made a home on my waist before drawing my attention back to him. "Is your hand comfortable?"

"Very much so," he says as he pulls me closer.

I don't resist when Knox pulls me into his chest. I glance around, half expecting to see someone I know gawking at us, but everyone's too engrossed in their own conversations to care. And I don't mind having this moment with him.

In fact, I'm enjoying it.

Knox keeps his arm around my waist as we mingle through the party. Every so often, he'll lean down to whisper something in my ear, his breath warm against my skin. It's usually some witty observation about one of his teammates or something he knows about someone. I find myself laughing more than I have in a while.

As the night wears on, the party starts to thin out. But no matter what, Knox stays by my side. At one point, Hailey catches my eye from across the room and gives me a knowing smile. I just shake my head at her.

Together, we move to a corner of the living room, and now that there aren't many people here, it allows us to talk quietly.

"I'm really glad you came tonight," he says, his eyes searching mine.

"Me too," I admit, surprising myself with my honesty. I'm not one to turn down a party, but this was different. What's happening between us is different. "I wasn't sure if I would, but...I'm having a good time."

"Even with me monopolizing your attention?" It's obvious that he's teasing me, but it feels as if he's actually making sure that I am okay with that.

"Especially because of that."

A slow smile spreads across his face, and he steps closer, crowding into my space. "Good. Because I don't plan on stopping anytime soon."

My breath catches in my throat. "Knox..."

"Selene," he murmurs, bringing a hand up to cup my cheek. His thumb brushes over my bottom lip, and I shiver. "Tell me to stop and I will."

But I don't want him to stop. I want him to keep going. I swallow hard and try to breathe deeply in hopes of calming my wildly beating heart. It doesn't work. "Don't stop," I whisper.

Thankfully, even with the music still playing in the background, I don't need to repeat myself.

Knox's eyes darken with desire as he leans in closer, his lips hovering just inches from mine. "Are you sure?"

I nod because words escape me. And then his lips are on mine. I melt into the kiss, no longer caring who might see us. He pulls me closer, deepening the kiss, and I can taste the faint bitterness of beer on his tongue.

We stay like that for a long moment, until the need for air becomes too great. Knox pulls back slightly, resting his forehead against mine. "Wow," he breathes.

"Yeah," I agree. I feel a bit hazy, and it has nothing to do with the cider I had.

He grins, looking equally affected. "Do you want to get out of here? Maybe go upstairs?"

"The last time I was up there, things didn't go so well."

"This time will be different, I promise."

And I believe every word.

"Okay," I say softly with a small nod. "Let's go."

23

SELENE

Knox puts his hand in mine, and we make our way to the stairs. His hand finds the small of my back, guiding me gently. I glance up at him and catch his eyes. He's watching me with an unreadable expression. I really want to know what he's thinking about, but I'm too nervous to ask.

As we walk the stairs, I try to calm every nerve in my body. That sense of déjà vu I had before our "outing" at Prosecco & Prose? It's back with a vengeance. The only thing I can focus on is Knox's warm touch and thinking of every outcome that can result from what is about to happen.

We reach the top of the stairs and Knox leads me down the hall to his room. Not that I don't know where it is. Once we are inside, he closes the door behind us and double checks that he locked it.

Knox turns to face me, and I still can't figure out what he's thinking. Part of me wonders if I'm making the same mistake again. Then again, if I get orgasms out of it, is it really a mistake?

Reframing things makes it a slightly easier pill to swallow.

"Selene," he murmurs, bringing my attention back to him. "Tell me what you want."

"I want you," I say with as much confidence as I pretend to have. "I want this, whatever this is between us."

His lips quirk into a small smile and he nods, trailing his fingers along my jaw and tilting my face up to his. "Good. Because I want you too. So fucking much."

And then his mouth is on mine again. I melt into him, losing myself and any sense of time because none of that matters. Just as we start tugging at each other's clothes, a loud thump sounds from downstairs. Knox breaks away and I can see the irritation in his face.

"Don't go anywhere," he says before unlocking the door and slipping out.

I take a moment to collect myself, running a hand through my hair and trying to steady myself. Maybe a small break is just what we need because things were growing hot and heavy quick.

The door creaks open and Knox steps back in. "It was just Wilder. He's fine. Where were we?" he asks, but he doesn't make a move to kiss me again. Instead, he strokes my hair back from my face. His touch is slow and soft, causing goosebumps to form on my arms.

"You were kissing me, and I was wondering if I'm making the same mistake again," I blurt out.

Knox's hand stills in my hair. For a moment, I think I've scared him off, that he'll tell me to leave, that this was all a bad idea. But then he sighs and sits on the edge of the bed, running a hand through his own hair in that way he does when he's frustrated or deep in thought.

"I'm nervous and I can't—"

I stop talking when Knox reaches for my hand and holds it in his. "I'm at least part of the reason you feel this way and it'll always be one of my biggest regrets. And that will never happen again. I swear."

Something clicks within me and settles the panic I have about what tonight will turn into. Sure, there's still some lingering hesitation about what he might think of my body even though he's seen all of me before, but I'm sure that will fade with time.

Time. As if we're going to be doing this over and over again. Now that is too much to think about.

"Okay, Knox. I believe you."

A soft smile appears on his lips just before he says, "Come here."

I hesitate for the briefest of moments and then take a step toward him. He pulls me gently onto his lap, and I straddle him, my hands resting on his shoulders. His eyes search mine, and for the first time tonight, I think I can read him. There's a tenderness there, mixed with something else that I can't pinpoint.

"We don't have to rush," he says. "We can take our time because we have all night."

"I like the sound of that."

"Thought you might," he says, the corner of his mouth tugging upward. He places his hands on my hips and lets them rest there for now.

"So," I say, trying to break the tension. "Do you have a game plan or are we just going to wing it? Get it? Wing it? Cause you're a left winger..."

He chuckles, a low rumble. "I see what you've done there. But back to the game plan, I was thinking I'd start with a PowerPoint presentation on seduction techniques."

I laugh. "Oh yeah? How many slides?"

"At least twelve. With graphs and charts."

"Sanchez, I didn't know you were an overachiever."

He shrugs. "I aim to please in every way, shape, and form."

"Every way, shape, and form?" I raise an eyebrow.

"Absolutely," he says, his voice dropping a notch. "But we could always just go with the flow, see where it takes us."

"Going with the flow sounds less stressful," I admit. "Though I'm still curious about those graphs."

"They're impressive," he says, his lips dangerously close to mine. "But I think you'd be more interested in the practical applications."

"You make it sound like you're teaching a class," I tease, though my voice is softer now.

"Maybe I just want an excuse to do some hands-on learning," he whispers as he draws his face closer to mine.

Our lips brush, but this kiss is slower, more deliberate. It's not as desperate as the one from earlier, and I can see that he's living up to his promise to take our time. My fingers end up in his hair, tugging slightly on the strands, and he responds with a gentle pressure against my hips.

Knox's hands begin to wander, tracing lazy patterns on my lower back. Every touch sparks like static electricity, making me hyperaware of every inch of skin he comes into contact with. His fingers find the hem of my shirt and play there for a moment, tossing a hint my way of where he wants the item to end up. I break our kiss long enough to pull the fabric over my head and toss it aside.

He takes me in, his gaze lingering on my breasts that are now only covered by a plum-colored bra. I try to read his mind, to see if he's judging or simply admiring, but before I can psych myself out, he leans forward and presses a kiss to the center of my chest, right where my heart is pounding its loudest.

"You're beautiful," he says.

I'm about to thank him when he flips us over gently. Now I'm on my back on the bed, and he's hovering above me, propped up on one arm. His free hand trails down my chest, then my stomach, stopping just at the waistband of my jeans. He looks up at me, seeking permission, waiting for a sign that I'm still with him. He's making sure that I still want this.

I nod, and he unbuttons my jeans slowly. I'm beginning to wonder if he's doing this to torture me. He tugs them down, and I lift my hips to help. The denim slides off and joins my shirt on the floor.

Knox's eyes never leave mine as he moves his head and drops a couple of kisses on my neck. Those must have been precursors to the real thing because it's as if a light switch goes off in his mind. Or the patience he has weakens a little because the intensity is kicked up several notches. And when he finds a particular sensitive spot on my neck, I find myself moaning before my brain even processes that I'm doing so.

The sound of my own voice startles me, but it seems as if it's music to his ears. Knox's kisses grow hungrier, his hands move to play with my bra straps. He shifts his head so that he can kiss the tops of my breasts that are now spilling out of the cups and while I might have been more insecure about this before, the thought doesn't cross my mind. I'm too busy enjoying myself and he seems to be too.

I arch my back, pressing myself closer to him, in an effort to convince him where all of his attention should be at the present moment. He gets the hint and bites down gently, then soothes the spot with his tongue. A rush of heat flies through me, and I can feel the dampness growing between my legs although he hasn't discovered it yet. My hands grip his shoulders because I need some-thing, anything to hang on to.

"Knox," I whisper, but I'm not entirely sure what I'm going to say next. Maybe to tell him to slow down again, or maybe to hurry up. I'm torn between wanting this to last forever and needing him right now.

He pauses and looks up at me and I can see the concern in his eyes. "Yeah?"

I take a deep breath. "Just... please don't stop."

A relieved smile spreads across his face. "Wouldn't dream of it. And I love hearing the word please fall from your lips like that."

I'm wiggling underneath him for a split second before I come to a stop. "What do you mean?"

He sits up and pulls off his shirt in one fluid motion. "Hearing you say it all...breathy-like is hot as fuck."

"I'm happy to be of service."

"Say it again."

"I'm happy to—"

My eyes widen slightly when Knox's eyes narrow because he knows damn well that I know what he wants me to repeat. It turns me on even more.

"Please, Knox. I want you to show me all of those hands-on techniques. For demonstration purposes only."

He doesn't need to be told twice. His hands are on me again, one sliding around to unhook my bra with an expert flick, the other cupping my breast as the fabric falls away. I lean into him and his touch because I'm absolutely desperate for more.

His thumb circles my nipple while his mouth leaves kisses along my collarbone. I close my eyes and let myself get lost in everything that is him.

I arch my back as he takes my nipple between his fingers, applying just enough pressure to make me gasp. My hips instinctively move against him because I'm ready for more, but I also don't want to rush. What a cycle to be in.

And that's before he looks up at me and puts my nipple in his mouth. A groan falls from my lips as he alternates between licking and sucking.

I find myself biting my lower lip to keep from crying out again, but I don't know how long that is going to last.

Knox switches to the other breast, giving it the same tender yet urgent attention. My skin feels as if it's on fire, and I'm loving every second of it. There's no way that Knox isn't affected by this too because I can feel how hard his cock is against me.

Although his mouth is currently occupied, one of his hands drifts down my side, light as a feather, toward my hips and thighs. He pauses at the edge of my panties, fingers slipping just underneath the plum-colored lace. My hips lift toward him involuntarily as if they have a mind of their own and the only thing they want to do is beg for his touch.

He releases my nipple with a soft pop. "You taste so

good," he says as his fingers continue exploring the rest of my body. I'm taken aback as he traces the hem of my panties. I can now say that I'm glad Isla and I went shopping because if we hadn't there's no way I would feel as confident as I do right now.

"However," he continues. "There's something else I want to try."

It doesn't take a rocket scientist to figure out what he's talking about. And I can't wait. His fingers hook into my panties and slowly slide them down my legs. I lift my hips to help him, watching as the lacy fabric joins the growing pile of clothes on the floor. Now I'm completely naked before him, while he is still clothed from the waist down.

Knox takes a moment to stare at me. "God, Selene, you're stunning."

"Thank you," I whisper because I'm not sure what else to say.

"No, thank you," he says just before he leaves a trail of kisses down my stomach. When he reaches my pussy, he dips his head and starts by leaving a kiss on each thigh. A smirk forms on my face just before his mouth descends on my pussy. I swear I've died and gone to heaven.

Knox takes his time, exploring, teasing, until I'm squirming beneath him. It feels as if his mouth is everywhere because of how quickly he's alternating between licking and sucking on my clit. I can't figure a rhythm to this madness, making it all the more unpredictable and all the more exciting because I don't know which way it's going to go next.

My hands don't know which way to turn but end up fisting the sheets as he continues on his quest to make me melt into a puddle on his bed. The explosion is building within me, and I know it's only a matter of time. He uses one hand to push my legs further apart while the other one lands on my stomach, lightly using pressure to keep me in place. The cries that I've given up on containing fall like an avalanche from my lips. I don't care who's in this house or if they can hear what Knox is doing to me, I can't be quiet.

I refuse to be.

When he slips in a finger to join the private party his mouth and my pussy are having, I swear I nearly levitate. Then he adds another, and after a few moments, I know this round is over. I come hard and he doesn't stop what he's doing until I'm finished. We're both left staring at each other as we're trying to catch our breaths.

Holy fuck. There's no way that was real. But there's no way this is over. Because it can't be. I need him. I crave him, and I'm not sure this will ever be enough.

Knox crawls back up my body, and when he reaches my face, his eyes land on mine and I can see that he's searching for something within.

"You okay?" he asks softly, brushing my hair back from my face.

I nod, not quite trusting my voice yet. The aftershocks

of my orgasm are still rippling through me, leaving me boneless and sated. But I know this is just the beginning.

"More than okay," I manage to say about a minute later. "That was... wow."

He chuckles. "I aim to please."

"And please you did," I reply, my hands trailing down his chest, enjoying the way he feels beneath my fingertips. "But now it's my turn."

I push on his shoulder, urging him to roll onto his back. He complies, and I straddle his hips, feeling his hard length pressing against me through his jeans. I grind down and receive a groan from him.

"These need to come off," I say, tugging at his waistband. "And you need a condom."

"Be my guest," he replies as he reaches over to get a condom from his drawer.

I make quick work of the button and zipper on Knox's jeans, tugging them down along with his boxer briefs. I find myself staring at his cock. It's thick and hard, and I can't help but lick my lips at the sight. I wrap my hand around him, giving a few slow strokes as I watch his reaction. His eyes flutter closed, and he lets out a hiss of pleasure.

"Picosita..." he groans as he thrusts up into my hand. The way he says the nickname he gave me sounds needy, as if he'll die without my touch. I find that hot.

I stroke him a few more times before reaching for the condom he retrieved. Tearing it open, I roll it onto his dick. I can't help but enjoy the way his muscles tense and relax under my touch. Once it's in place, I position myself over him, the tip of his cock brushing against my entrance.

The first time we had sex, there's no way I would have been comfortable with being on top. But now I feel empowered. We lock eyes, and in that moment, an understanding passes between us. This isn't just sex. It's something more, something deeper that neither of us can quite define yet. But the intensity of the connection is undeniable.

Slowly, I sink down onto him, taking him inch by delicious inch. The stretch and fullness is something I can't explain. I have to stop to adjust once he's fully inside me. Knox's hands come to rest on my hips, his fingers digging in slightly.

"Fuck, you feel incredible," he pants out. The sound of his strained voice makes me smirk.

"Now who's in control?"

"It's you. It's always been you."

His words startle me, but before I can fully process their meaning, Knox sits up, wrapping his arms around me and capturing my lips in a searing kiss. The new angle causes him to go even deeper, and I moan into his mouth. We start to move together, finding a rhythm that has us both gasping.

I break the kiss to tilt my head back. Knox's mouth finds my neck as his hands roam my back, my sides, my breasts, like he can't get enough of touching me. And I can't get enough of him period.

I rock my hips, riding him as if this is something that comes naturally to me. No more concerns about how I must look in his eyes from this view or my own self-consciousness. The only thing that matters is the pleasure that both of us seek. The room fills with our panting and groans. Knox's fingers dig into the flesh of my hips, guiding my movements as well as urging me on.

"That's it, baby," he says in between harsh breaths. "Just like that."

His praise spurs me on, making me feel sexy and desired in a way I've never experienced before. I tangle my fingers in his hair, tugging lightly as I grind down harder.

"I'm close," I gasp out as my movements becoming more erratic. "Knox, please…"

He seems to know instinctively what I need. One of his hands slides between our bodies, his fingers finding my clit and rubbing in tight circles. The added stimulation is almost too much, and I swear I'm beginning to see stars. I cry out, my inner walls starting to flutter around him.

"Come for me, picosita," he demands. "I want to feel all of you."

And who am I do deny the both of us? His words are my undoing. I come apart in his arms as my orgasm crashes over me. Knox holds me tight, thrusting up into me a few more times before he finds his own release while moaning my name.

We collapse onto the bed together. For however long we simply lay there, holding each other as we come down from the high. Knox gently brushes my damp hair back from my face, his touch tender and intimate.

"That was..." he starts, then seems to struggle to find the right word.

"Yeah," I agree breathlessly, knowing exactly what he means. "It really was."

A smile is stationed on his lips as his fingers continue to stroke my hair. I let my eyes drift closed, enjoying the feeling of his touch in a completely different way than I had just moments ago. Something has shifted between us, and it puts me so much more at ease.

Eventually Knox moves, and I feel the loss of his warmth immediately. I watch as he disposes of the condom, but thankfully, he's back in an instant. He pulls me into his arms again and I rest my head on his chest. The steady thumping of his heartbeat in my ear relaxes me further as his fingers trace lazy patterns on my back.

"Stay with me tonight," he whispers, pressing a kiss to the top of my head.

It's phrased like a statement, but I can hear the underlying question. He wants me here, in his bed and in his arms. And there's nowhere else I'd rather be.

"I'd love to."

24

KNOX

I can't remember the last time I've felt this relaxed, on or off the ice. It's like a fog has lifted, and the world is clear. I make another crisp pass down the length of the rink and watch it glide perfectly to Levi's stick. He looks almost surprised before grinning and giving me a thumbs up.

"Nice one, Knox!" he shouts, forever stepping into his role as captain and helping keep team morale up.

I nod, acknowledging his comment. I can't fight the smirk that appears on my face. The praise means a lot, but more importantly, I know I've been on fire all session and I'm glad my teammates are taking notice. It's like every drill, every pass, every shot has just clicked today.

Coach Johnson blows his whistle, and my attention is on him. "Alright, bring it in!" he yells.

We all skate toward the bench, quickly forming a loose

huddle. Several of us have already grabbed water bottles and towels as we try to calm ourselves down.

"Great practice today," Coach says. "We're really starting to gel as a unit. Keep this up, and we'll be unstoppable." He reaches for the glasses that are sitting on top of his head as if to double check that they are still there before he turns to me. "Levi, Knox, fantastic chemistry out there, especially at the end."

Coach's words linger in the air, and I allow them to sink in. Chemistry. It's what I've been missing, not just with the team, but in life lately. Maybe things are finally starting to click.

Asher slaps me on the back. "And your shoulder looks to be as good as new now, so we've got this season in the bag."

"Hell yeah," I reply in return.

"Alright, hit the showers," Coach Johnson says, breaking up our huddle. "And remember, team dinner tonight. Mandatory."

In the locker room, the guys are already stripping off their gear and cracking jokes. It's loud and chaotic, but in a way that's comforting. I take a seat at my stall and start unlacing my skates.

Asher sits down next to me, his blond hair a sweaty mess. "Dude. Knox, that was the best I've seen you move in weeks, not including when you clutched that win for us a few games ago. What was that?"

I shrug, trying to play it cool. "Just feeling good, I guess."

Asher raises an eyebrow, skepticism written all over his face. "Oh really? Just 'feeling good'? Come on, spill it. Does it have something to do with a particular redhead that is also best friends with my girl?"

I pause, the lace in my hand tightening into a knot. Asher's not wrong; Selene has a lot to do with my improved mood. It's been nice getting to talk to her again and getting to know her in...other ways, but I don't really want to talk about it with the guys if I can avoid it.

At least not yet.

But given that Isla and Selene are best friends, it looks like I might be forced into a corner. I glance over at Asher, weighing my options. Before I can come up with a response that nicely tells him to fuck off, Wilder strolls over, towel slung around his neck and smirking like he already knows the punchline to a joke we haven't heard yet.

"Don't tell me it's love that's turned you into frickin' Wayne Gretzky," Wilder says, crossing his arms. "Because if that's the case, maybe I need to find myself a cute girl too."

The locker room falls silent, all eyes on me. I can almost hear the unspoken "Ooooooh" hanging in the air.

I laugh, trying to defuse the sudden tension. "You'd have to develop a personality first, Wilder."

He holds a hand to his chest, pretending that I actually hurt him. "Touché."

The room erupts in noise again as soon as they realize that nothing else is going to come of this. I go back to untying my now double-knotted laces.

"Seriously though," Asher says, leaning in closer so only I can hear. "I'm happy for you, man."

"Thanks, but what did Isla say about Selene and me?"

Asher leans back, stretching his arms over this chest. "She may have mentioned that Selene and you are doing better this time around," he says with a casual nonchalance that I don't buy for a second. "And that you two have been spending some time together. Dude, it's not like we're blind. We can see that you've been way happier recently. Hell, Wilder even mentioned that someone must have dislodged the stick from your ass."

I roll my eyes as I finish with my laces and start peeling off my pads. "That's all accurate. It's been really good."

Asher stands, starting to strip off his own pads. "So it's official then? You two are together?"

I hesitate, choosing my words carefully. "We're taking it slow. Seeing where things go."

"Yeah, sure," Asher says, standing up and starting toward the showers. "Just remember, if you hurt her again, Isla will kill you. And then I'll have to kill you again for good measure."

"Just know that goes both ways, *roomie*."

Asher waves a hand dismissively but doesn't turn around. "Yeah, yeah. We're all one big, happy, murderous family."

I watch Asher disappear into the showers, his playful threat still lingering in my mind. He's right, of course. If things go south with Selene again, it's not just my relationship with her that's on the line—it's my friendship with Asher and Isla, and potentially the entire team dynamic.

I strip down to my towel and head toward the showers, letting the hot water work its magic on my sore muscles. The team cycles in and out, some guys finishing up quickly while others take their time. By the time I'm back at my locker, most of the guys are dressed and making plans for the afternoon.

Levi walks by and points a finger at me. "Don't forget about dinner tonight."

"I'll be there," I say, toweling off my hair.

Levi pauses, as if he's about to say something else, then just nods and walks away.

As I'm getting dressed, my phone vibrates in my duffel bag. I reach for it and see a text from the woman of the hour.

Selene: How was practice?

I type a response, then delete it. Type another, then delete that too. Why is it so much harder to talk to her through a screen?

Me: Good. Exhausting. How are you?

I hit send and start dressing. My phone buzzes again.

Selene: Just finished class. Tired, but I'll
be okay.

I can picture her, red-faced and sweaty but glowing with that post-workout energy. Another text comes in before I can respond.

Selene: Want to grab lunch?

I bite my lip, conflicted. I do want to see her, but if I don't go home and rest now, there's no way I'll survive the team dinner.

Me: Can't unfortunately. I have class in
30 and then a team project meeting.
Then there's this team thing tonight.

Selene: No worries! I'll catch you later.

For some reason, her dismissal doesn't sit well with me, so I don't end the conversation there.

Me: Are we still on for Thursday?

I stare at the phone screen, waiting for those three little dots to appear, signaling that she's typing. When they finally do, my chest tightens.

Selene: Of course ☺

The smiley face eases the tension in me a bit. I shove the phone back into my duffel and finish getting dressed. Once I've gathered my things, I leave the rink and head to my car. I pop my trunk, put my hockey gear inside and grab my book bag. Then I hop into the driver's seat for a moment and turn my car on. As I'm letting it warm up, my phone buzzes again.

Selene: If you're too busy we can reschedule...

Shit. That isn't the impression I wanted her to have. I quickly type out another message.

Me: No way. I'm really looking forward to it.

Selene: Okay.

As I'm about to put my phone down so that I can drive, it vibrates in my hand again. I expect it to be a text from Selene, but it's from Willow.

Willow: Mom really wants to know what day we're going to be home for Mamita's party so she can organize stuff.

Shit. I haven't forgotten about the party, but I still haven't figured out when would be the best time for us to leave. A lot of it was dependent on my schedule and things have just been so hectic with everything. I'll think about it when I get back home.

As I'm about to throw my car into drive, I freeze in place because of a sudden tapping on my window. I turn my head slowly only for my stomach to drop the second I see her.

Tessa.

Lowering my window halfway, I brace myself. "What do you want?"

"Why haven't you answered my texts?" she demands without an introduction, crossing her arms over her chest. Can't blame her for that since I tossed any sort of manners, I had out the window.

"What texts?" It's a lie, but I just want her go away.

"Don't play dumb, Knox. I know you've seen them."

"I haven't—" I start, but she cuts me off with a sharp shake of her head.

"I texted you a while ago." Her eyes narrow as she studies me. "You had no problem liking my comment on your post, but you can't respond to a simple text?"

I do a double take. Because what in the actual fuck? "I didn't like your comment."

She snorts in response. "Whatever. It's not like you haven't answered before. So what, now you're too busy to talk to me?"

"I never said that," I reply, gripping the steering wheel a little tighter. "I didn't like your comment and if I don't want to respond to anything you've sent me that's my prerogative. We are over and have been for years. I thought I made that clear numerous times."

Her eyes flash with something that I can't place. I don't know her anymore and she doesn't know me so I'm glad I don't know what she's feeling.

She flips her hair over her shoulder. "Yeah, well... I just thought you'd at least respond. We were together for a long time, Knox. You can't just pretend none of that mattered."

This is why I shouldn't have lowered my window.

"I'm not pretending anything," I say, forcing my voice to stay level. "But whatever you're trying to do? Cut it out. We have nothing to say to each other."

"Fine," she mutters. "Whatever, you say, Knox."

Before I can respond, she spins on her heel and walks away. I watch her disappear around the corner of the building before leaning back against the headrest.

What the hell was that? And how did she know I was here?

It's not like it matters now because she already achieved one of her goals: seeing me. I rub the back of my neck and try to stop thinking about Tessa. The whole interaction leaves a bad taste in my mouth, but there's not much I can do about it now.

I glance at my phone still sitting in the cupholder, the earlier texts from Selene and Willow staring back at me. My thumb hovers over Willow's message, but my mind shifts to something else entirely—something I have no business thinking about right now.

What if I invite Selene to Mamita's birthday party?

The idea is insane. I know it. Selene and I aren't even solid yet and bringing her into the hurricane that is my family could either solidify us or completely tear us apart. But if I don't invite her, I'll be gone for the whole weekend, right when things are starting to click.

My phone slips out of my hand and onto my lap. I pick it up and find the text messages that Selene and I have sent to each other. The thought of inviting her still feels reckless, but why does it sound like such a good idea at the same time?

Since I need to get to class, I flip back to the texts that my sister and I have shared with one another and hastily type out a message to her.

Me: I'll let you know later this week.

With that still lingering on my mind, I put my phone in my cupholder and pull out of the parking lot.

25

SELENE

A s I pull up to Knox's house, I see the front door swing open. It's as if he was waiting by the window for me to arrive. I turn off my car and pop the trunk as Knox walks down the stairs of his front porch to approach my vehicle. I step out and greet him with a grin.

"Is everything back here?" he asks, gesturing to my car.

"Yes, it is. I might have gone slightly overboard, but I wasn't sure what you guys had and didn't have."

Knox shakes as he leans into the trunk, surveying the mountain of grocery bags as I walk to the trunk.

"We've got salt, pepper, and beer," he says, lifting a bag to test its weight. "Maybe some expired ketchup."

I swat at his arm playfully. "Ridiculous. A well-stocked kitchen is essential for culinary success. You are in the hands of a professional here."

"I'm sure I am, picosita," he says, and I don't hear an ounce of sarcasm in his words.

I feel my cheeks grow warm at the nickname he's given me. "You know, I've been meaning to ask you. What does that mean?"

"It means spicy."

My hand lands on my chest before I point at my hair. "Is it because I'm a redhead?"

"No, it is because of our banter, but the hair color is the cherry on top."

I swat at him again and all he does is laugh as he takes the groceries into his place.

I follow Knox up the steps of his porch and through the front door, taking in the familiar sight of his living room. We continue down the hallway until we reach the kitchen. He sets the bags on the counter and turns back to me for further instructions.

We both start to unpack the groceries, pulling out fresh vegetables, various types of cheese, and an assortment of spices. Knox watches me with mild curiosity as I organize everything.

"So what are we making?" he asks.

"Tortellini soup. It's something I've always wanted to try, so we shall see how this goes."

Knox opens the fridge and grabs a beer. "Sounds legit." He holds up another bottle, offering it to me.

I hesitate for a moment but then take it from him. He

pops the caps off with a bottle opener that's magnetized to his fridge and clinks his bottle against mine.

"To culinary adventures," he says.

I take a swig and let the cold liquid wash down my throat. It's so refreshing and might help me remain calm throughout this whole ordeal. I set the bottle down and reach for a cutting board, pulling a knife from the block on the counter.

"Okay, first we need to chop these veggies." I slide a bell pepper and an onion toward Knox. "Think you can handle that?"

He grabs the knife and examines it like it's a new toy. "I'll give it my best shot. Just don't yell at me if I ruin them."

I laugh. "I'm more concerned about you losing a finger. Don't want Crestwood University suing me because one of their star players can't play anymore."

With slow and deliberate movements, Knox starts to slice the bell pepper. I watch for a second, amused by his concentration, then turn to the bag of fresh tortellini and start to inspect it. The whole situation feels surreal. Here we are, standing in Knox's kitchen, preparing food together. If you'd told me a few weeks ago that I'd be here, I would have laughed in your face.

I glance over at Knox. His usually confident demeanor is replaced with the utmost focus as he struggles with the vegetables. It's adorable, and I can't help but smile. He catches me looking and raises an eyebrow.

"What?" he says, defensive but playful.

"You're actually doing a pretty good job," I admit, taking another swig of my beer. "Maybe there's hope for you after all."

He grins, pleased with himself, and finishes off the bell pepper with a flourish. "Told you I could handle it."

"Don't get cocky. We still have the onion."

Knox grabs the onion and starts peeling it with his fingers, making a mess of the outer layers. I open my mouth to give him a tip but decide against it. There's something nice about watching him figure it out on his own. Instead, I turn to the stove and start heating up a pot with some olive oil.

"So where are the other guys?" I ask, trying to sound casual.

Knox shrugs. "Who knows? I wouldn't be surprised if someone is here, just hanging out in their room."

I turn my attention back to the pot, swirling the olive oil around. The warmth of the stove combined with the beer is making me a little flushed. Or maybe it's something else.

"Don't worry," Knox says, breaking the silence. "You're safe with me."

I look back at him, confused. "Safe?"

He smirks. "I mean from starving. In case this cooking adventure goes south."

I let out a belly laugh. "Oh, thanks for the vote of confidence."

Knox has managed to slice into the onion, and tears are starting to well up in his eyes. He wipes them with the back of his hand, smearing a bit of onion juice on his cheek. It's almost too much; I have to bite my lip to keep from laughing out loud again.

"Here," I say, taking pity on him. I walk over and take the knife from his hand. "Run your hands under cold water. It'll help with the sting."

He doesn't argue, which surprises me. As he moves to the sink, I take over on the onion. I manage to get it cut in record time, but that doesn't mean I don't appreciate Knox's help.

"I never asked," Knox says over his shoulder. "How did your presentation go?"

I'm taken aback that he remembers. "It went well," I say, trying to hide my surprise. "Better than I expected, actually. Thanks for asking."

Knox turns off the water and dries his hands on a towel, then leans against the counter and takes a long pull from his beer. "I knew you'd kill it. You're always so prepared."

I'm not sure quite how to respond. Compliments from Knox are something I'm still getting used to. The banter, the teasing—those come naturally. But this? This is different.

"Thanks," I say just before I clear my throat and hold up the chopped onion. "See? No tears."

He wipes at his cheek again, grinning. "Yeah, yeah. So what's next, Chef?"

I like the way he's deferring to me in this setting, letting me take the lead. "Next, we need to sauté these with some garlic," I say, moving toward the stove. "Can you get me another cutting board? We need to slice the zucchini next."

Knox rummages through a cabinet and pulls out a cutting board, sliding it across the counter to me. I start slicing the zucchini into thin rounds as he watches over my shoulder.

"You make it look so easy," he says.

I shrug. "It just takes practice. Cooking is like anything else—you get better the more you do it."

"Maybe you can teach me," he says.

I look over at him. "Just like you're teaching me how to work out more efficiently?"

"Exactly," he says. "We can do a skills swap."

"Deal," I say, turning back to the zucchini. "But don't blame me if you end up as ripped as me."

He chuckles, a deep and genuine sound that fills the kitchen. "I think I can handle it. Not to mention, I absolutely love your body."

My knife freezes in the air mid-slice. Did he just—?

I turn slowly to face Knox. His eyes lock on mine and a thousand thoughts sprint through my mind.

He steps closer, closing the space between us. I put the knife down to prevent cutting myself or him.

"You what—"

"And I mean it. Every word. You're stunning." He takes another step and places his finger under my chin, tilting my face toward his. His eyes study my lips for a moment before his lips meet mine.

The kiss is soft at first, tentative, as if he's testing the waters. Then it deepens, a surge of warmth and electricity that makes my knees threaten to give out. I can taste the mix of beer and something inherently Knox on his breath.

My hands land on his chest and I find that his heart is pounding just as wildly as mine. I love that I have this effect on him.

He pulls away slowly and I'm left breathless. My lips are still tingling as a result of his kiss.

I take a shaky breath and respond with, "Thank you for saying that. And I want to thank you for the kiss, but that might be weird."

That makes Knox chuckle. "It was my pleasure, both things."

I pick the knife back up and get back to work on dinner. The comfortable silence that follows is punctuated by the sizzle of vegetables hitting hot oil and the occasional clink of glass as Knox finishes his beer. I half expect him to open another, but instead, he just leans against the counter, content to watch me work.

"So why tortellini soup?" he asks after a while.

I stir the pot, inhaling the aroma of garlic and onions.

"Just found the recipe randomly. It's comfort food. Plus, it's getting colder out, so soup just sounded right."

"Good choice," he says. "I'm looking forward to it."

"Can you hand me the broth?" I ask, trying to focus on the task at hand. He obliges, and I pour it into the pot just before he asks another question.

"Do you cook a lot when you're home?"

"Not as much as I'd like," I admit. "When school is out, either my mom or dad cook. Sometimes I'll throw something together quickly, but I'm hoping all of that changes once I graduate."

"Oh yeah? What's the plan?"

"I want to get my own place, maybe a tiny apartment with a nice kitchen. Somewhere I can experiment and not have to worry about washing fifteen different pots and pans every night."

"Sounds nice," Knox says, almost wistfully. "I can't imagine living alone though. The silence would drive me nuts."

I smile, thinking of the controlled chaos that is my family. "Silence has its perks. But yeah, I'd probably miss the noise after a while."

Knox stretches, his shirt lifting slightly to reveal a sliver of his abdomen. My eyes flicker to it, then quickly away. "So," he begins, and there's a note of hesitation in his voice that catches my attention. "Can I ask you a question?"

"You've been doing that. Why are you asking? Or should I say, what would you like to ask?"

Knox rubs the back of his neck, and I can see that he's nervous. That increases my curiosity even more. "Would you want to come to my abuela's birthday party next weekend?"

I find myself staring at him as I process the question. My first instinct is to say no. Not because I don't want to go, but because meeting someone's family is a big deal, and I'm not sure where Knox and I even stand.

"Selene?" he says, and I snap back to the present.

"That sounds… nice," I say slowly, trying to buy time for my brain to catch up. "But are you sure? I mean, it's your family."

He shrugs, though his eyes are more serious than his posture. "You're important to me. They should get to know you."

Important to me. Those three words hit me harder than the kiss, than any of the compliments tonight. *They should get to know you.* This is more than just an invitation; it's an opening into his life, his world.

"I don't want to intrude," I say, though my resistance is weakening.

"You wouldn't be," he says firmly. "Besides, there will be tons of people. It's a big celebration with enough chaos to make you feel right at home." He gives me a hopeful smile, and I can see how much this means to him.

I bite my lip, torn. This could be a chance to see a different side of Knox, but this is serious.

"Okay," I say at last, and his face lights up. "I'll come. But if it gets too overwhelming, I reserve the right to make a quick escape."

"Excellent," he says, and I can almost hear the relief in his voice. "You're going to love Mamita. She's a firecracker."

"I'm sure she is," I say, stirring the pot again. The confession of his feelings and the kiss have already left me off balance. Now this invitation is making me feel as if I'm teetering on the edge of a cliff.

The vegetables have softened, and I add the tortellini to the pot. "It needs a few more minutes," I say, turning to face him. He's closer than I expected, and I take an involuntary step back.

"Selene," he starts, but I cut him off.

"So what should I wear? To the party, I mean."

He pauses, clearly switching gears in his head. "It's casual. Just come as you are."

As I am. "Got it," I say. "Casual."

The tortellini swirls in the pot, and I watch it like a crystal ball, hoping for some glimpse of the future. What will it be like, meeting his family? Will they welcome me with open arms? More than that, what does this mean for us? Are we a thing now?

I'm so lost in thought that I don't notice when Knox

reaches for me. His hand lands gently on my shoulder, and I look over at him.

"Hey," he says softly. "You don't have to overthink it. Just come and have fun."

I nod, though I know that overthinking is my default setting. He means well, but he doesn't realize the whirlwind he's unleashed in my mind.

"Let's eat. Can you grab some bowls?"

Knox releases my shoulder and moves to a cabinet. He pulls out two ceramic bowls. He hands them to me, and I give us both generous portions of the steaming soup. The rich aroma of parmesan fills the kitchen, mingling with the warmth of the broth.

We take our bowls to the dining table. Just as we are sitting down, I hear a door open and look up and find Wilder walking into the room. He scratches his head as he takes in the scene before him. "Am I interrupting something?"

Knox and I exchange a quick glance. "Not at all," Knox says, leaning back in his chair. "Just having some dinner. Tortellini soup. Want some? Selene made enough for an army."

Wilder's eyes flicker with a mix of emotions. "Tortellini soup?" he asks, as if he doesn't quite believe it.

"Yeah," I say, trying to sound casual. "There's plenty if you're hungry."

Wilder shrugs, but I can see the wheels turning in his

head. "Sure, why not?" He walks over to the stove and scoops himself a big portion into a bowl.

As Wilder takes a seat at the table, I notice the tension in Knox's posture. This was supposed to be our time, but now we have an audience. Maybe that's for the best, I think. It gives me a little more time to process everything without the immediate pressure of Knox's attention solely on me.

"So," Wilder says, blowing on his soup. "What's the occasion? You two celebrating something?"

"Selene wants to cook more, and we have a kitchen that we barely use," Knox says smoothly. "We are just catching up."

"Just catching up," Wilder repeats and I can tell he doesn't believe Knox. He takes a large, deliberate spoonful of soup and chews slowly. "This is really good," he says, directing the compliment at me. "You should cook for us more often."

"Thanks. I'm glad you're enjoying it," I say.

"Yeah, Selene, this is delicious, but I didn't expect anything less."

Knox's compliment makes me smile and I try to hide it by taking another spoonful of the soup. It doesn't work.

"You know, Selene, if you're going to start cooking for the team, we should set up a schedule. Maybe a weekly thing?"

Wilder's joke doesn't land like he thought it would

because Knox is quick to respond. "Leave her alone," he says low enough that it almost sounds like a growl.

Wilder raises an eyebrow and lets out a low whistle. "Well, don't let me get in the way of your dinner." He shovels a bit more soup into his mouth and stands up. "Thanks for the soup, Selene. I'll take this to my room."

With that, he leaves Knox and I alone, and I'm left looking at Knox like he's grown another head. "What was that all about? Wilder was obviously joking."

Knox studies his soup for a moment. "I know he was joking. Sometimes he doesn't know when to stop. I don't want you to feel obligated to do anything that you might not want to do."

I open my mouth to argue, but close it just as quickly. I can see how that can become a problem and I'm not going to lie to myself and say I didn't enjoy that he defended me.

In fact, I more than enjoyed it. I loved it.

26

SELENE

I flip another page of my textbook, the same book I'm supposed to be using to help me study for an exam in a couple of days. I'm convinced that the words are blurring together versus it being a result of my exhaustion. Normally, being up late for my shift at the library is easy peasy, but tonight I'm struggling.

As I fight the urge to yawn, my mind keeps drifting back to Knox's invitation from several days ago. I'm still trying to figure out why he thought it was a good idea to invite me to his grandmother's birthday celebration. Things have been great, but still, it caught me off guard.

This feels like a massive step and while I want to go, I'm left wondering what the hell all of this means. Are things moving too fast between the two of us?

Maybe? Probably? Yolo?

As I debate what all of this might mean, I turn the

page again and I notice a folded note. I stare at it for few seconds because I'm confused by what I'm looking at. This wouldn't be the first time I've found little notes or mementos in my college books, but it's also super random. I unfold the note and immediately recognize the handwriting. It's because I have another letter with similar penmanship. However, this note is much more uplifting than the one I received previously.

Just thinking about you and wanted to leave you a little something. You're going to kick that exam's ass.

Yours

-K

A small smile tugs at the corners of my lips as I reread Knox's words, It's such a simple gesture, but his reassurance feels like a warm hug on a cold winter night.

It's strange how a few scribbled lines can shift my entire mood. The stress of this exam, my exhaustion, the confusion over our relationship fades for a moment. For these precious few moments, they don't matter. His words have managed to muffle all of the other noise in my brain, giving me a chance to just exist.

I fold the note carefully and tuck it into my wallet for safe keeping. I try to remove the tiredness from my body by standing up and stretching. It helps somewhat, but I could still fall asleep at this desk with no problem.

When I sit back down at the circulation desk, I pull out my phone to send Knox a quick text message.

> Me: Found your note. That was really sweet, thank you.

I wait about ten seconds to see if Knox is going to respond. When he doesn't, I force myself to focus back on my textbook. I need to make at least a small dent in this material before my shift ends.

I manage to read a few more pages before my phone vibrates with an incoming text. My heart skips a beat as I grab it, hoping it's Knox. Sure enough, his name lights up the screen.

> Knox: Anytime and I meant every word. You've got this.

I can't stop the grin that spreads across my face. Seriously, what is this life that this is now happening to me?

> Me: Thanks for the vote of confidence. I needed that tonight.

> Knox: Rough shift?

> Me: I'm just tired. And studying for this exam is kicking my ass.

> Knox: I'm sorry. Wish I could be there.

I stare at Knox's last message and sigh. He has an early

morning practice and shouldn't even be texting me right now, if I'm being honest.

> Me: I wish you were here too. It would make this night a lot better. But also, go to sleep.

> Knox: You're right. And Coach will have my ass if I'm not bright eyed and bushy tailed. Night, picosita.

> Me: Haha goodnight.

I put my phone away, still smiling as I eye my textbook. Who would have thought that all I needed was Knox's thoughtfulness to get me through the rest of my shift? I manage to review quite a few pages and am pleased that the concepts are finally starting to click into place.

After I do my routine of making sure that everyone is out of the library, I make my way to the entrance to lock those doors. But what greets me leaves me stunned.

There, standing outside the library doors, is Knox. He's leaning against a brick wall, one hand tucked into his pocket, the other holding onto what looks like a cup of coffee. When he sees me, a slow smile spreads across his face.

I push open the door, my heart doing a little flip in my chest. "What are you doing here?" I ask, trying to keep my voice steady. "I thought you had an early practice."

"I do. But I couldn't stop thinking about you and figured you could use some midnight fuel."

"You didn't have to do that," I say as I reach for the cup. Our fingers brush, and goosebumps appear on my arms.

"I wanted to," Knox says simply. "I know how hard you've been working."

I take a sip of the coffee, and I swear it's like everything makes sense again. "Thank you," I say softly. "This is exactly what I needed."

"You're welcome."

Together, we walk to the parking lot, and I quickly realize that my car is the only car there. "Where's your car?"

"Wilder owed me a favor."

"And you made him pay you back at midnight? By helping you bring me coffee?"

Knox shrugs. "It was worth it."

I chuckle. "You're something else, Knox Sanchez."

"And I'll take that as a compliment."

I wave him off. "Of course you would. But I'll allow it since this coffee tastes delicious."

When we reach my car, I turn to face him. "Did you want to come back to my place, or should I drop you off at yours?"

"Well, as much as I'd love to come back to your place, I should probably get some sleep before practice. I didn't bring my gear, but... that doesn't mean you can't come back to my place. You can use my desk and sleep in. I want to have you in my arms, even if it's for an hour."

"That's...not a bad idea. I can pack a quick bag, so if you're cool with me stopping at my dorm, I can make that work."

Knox nods. "I'm more than cool with that. Let's swing by your dorm so you can grab what you need."

The drive to my place is quick, and I dash inside to throw some clothes and my toothbrush into a bag. When I return to the car, Knox is fiddling with the radio, settling on a soft indie station.

As we make our way to his house, a comfortable silence settles between us. It's late, and the streets are quiet, the world feeling still and peaceful. Knox reaches over and takes my hand, his thumb brushing over my knuckles. The simple touch makes me feel even more at peace.

When we arrive at the hockey house, all the lights are out. Knox leads me inside with his hand resting gently on the small of my back. When he closes the door behind us, I realize just how quiet it is. And it feels so strange. I've been here when there are no parties going on, but this still feels weird.

Knox takes my bag from me, and I follow him up the stairs to his bedroom.

"It's so quiet," I whisper. "I don't think I've ever heard it this silent before."

"That's because everyone's actually asleep for once," he says as he closes his bedroom door, shutting us off from the rest of the world. Thankfully, he left his desk lamp on so we can still see.

"And yet here you are, awake at an ungodly hour, all to bring me coffee and let me invade your space."

He reaches out, tucking a stray strand of hair behind my ear. "Invade away. I just like being around you whenever I get the opportunity. And that's something I thought I would never say again."

"A lot of things are changing, I guess."

Knox nods and gives me a small. "That they are. That they are..." His voice trails off. "Okay, let's get you all set up so that you can study."

"And you can go to sleep. Don't forget that part."

Knox chuckles softly as he sets my bag near his desk. "I won't forget. But first, let's make sure you have everything you need."

He clears some space on his desk, stacking his own textbooks and papers neatly to the side. Then he pulls out the chair, gesturing for me to sit.

I do as he wants and set my now-cool coffee down on the surface. I pull out my textbook and notes, preparing to get at least a couple of more hours of studying in.

"Is there anything else you need?" Knox asks, his voice low. "A blanket?"

I glance up at him. "I think I'm good. But thank you."

"Okay. I'll let you get to it then."

As he turns to head toward his bed, I reach out and catch his hand. "Knox?"

He looks back at me with an eyebrow raised.

I give his hand a gentle squeeze. "Thank you. For everything tonight. It means a lot."

"Stop thanking me. I'm happy to do this for you." With a final squeeze of my hand, he lets go and makes his way to the bed.

I watch as he strips off his shirt and jeans, leaving him in just his boxers. Even in the dim light, I can't help but admire his body. Knox catches me staring and smirks, making me quickly turn back to my textbook.

I hear the rustle of sheets as Knox climbs into bed. "Good night. Wake me if you need anything."

"I will. Sweet dreams," I whisper back.

The room falls quiet except for the sound of Knox's even breathing and me occasionally turning a page. I manage to review a couple of chapters before I can feel the crash that's about to happen.

When it's hard for me to keep my head up, I decide to call it quits. I make my way to the bag that I packed, quickly change into my pajamas, turn off the lamp, and manage to crawl into Knox's bed without stubbing my toe.

As if he knows that I've joined him in his bed, he turns his body, molding it around mine. I hear what sounds like my name mumbled under his breath, and I can't help but release a sigh of relief.

I'm at peace here and his arms. It's when I come to the realization that I'm making the right choice by going to meet Knox's family this weekend.

27

KNOX

The soft sound of Selene's fingers tapping against the dashboard draws my attention to her briefly before I turn my eyes back to the road. She seems to be intently focused on the landscape out of the window versus anything else. I'm not sure if it's nerves about meeting my family or something else entirely.

"You're not second-guessing this, are you?" I ask. I keep my tone light so as not to freak her out.

"Um...no, I'm not second-guessing. Just... thinking."

I accept that answer instead of pushing for more. The last thing I want is to make her feel cornered, especially when she's walking into a situation that is as over-whelming as this. It's only a couple of more minutes before I'm putting my car into park as Willow is walking down the stairs with her phone in hand and a small bag in the other.

"There she is," I say.

Selene looks up, and the second her eyes land on Willow, she looks back at me with her mouth open wide. "Wait... is that Willow?"

I frown, glancing between the two of them. "Yeah? Why?"

Willow notices us then, shoving her phone into her pocket and heading toward the car. The moment she opens the door and spots Selene, her mouth falls open. "What the hell?"

"Oh shit, I forgot you two met each other..." I can't remember where it was.

Willow slides into the backseat, still staring at Selene. "Hiking. Hailey, Jade, and Isla were there too." She pauses for a split second before a smirk appears. "This weekend just got a whole lot more interesting."

"You could say that again," Selene mumbles. "Knox didn't say anything besides that his sister was coming with us."

"And he mentioned that he was bringing a friend home with us, but I thought it was one of his teammates." Willow's eyebrows shoot up as she puts on her seatbelt, and then she bursts out laughing. "You've been hanging out with my brother to the point where he invited you to Mamita's birthday party and you didn't even know? Oh, this is too good."

"I didn't exactly think it was relevant," I mutter, putting the car back into drive and starting the journey to home.

"Not relevant?" Willow says. "Oh, Selene, you're in for a treat. This guy is a disaster."

"I'm sitting right here," I point out, but it doesn't matter because they're already ignoring me.

"Big brother, this was a mistake on your part because I have so many stories that I can tell."

Out of the corner of my eye, I see Selene turn in her seat to face Willow. "Oh, do tell. I'm always up for some good Knox stories."

"Oh my fucking—" I start, but I'm quickly cut off.

"Do you hear something? Maybe it's just the wind," Willow says. When I meet her gaze in the rearview mirror, she sticks out her tongue and I return the sentiment by giving her a one finger salute.

Selene giggles, a sound that somehow manages to ease some of the tension in my shoulders over how this whole car ride is going so far. "I think it was just the wind," she agrees.

I let out a heavy sigh, resigning myself to my fate. "All right, you two, get it out of your system now. Just remember, Willow, I've got plenty of dirt on you too."

Willow scoffs. "Please, I'm an angel compared to you."

"An angel? Really? So that time you got caught sneaking out—"

"Okay, okay!" Willow cuts in. "Let's not get carried

away. I'm just saying, Selene, if you want to know anything about Knox, I'm your girl."

I glance at Selene has her gaze darts between us. "I might just take you up on that."

I groan, focusing on the road ahead. "I'm starting to think this was a terrible idea."

"Too late now," Willow sing-songs from the back seat. "You're stuck with us."

The rest of the drive passes in a blur filled with Willow's embarrassing stories and Selene's laughter. I try to interject in an effort to defend myself, but it's a losing battle. By the time we pull up to the house, I'm seriously questioning my life choices.

"Home sweet home," Willow declares as she hops out of the car. "Ready for the chaos, Selene?"

Selene glances at me. I can see her nervousness before she covers it with a grin. "As ready as I'll ever be."

"Wills, can you give Selene and me a moment?"

Willow raises an eyebrow, glancing between us with a knowing smirk. "Sure thing. I'll just be inside, waiting to embarrass you further." She grabs her bag and heads for the front door, leaving Selene and me alone in the car.

I turn to face Selene "Hey, you doing okay? I know this is a lot."

She takes a deep breath and throws a small smile my way. "Yeah, I'm okay. Just a little nervous, I guess. Meeting the family is kind of a big deal."

I reach out and take her hand in mine. It's done to

soothe her nerves, but it helps me as well. This is the first time I've brought anyone home since Tessa. "You've got nothing to worry about. They're going to love you." I pause, a grin tugging at my lips. "Well, maybe not as much as Willow seems to."

Selene laughs, squeezing my hand. "I can handle Willow. It's your grandmother and mom I'm worried about impressing."

"Trust me, just be yourself and they'll adore you." I lean in and press a soft kiss to her cheek. "You ready?"

She nods. "Let's do this."

We climb out of the car, and I grab our bags from the trunk. The sound of music and laughter grows louder as we walk toward my front door. I can feel Selene's hand tighten in mine as we climb the porch steps.

Before I can knock, the door swings open, revealing my mom's beaming face. "Knox! Finally!" She pulls me into a tight hug before turning her attention to Selene. "And you must be Selene! We've heard so much about you."

Selene throws me a surprised look before smiling at my mom. "It's so nice to meet you, Dr. Sanchez. Thank you for having me."

"You're welcome," Mom waves us inside. "Come in, come in! Just about everyone is here."

The first thing I notice is the smell of Mamita's cooking filling the air. It feels so much like home that I'm taken back by how much I actually missed this.

In the kitchen, we find Mamita watching the last of the cooking . Mom walks over to her, taps her on the shoulder and points at us. As soon as her eyes meet mine, her face lights up. "Mijo! There you are!" She pulls me down for a kiss on the cheek before turning to Selene. "And who is this beautiful girl?"

"Mamita, this is Selene. Selene, this is the birthday girl herself."

Selene extends her hand, but Mamita pulls her into a warm embrace. "Welcome. We're so happy to have you here."

Selene returns the hug. "Thank you so much. It's wonderful to meet you. Happy birthday!"

Mamita pulls back, patting Selene's cheek affectionately. "Thank you. Now, let me get a good look at you." She studies Selene appraisingly, then nods in approval. "Beautiful and polite. Knox, you've done well."

I feel my cheeks warm at the praise. "Thanks, Mamita. I think so too."

Selene blushes, her eyes meeting mine briefly before she looks away.

"Now, you two go get settled," Mamita commands. "Dinner will be ready soon, and then the real party begins!" She shoos us out of the kitchen.

Since I need to bring our bags upstairs, I decide to give Selene a quick tour of the house and show her where she'll be sleeping for the night. The stairwell leading up is packed with framed photos, several of them featuring a much younger me with different hockey teams. Selene pauses to look at a few.

"You were such a cute kid," she teases, pointing at a photo of me missing my two front teeth.

"Were?" I pretend to be offended.

"Cute isn't exactly how I would describe you now. Handsome and hot are what come to mind first."

"Excellent save."

She rolls her eyes but smiles as she moves on to the next set of pictures. "Your family is really tight knit, huh? It must have been nice, moving around together like that."

"It was," I say. "Hockey gave me a constant, something to hold onto no matter where we ended up. And we had to rely on each other more because of the constant moving."

We continue the tour, and I show her the office where my dad keeps his military memorabilia, then the sunroom that my mom has turned into her craft space.

Finally, I open the door to the guest room. "This is where you'll be crashing."

Selene walks in and I can see that she's taking in the cozy space with its soft blue walls and floral bedspread. "It's perfect. Thanks, Knox."

I set her bag down near the bed. "I'm just across the hall if you need anything."

"Good to know."

I'm about to say something else when Willow appears in the doorway. "There you two are! Come on, everyone's waiting to meet Selene."

I glance at Selene, trying to figure out what she's thinking, but she has a grin plastered on her face. "Lead the way."

We head back downstairs where the party is in full swing. Music blares from the speakers as my younger cousins are having a dance-off in the middle of the floor. The dining room table is filled with a spread of food that would make any restaurant jealous—tamales, enchiladas, and tostadas—all of it homemade. Various family members are hanging out, balancing plates and glasses, shouting to be heard over the music. I spot my dad in the corner, deep in conversation with one of his old military buddies, and Willow is already making a beeline for the kitchen, probably to snag a soda or some dessert.

Selene slows as we reach the bottom of the stairs, her eyes wide as she takes in the scene. I can tell she's a little overwhelmed, but I'll be there with her every step of the way.

As soon as we enter the main hallway, all eyes turn to Selene. I can feel her body grow tense beside me, so I place a reassuring hand on the small of her back. The music volume drops, giving me the opportunity to speak without having to yell.

"Everyone, this is Selene," I announce. That's all it takes for my family to rush over and introduce themselves. Selene is instantly surrounded by a sea of smiling faces. My aunts are the first to reach her, pulling her into tight hugs and peppering her with rapid-fire questions.

Once the introductions wind down, I guide Selene through the crowd toward the dining room. "You're doing great," I whisper.

She returns the smile, but I can still see the nerves in her eyes. "Thanks. It's just a lot all at once. It also reminds me that I should probably call my parents."

That makes me chuckle. "I know it's a lot. But they already like you, I can tell."

We reach the dining room table, and I hand Selene a plate. "Here, dig in. Mamita's tamales are legendary."

"This all looks amazing," she says as she starts filling her plate, and I do the same.

When we're done, we find a spot in the living room to eat. Selene takes a bite of a tamale, and her eyes widen. "Oh my god, Knox. This is incredible."

I grin. "Told you. Mamita's tamales are the best."

"I'm never eating anything else ever again," she declares, taking another huge bite.

I chuckle to myself. Seeing her enjoy my family's food, fit in with my relatives, and having this all go better than I thought is amazing. It feels right in a way I wasn't expecting.

And that's more than I can ask for.

28

KNOX

It's a few days after Abue's party and I find myself somewhat spiraling. I usually rely on logic instead of emotions when it comes to most aspects of my life, but unfortunately, this isn't working. As a result, I pace restlessly in my living room because I can't turn my brain off.

I'm so fucked.

My mind races as I walk back and forth. My hands alternate between hanging at my sides and nervously running through my hair. I can't remember the last time I felt this on edge.

I try to distract myself by grabbing my phone and scrolling through sports highlights. My eyes glaze over as I swipe aimlessly. I can't focus on any single post before my mind wanders back to Selene and the question I'm terrified to ask her. My attempt to distract myself fails after thirty seconds and soon my anxiety comes crashing back in.

From the corner of my eye, I catch Blaise looking at me from where he's messing with the Wi-Fi router. I assume he's improving it in some way, but don't ask me exactly what he's doing. He tilts his head at me.

"Dude, what's up with you? You're making me dizzy with all that pacing."

I brush it off with a shake of my head. "Nothing. Just thinking about practice."

Blaise's eyebrow arches, his expression making it clear he's not buying it. "Right. Practice. That's why you look like you're about to throw up. Makes total sense."

I've never been good at this whole 'talking about feelings' thing. I try to shrug it off, but my shoulders feel tense as hell. "It's nothing, seriously. Just... a lot on my mind."

Blaise snorts, clearly not convinced. He leans against the wall, arms crossed, mirroring my posture. "Knox, I've known you for years now. It's obvious something's up. Spill."

"It's Selene, man. I think... I think I want to ask her to be my girlfriend. Like, officially."

Blaise sits up straighter. "First of all, is that what has you so screwed up right now? Second of all, you haven't done that yet?"

I stop pacing and turn to face Blaise. I try to unclench my jaw, but I fail. "No, I haven't. And yes, it's messing with my head." I let out a heavy sigh, sinking into the armchair across from him. "I don't know, man. This feels different from anything I've done before. I haven't had a girlfriend since high school."

Blaise nods slowly. "I get it. She means something to you. But why are you so nervous about making it official? From where I'm sitting, it seems like a no-brainer."

I lean forward, resting my elbows on my knees. "Because I don't want to screw this up. And I'm really good at screwing things up."

"Okay, I have a question. Since when does Knox Sanchez second-guess himself?"

A smile tugs at my lips. "Since now, apparently. I'm glad my existential crisis is amusing to you."

Blaise holds up his hands in mock surrender. "Hey, I'm just saying, this isn't like you. The Knox I know is confident and decisive. He sees what he wants, and he goes for it."

I run a hand over my face, feeling the rough stubble on my jaw. "Yeah, well, maybe that Knox is an idiot who doesn't know what's good for him."

"Or maybe," Blaise counters, "that Knox is exactly who Selene fell for in the first place. You can't tell me that she doesn't care about you too."

I sit back in the chair and think about what he said. He has a point. Selene and I didn't get to this place by me second-guessing every move. I screwed up in the beginning, but I think I've made an excellent comeback. I'm grateful that Selene forgave me and gave me another chance.

"There he is. There's the Knox I know." Blaise sets down the router, giving me his full and undivided attention. "Look, man. You can't let your past experiences dictate your future. Selene isn't Tessa. And you're not the same guy you were back then either."

I hate to admit that he's right. I've grown a lot since high school, and my relationship with Selene is on a whole different level.

"I can't let my fear of messing up keep me from taking this step with her. She deserves better than that. We both do."

Blaise leans over and claps me on the shoulder. "Damn right. So what's the plan? How are you going to ask her?"

I shrug. "I don't know yet. I want it to be right, you know? Not some half-assed, spur of the moment thing."

"Makes sense. But how..."

That is the question of the day.

I stand up from the chair and start pacing again because why not? I see Blaise smirking at me out of the corner of my eye. He can laugh at me, but at this point, I don't care.

"I need to plan this out. Maybe take her somewhere nice for dinner first? Or do something more casual, like a movie?"

Blaise responds quickly. "Those are both viable options."

But are they really? Each idea seems more cliché or inadequate than the last. Selene deserves something thoughtful, something that shows her how much she means to me. Going to Prosecco & Prose again would be nice as a redo, but it's something we've done before. Then I think about asking her after a shift at a library. But we'd both be exhausted.

My frustration builds as I realize I'm shooting down every possible scenario. Why is this so hard? It was never this complicated with Tessa. But then, with Tessa, we were in high school, and everything was easy until it wasn't.

"You're overthinking it, bro," Blaise interrupts my spiraling thoughts.

I shoot him a glare. "Oh really? Tell me something I don't know."

He chuckles and shakes his head. "Alright, how about this... keep it simple and sincere. Selene likes you for you, not for some grand gesture or fancy dinner. Just find a moment when it's just the two of you and speak from the heart."

"You might be onto something there. But what if I freeze up or say the wrong thing?"

"Then you apologize, laugh it off, and try again. This isn't a marriage proposal," Blaise says with a shrug. "Dude, you've faced down guys twice your size on the ice.

You can handle telling a girl how much you care about her."

The words 'marriage proposal' make me pause, but I quickly recover. "Not even remotely the same, but okay," I say.

"I know, but I still think you're overthinking all of this."

"You're right, but I can't turn my brain off. She and I are doing an ice skating lesson tomorrow and—"

Blaise does a double take before he responds, "And that would be the perfect time to ask her!"

"Fine. I'll figure out a way to do it there. You're a genius."

Blaise grins, clearly pleased with himself. "I know I am. But seriously, everything is going to go fine. Now, can we please talk about something else? I can only handle so much emotional turmoil in one day."

"Yeah, yeah, yeah," I say as I roll my eyes. "Thanks for the pep talk, Coach."

"Anytime, man. That's what I'm here for." Blaise returns to the router.

"What are you up to?"

Blaise turns the router over in his hands. "Trying to boost the signal. The connection's been spotty in my room." He gestures to the various wires and gadgets spread out on the coffee table. "Figured I'd see if I could fix it myself before calling to have someone come out."

"Isn't it illegal to do that? Like it voids a warranty or something?"

"What they don't know won't hurt them."

I snort, more amused by Blaise's nonchalant attitude than I expected to be. For as long as I've known him, he's always been into taking things apart and putting them back together, so I can't even be surprised by what he's doing right now.

"Just don't burn the place down, alright?" I say, only half joking. "I'd prefer not to have to explain to the land-lord why our house suddenly reeks of melted plastic."

Blaise laughs, waving off my concern. "Ye of little faith. Have I ever steered you wrong before?"

I raise an eyebrow. "Do you really want me to answer that?"

"Fair enough. But seriously, I've got this under control. No fires, no explosions, no angry calls from the internet provider. Scout's honor."

"You were never a scout," I point out.

"Doesn't matter," he says and soon his attention is back on the router. "Now, are you going to stand there and critique me, or are you going to make yourself useful and grab me a beer from the fridge?"

I flip him off. "Fuck you."

Blaise just laughs, completely unfazed. "Love you too, bro. Now seriously, beer me."

I roll my eyes but head to the kitchen anyway, grabbing two cold ones from the fridge. I can be nice this one time because he did talk me off a ledge. I return to the living room, handing Blaise his beer before sinking back into the armchair. He takes a long swig, then sets the bottle aside and refocuses on the router.

29

SELENE

A s I walk up to the Crestwood Red Wolves' rink, I'm feeling both confident and nervous at the same time. I'm proud of myself for deciding to try something new but also wondering what the hell was I thinking. Why did I think it would be a good idea to learn how to skate?

Because of the man standing next to me. Holding a bag with our skates in it.

"So the arena is closed today?" I ask as we walk up to the entrance.

A smug grin spreads across Knox's face. "Yep, just you and me, picosita. I pulled some strings to get us private ice time."

I raise an eyebrow at him. "Wow, using your hockey star status to impress a girl? How original."

He just laughs, completely unfazed. "Hey, it worked, didn't it? You're here."

I can't help but smile back. He's not wrong.

When we enter the arena and make our way toward the ice, he does this very exaggerated gesture that includes a mock bow and says, "Welcome to my world."

I laugh at his antics, and it makes me feel a little better. "Wow, this is...intimidating."

Knox grins. "Nah, you got this. It's just frozen water." He sits on a bench and pulls out his own skates and then the ones I borrowed from Isla. Thankfully, we are the same shoe size.

"Nervous?" he asks, glancing over at me.

"No," I lie. Truth is that my stomach is in more knots than I should put these laces in.

"Ice skating is easy once you get used to it."

I snort as I watch him start tying his laces. I try to follow suit, but I'm not nearly as comfortable obviously. "Easy for you to say, Mr. Hockey Hottie. Some of us weren't born with blades attached to our feet."

"Hockey Hottie?" He raises an eyebrow. "I like it. Has a nice ring to it."

"And I immediately regret saying it. Your ego definitely doesn't need any more stroking." I finish tying my laces and stand up unsteadily. I move too quickly and end up flailing my arms like a chicken.

Knox reaches up and catches my arm, steadying me

with a strong grip. "I know something that would love some more stroking...Whoa there, Bambi. Take it easy."

I feel a blush creeping up my cheeks just before I narrow my eyes at him. "Did you just compare me to a cartoon deer?" I intentionally ignore what we both know his first sentence was hinting at.

"If the skate fits." He shrugs unapologetically. "But don't worry, by the end of this lesson, you'll be skating circles around me."

"Doubtful," I mutter, but I can't help but smile at his confidence in me.

Knox finishes lacing up his skates and stands as if he's spent more time on the ice than on solid ground. Because he probably has. He offers me his hand. "Ready to kick this ice's ass?"

I eye his outstretched hand warily. "I'm pretty sure the ice is always going to kick my ass, but I guess there's only one way to find out." I place my glove-covered hand in his and enjoy the feeling of his hand holding mine once more.

We wobble-step our way to the rink entrance and I pause. Holy shit, this is big. I smirk when I mentally say, *That's what she said.*

Sensing my hesitation, Knox squeezes my hand. "Hey, I've got you. We'll take this as slow as you need."

I nod and let him guide me onto the ice. The moment the blades touch the slick surface, my legs start to tremble.

Knox glides backward, holding both of my hands now, his eyes locked on mine. "That's it, nice and easy."

I try to mimic his movements, but my skates seem to have minds of their own. I end up falling into his solid chest. "Sorry!" I yelp, my face burning with embarrassment against the cool fabric of his sweatshirt.

Knox chuckles, the sound rumbling beneath my cheek. "No worries, I like you throwing yourself at me."

I pull back and glare at him. "In your dreams, Sanchez."

"Every night, Davis." He winks, then starts skating backward again, pulling me along with him. "Now, bend your knees a bit and try to find your center of gravity."

I do as he says, focusing on keeping my legs steady. It's not easy, especially with the way he's looking at me. It's as if I'm the only person in the world that matters. "Like this?"

"Perfect." His praise makes me feel things I shouldn't feel while ice skating. "You're a natural."

I snort. "Hardly. But I guess I have a decent teacher."

"Just decent?" He clutches his chest in mock offense. "I'm wounded."

"I'm sure your ego will survive." I manage a small glide forward, feeling more than relieved when I don't immediately faceplant.

Knox matches my pace, his hands still anchoring me. "There you go! See, I knew you could do it."

We continue like this, him skating backward while

giving me tips and encouragement, me focusing on staying upright and not making a complete fool of myself. Before I know it, we've made a full lap around the rink.

"I think I'm actually getting the hang of this," I say, surprised at how much I'm enjoying myself.

"Told you." Knox slowly releases my hands, moving to skate beside me instead. I feel momentary panic at the loss of his support, but I manage to keep my balance. We glide together, our movements becoming more in sync as if we've done this a thousand times before.

As we complete a few laps, I'm beginning to feel more confident. The fear I had when I first stepped onto the ice has melted away, and in its place is a giddy sense of accomplishment. I'm actually doing this!

Knox must sense the change in my demeanor because he turns to me and says, "Ready to try it on your own?"

My stomach does a little flip at the thought, but I nod. "I think so. Just don't go too far, okay?"

"I'll be right here," he assures me, gradually slowing his pace until he's a few feet behind me.

I take a deep breath and focus on the rhythmic glide of my skates against the ice. Left, right, left, right. I wobble a bit, my arms instinctively reaching out for balance, but I manage to stay upright. A laugh bubbles up from my chest as I realize that I have this.

"You're killing it," Knox calls out from behind me.

His encouragement fuels me, and I pick up speed, loving the cool rush of air against my face. I feel free. Of course, that's when my left skate decides to revolt, sending me forward with a yelp.

But before I can hit the ice, strong arms wrap around my waist, pulling me back against Knox's chest. I can feel his heart beating rapidly against my back, matching the frantic pace of my own.

"Whoa there," he says, his warm breath tickling my ear. "I've got you."

I let out a shaky laugh, adrenaline still coursing through my veins. "My hero," I say, only half joking.

He helps me regain my balance but doesn't let go right away. We stay like that for a moment, his arms around me, my hands resting on his forearms. It feels intimate. Safe. Like this is exactly where I'm supposed to be.

"I think that's enough excitement for one day," Knox says, his voice low and husky. He slowly releases me but takes my hand.

I nod in agreement. My heart is still pounding from both the near-fall and the feeling of Knox's arms around me. "Yeah, I think my legs have turned to jelly."

He laughs and begins guiding us toward the rink exit. "You did great though, seriously. I'm impressed."

I shrug, trying to play it cool even as a grin spreads across my face. "Well, I had a pretty great teacher."

"Pretty great, huh?" The smirk on his face tells me where this is going.

"Okay, fine. An amazing teacher. The best." I roll my eyes dramatically. "Happy now?"

"Ecstatic." He helps me off the ice and to a nearby bench.

We sit down and start unlacing our skates. As we remove them, I catch Knox watching me with a soft expression. He reaches over and runs his fingers down the side of my face, allowing them to linger on my cheek.

"Selene, I..." He pauses, as if searching for the right words. "I've been wanting to ask you something."

My brain is trying to process if this is a good thing or not. "What is it?"

He takes my hand, his thumb tracing gentle circles on my skin. "These past few weeks, getting to know you, spending time with you... It's been incredible. You're unlike anyone I've ever met."

A nervous giggle falls from my lips. "Knox..."

"Let me finish," he says with a small smile. "I know we started off well, then it quickly got messed up, and we've spent a lot of time building this into something special. At least, I think so. Just everything about you and the way you challenge me to be better. I don't want to imagine my life without you in it."

I swear I'm almost frozen in place, but at least I'm still able to speak. "What are you saying?"

He takes a deep breath, his brown eyes locking onto mine. "I'm saying that I want to be with you, Selene. Officially. I want you to be my girlfriend."

My heart skips several beats at his words. Did I hear

him right? I realize I've been silent for too long when I see a flicker of uncertainty cross his face.

He starts to pull his hand away. "If you don't feel the same way, I understand. I just thought—"

"No!" I blurt out, grabbing his hand and lacing our fingers together. "I mean, yes. Yes, I want to be your girlfriend."

The smile that spreads across his face is blinding. He tugs me closer, his free hand coming up to cup my cheek. "Yeah?"

I nod, feeling giddy again and lightheaded in the best possible way. "Yeah. I want this, Knox. I want you."

He leans in, resting his forehead against mine. "You have no idea how happy I am to hear you say that."

"I think I have an idea," I whisper, my gaze dropping to his lips.

He closes the distance between us, capturing my mouth in a slow, deep kiss. I melt into him, my hands sliding up his chest to loop around his neck. The kiss starts off gentle, but soon the intensity builds, and I find myself getting lost in the feel of Knox's lips moving against mine. His hands slide down to my waist, pulling me closer until there's no space left between us.

I tangle my fingers in his dark hair, and he lets out a low groan that sends shivers down my spine. When we finally break apart, both of us are breathing heavily.

Knox rests his forehead against mine again. "This is the best feeling in the world."

"I completely agree. I guess that means I need to come to your games when I can, huh?"

Knox moves back slightly and nods. "Absolutely."

I grin at him. "Well then, you better put on a good show for me, Hockey Hottie. I expect to be impressed."

"Oh, I'll impress you alright. Just try not to swoon too hard when I score a goal and point at you in the stands."

I shove his shoulder playfully. "You're so full of yourself. I take it back, I don't want to be your girlfriend anymore."

He captures my hand and brings it to his lips, placing a gentle kiss on my knuckles. "Too late, you're stuck with me now."

I smile as I stare into his eyes. "I guess I can live with that."

30

KNOX

I pull Selene closer to my body as the cool wind sweeps past us in an effort to keep her warm. We are just completing another date at Prosecco & Prose. I suggested we visit again because it was a no-brainer, and I wasn't surprised she couldn't resist. She exercised some impressive restraint this time, not buying every book that caught her eye, but we still managed to fill up a good portion of the bookbag I brought along.

As we approach my black and white motorcycle, she asks, "Where are we going now?"

I grab the spare helmet, hanging the book bag on the bike, and meet her gaze. I take my time fitting the helmet snugly on her head and securing it under her chin. "You'll see," I reply.

I hand her the bookbag since she'll be riding as my "backpack" for the journey ahead. Once I mount the motorcycle, she swings her leg over and settles in behind me. I look over my shoulder to find her adjusting the book bag straps just before wrapping her arms securely around my waist.

I rev the engine, enjoying the way it comes to life under my fingertips. Selene's arms tighten around me as we take off, accelerating through the alleyway and headed toward Main Street, quickly leaving Prosecco & Prose behind. The exhilaration of the ride floods through me, heightened by her warm presence pressed against my back.

We ride through the now quiet streets of downtown Crestwood and soon we are leaving all of that behind. The road opens up before us as we leave our college town behind. It becomes even more noticeable as the street-lights becoming fewer and farther between. I guide my bike onto a winding country road, and I enjoy the feeling of Selene relaxing against me.

After a while, her hands begin to wander, sliding from my waist to my thighs. I suck in a breath as her fingers make their way to one particular area of my jeans. She presses herself more firmly to my back and I can already imagine the feel of her breasts in my hands as I'm pounding into her.

"Selene..." my voice trails off, giving her a halfhearted warning.

"What?" Her voice comes through slightly muffled

through my helmet's speakers, but it doesn't hide her attempt to appear innocent. We both know that's bullshit.

My heart beats faster as her hand drifts to my zipper, her palm rubbing over the growing bulge there. I'm finding it harder to concentrate on the road, my grip tightening on the handlebars. She grows bolder and I already know how this is going to go down....

I veer the bike onto a dirt side road, easing to a stop under a bunch of trees. Before the engine grows quiet, I'm hopping off my bike at the same time and turning to face my girl, who is already pulling off her helmet.

"What are you doing besides being a fucking little tease?" I growl.

Selene steps off the bike, places her helmet on the ground and runs her fingers through her now messy red hair. "What can I say? I couldn't help myself."

I step closer to her, my hands gripping her hips and pulling her body against mine. "Is this really a game that you want to play, picosita?"

A shiver runs through her, and I know it has nothing to do with the cold. "Hell yeah. What are you going to do about it?"

"Fuck you until you're begging for mercy."

"Then, do it."

That's the only incentive I need.

I immediately turn her around and Selene is forced to lean on my motorcycle seat. I lean forward so that she can hear every word I say. "I wonder how soaked your panties are right now."

Selene's hair slightly covers her face as she looks over her shoulder. "Who said I'm wearing any?"

I reach around her and shift her coat out of the way to find the waistband of her leggings. I slip my hand beneath the protective layer to find out that while she's wearing underwear, she might as well not be. The lacy fabric does little to hide the fact she wants this as bad as I do. "Damn, baby. You're practically dripping for me."

I move her panties to the side so that I can properly tease her pussy. I can't fight the grin that covers my face behind this helmet as she moans while my fingers explore her thoroughly except to give her what I know she's craving. She can't have that yet.

"Knox, please," Selene begs. And I love the sound of it.

I chuckle. "Patience, picosita. I'm not done with you yet. And this is payback for the stunt you pulled maybe five minutes ago."

My free hand tugs at her leggings, yanking them down to her knees along with her soaked panties. The cool night air kisses her skin, and I can feel the goosebumps forming. I'm not sure she even knows she's exposed. I take a small step back so that I can admire the view. Her perfect ass is on display for my entertainment.

Unable to resist, I deliver a sharp smack to her right cheek, and I smile at the yelp that escapes her lips. I soothe the sting by gently caressing the area before I slap the other cheek.

Selene's breath comes in ragged gasps as I continue to drive her wild. I alternate between gentle caresses and sharp smacks, causing her to tremble and drawing her closer to the edge.

"Are you enjoying this?" I ask as I try to maintain some semblance of control.

Selene nods. "Yes, fuck yes. Don't stop."

I deliver another firm smack to her ass. "I didn't quite catch that, picosita. You'll have to speak up."

She moans loudly, arching her back and pressing herself against me. "Yes, fuck yes! Please, Knox, I need more. I need you."

Her desperate cries are music to my ears. I push her forward so that she's bent over my bike and slip two fingers deep inside of her. "Is this what you want, baby? You want me to fuck you right here on my bike, where anyone could see?"

"Yes!" she cries out as I pump my fingers faster, curling them to hit that sensitive spot that I found. "Please, I don't care. I just want to come."

I'm all too happy to oblige. I play with her clit and begin rubbing tight circles while I continue thrusting my fingers inside her. Selene's moans grow louder, fueling my desire to make sure she comes and that I'm the one to get her there.

"That's it, baby," I encourage her. "Let go for me. I want to feel you come all over my fingers."

My words seem to push her over the edge. Her inner walls clench around my fingers as she groans. But I'm not done yet.

"There it is. I got you, sweetheart," I say as I work her through it. "Take everything you need and more."

I slowly withdraw my fingers, bringing them to her lips so that she can taste herself. Selene hesitates for a moment before she parts her lips and takes my fingers into her mouth. The sight alone is enough to make me even harder than I already am. I quickly undo my helmet and toss it on the ground somewhere in the vicinity of us.

"Fuck, baby, you don't know how hot that is," I groan. My other hand starts fumbling with my zipper.

Selene releases my fingers with a pop. "I need your cock inside me, now."

I don't need to be told twice. In one swift motion, I grab the condom out of my back pocket and tug down my jeans and boxers just enough to pull out my cock. I stroke myself a few times, spreading the precum that's already leaking from the tip.

I slide the condom on and position myself at her entrance. I take a moment to catch my breath and watch as we're both anticipating my next move. Then with one thrust, I bury myself deep inside of her.

"Fuck, Selene," I say just before gripping her hips. She

feels incredible and I say a silent thank you every day that she's mine.

She moans as I begin to move. I quickly know that this won't be anything but fast and she has no issue meeting my pace. Her body rocks against the motorcycle as I grip her hips tighter. I find myself pulling her back to meet my strokes and I can't help but marvel at how well she's taking me.

"Yes, just like that," Selene says with a hint of raspiness in her voice. "Don't stop, Knox. Please don't stop."

I lean over her, pressing my chest to her back as I continue to pound into her. One hand reaches around to play with her breast through her shirt. It's just my luck that my earlier ministrations, must have forced her tits out of her bra because it makes my job very easy. My other hand remains anchored to her hip, guiding her body to meet mine. "You like that, picosita? You like being fucked out here where anyone could catch us?"

"God yes," she pants, turning her head to capture my lips in a searing kiss. It's the first time we've kissed since we left Prosecco & Prose, and it didn't occur to me how much I missed her sweet lips until just now. The kiss is anything but neat and I wouldn't have it any other way.

"Harder," she gasps out right after breaking our kiss. "I need it harder."

I'm all too happy to give her what she wants. I withdraw almost completely before slamming back in. The motorcycle rocks beneath us with each thrust as her groans grow louder. The intensity in me builds as I drive into her relentlessly, chasing the release we both crave.

"That's it, baby," I manage to get out. "Take every fucking inch. You feel so goddamn good."

"Knox...I'm going to—"

I stop her sentence in its tracks as I slide my hand from her breast down between her legs, my fingers finding her clit once more. I rub in time with my thrusts, determined to send her over the edge. "You're going to fucking come for me again. This time, I want to feel you come all over my cock."

Selene turns her head, and I captured her lips once more, swallowing her cries. Her body shudders against me as her orgasm crashes over her. Her pussy clenches around my cock and the sensation nearly pushing me over the edge with her. I pull away from her to grit my teeth, determined to prolong this for as long as I possibly can.

I continue to fuck Selene as she rides out the waves of her orgasm and that's when I feel what I think is a drop of rain. The feel of her pulsing around my cock is indescribable. I don't bother with slowing down my pace because I know for a fact that I'm going to make her come again and it will be followed by my own release.

"I can't come again," she says as she's gasping for air.

"Yes, you can. And you will. One more time for me."

I feel another drop of rain, then another, but I barely register it. My focus is solely on Selene, on bringing her to the brink once more and following her over the edge. I redouble my efforts, thrusting harder, deeper as my fingers play with her pussy.

Selene's moans escalate as it starts to rain harder, but it does nothing to cool us down.

"Knox," her voice cracks. "I can't be ready to come again already!"

If I could give myself a pat on the back, I would.

"You're so fucking incredible. You can come for me again, I know you can. Let go, baby. Give me one more."

"Oh my...please, fuck—"

I grin as I realize that Selene is so far gone and that I've kept my promise of making her beg for mercy. It's then that she sails over the edge for a third time, but who's counting? The sensation is too intense for me to resist any longer, and with a guttural groan, I let go, emptying myself inside her. For a moment we stay like that. Selene is so still that I wonder if she's gone into shock.

"Are you okay?"

Selene slowly nods. "Yes, but I might have lost feeling in my legs."

That makes me chuckle and another raindrop falls on my forehead. Reluctantly, I pull out of her and dispose of the condom. We both quickly get dressed because there's no time for kissing and hugging with a rainstorm about to begin.

The rain picks up as we finish getting dressed. I grab our helmets from the ground and hand Selene hers. She takes it with a shaky hand, and I know it's because she's still coming down from the high of her orgasms.

I can't resist pulling her close for one more kiss, the rain mingling with the taste of her lips. "You're amazing, you know that right?" I murmur against her lips.

She smiles up at me. "As are you. You really know how to show a girl a good time, Sanchez."

"Anytime, picosita. Now let's get on the road before this turns into a downpour."

We quickly put on our helmets and Selene grabs the bookbag before we climb back on the bike. She wraps her arms around my waist once more, hugging me close as I start the engine.

"Ready?" I look over my shoulder as I ask through my helmet's microphone.

Selene gives me a quick nod. "More than ready."

And with that, we take off back down the dirt road and head back to campus.

31

SELENE

The excitement that I feel around me is electric. I can't help but embrace it as Hailey, Jade, and I make our way through the sea of red and white jerseys. Hailey leads the way; I assume she's scanning the ice for any sign of Levi. Despite her usual grumpy demeanor, there is no doubt in my mind that she's happy to be here.

"There they are!" Jade squeals, pointing to a cluster of players warming up near the goal. I follow her gaze and spot the guys.

My eyes immediately find Knox. I saw small aspects of the moves he showed off during our private skating lesson; however, watching him warm up and prepare for this game has me thinking so many different thoughts.

My gaze lingers on Knox as he goes through his pre-game stretches. Heat rises in my cheeks as I watch him transition into a deep lunge. I watch as his hips thrust forward while he extends his arms over his head. Part of me wants to look away, but there's no chance in hell that I would. When he drops into a groin stretch on the ice, I nearly lose my mind.

I'm so entranced by Knox's movements that I barely register Jade's elbow digging into my side. "You might want to close your mouth before you start drooling," she says.

I snap my jaw shut, feeling the heat in my cheeks intensify. "I wasn't—I mean, I was just—" I stammer, trying to find an excuse for what I was doing but failing epically.

"Uh-huh," Jade says with a smirk.

Hailey saves me from further embarrassment. "Come on, let's find our seats before the game starts." She tugs on my arm, and I follow without hesitation.

As we settle into our seats, I can't help but let my gaze drift back to the ice. Knox is still going through his warm-up routine, and I'm still mesmerized by his movements. My eyes drift away from him for a moment until I see Isla's blonde ponytail. She has her camera up to her face, snapping shots of the Red Wolves as they get ready to play.

The buzzer sounds, jolting me out of my daydream. My eyes are drawn back to Knox as he is now standing with his team, tapping the blade of his stick against the ice. His head tilts slightly as he listens to Coach Johnson. I wonder what's going through his mind right now. He looks calm, focused, but there's an intensity in his stance that I remember seeing just before the start of the game I watched from Hailey and Jade's apartment.

"Ready for this?" Hailey asks me, breaking my thoughts.

I nod as I smooth my hands down Knox's jersey, which he insisted I wear tonight. However, I'm not sure if I'm nodding because I'm referring to the game or the fact that watching Knox play is already doing something to me. Things like making me cross my legs tightly in an attempt to maintain some form of control.

Before I know it, the game begins, and I already feel like I'm on the edge of my seat. At first, it's hard to follow what's happening. The players move so fast it's a blur, and the announcer's voice over the loudspeaker only adds to the noise. Hailey and Jade are shouting, but I can barely make out what they are saying because their cheers are blending in with the roar of the crowd. But all I can do is watch Knox. I swear he's everywhere. Racing across the ice, weaving between defenders, and crashing into the boards with a sound that makes me wince. Every time he moves, it's like watching something that has been choreographed to perfection but is also chaotic at the same time.

I zero in on Levi, who is in the center of it all as he snatches the puck. Hailey lets out an uncharacteristic yell of triumph as he passes it to Knox, who streaks down the left side of the ice.

My heart jumps into my throat as Knox dodges around one of the opposing players, his movements as smooth as the ice he's skating on. I think he's on the attack now, working with Asher, who is near him on the right.

"They're setting it up," Jade whispers, but her eyes never move from the action in front of her.

Setting what up? I want to ask, but the crowd erupts as Knox fires the puck toward the net. The goalie blocks it, but Levi's already there, scooping up the rebound and sending it back where it belongs.

Hailey jumps out of her seat, screaming, "Yes!" while Jade claps loudly. I can't help but smile, even if I don't entirely understand how it all came together.

As the first period continues, I find myself getting caught up in the excitement. The Red Wolves are playing well, and Knox is a force on the ice. Every time he gets the puck, I grab Jade's arm because I'm so nervous. Over time, I assume I'll get better, but for now, Jade doesn't seem to mind.

During a break in play, I let my gaze wander and that's when I notice a familiar person standing a few rows behind us. My eyes have to be messing with me right now.

It's Tessa. Isla's roommate. And Knox's ex-girlfriend.

My stomach twists as her gaze meets mine. There's a flicker of recognition in her eyes, followed by something else. Surprise? Curiosity? She tilts her head slightly, as if piecing together the puzzle of why I'm here. It doesn't help that I'm wearing Knox's jersey.

Not that I'm the only one wearing his jersey in the arena, but given the warning she gave me weeks ago about how I shouldn't put him on that fake list as a guy to rebound with, I'm sure she's probably trying to figure out what this is all about.

I quickly look away, trying to focus on the game again. But I can feel Tessa's gaze lingering on me like she's staring a hole through me. Hailey must notice my discomfort because she leans in closer to me to say something in my ear.

"Everything okay?" she asks.

I debate brushing it off, but decide honesty is the best policy. "Knox's ex-girlfriend, who wants him back, is here," I murmur. "A few rows back."

Hailey's eyes widen and she casually glances over her shoulder. When she turns back to me, she rolls her eyes, but not at me. "Ignore her," she says firmly.

I try to but there's also a small urge to see if she tries something. I think back to how she treated Isla when we were hanging out in common area of their dorm. I'd wanted to hit her then and I'm not all that afraid to do it now, if I'm being honest.

"I will. Plus, Knox and I are officially dating, so she's going to be even more pissed."

This time Jade grabs my arm. "Excuse me, what?!"

I turn to face Jade, and I can't help but smile. "Knox and I made it official yesterday," I confess.

Jade's eyes widen, her mouth forming a perfect 'O' before breaking into a grin. "Selene! That's huge! Why didn't you tell us sooner?"

I shrug, glancing back at the ice where Knox is lining up for a face-off. "I didn't have a chance to?"

"I'm so happy for you," Hailey says, but her face doesn't look it. That's what happens when you have a resting bitch face.

The buzzer sounds, signaling the end of the first period. The Red Wolves are up 1-0, thanks to Levi's goal off Knox's rebound. As the players skate off the ice, I can't help but feel so proud. My boyfriend just helped his team take the lead. My boyfriend. The words still feel new and exciting on my tongue.

Jade turns to me, her eyes sparkling with mischief. "So, tell us everything! How did it happen? Who asked who? I need details, Selene!"

I laugh, shaking my head. "It wasn't some big, dramatic thing. He gave me an ice skating lesson and he brought it up."

Hailey nods approvingly. "Good. You two are good together. Also explains why you're wearing his jersey."

"Yeah, he made sure that I had one for today," I respond.

We continue to chat until the second period starts. Once it does, I try to focus on the game and it's very difficult. It looks as if Knox is playing even more aggressively now, but my attention is divided because of Tessa's presence behind me. It helps that Knox is playing exceptionally well and I get swept up in my own and the crowd's excitement. But even as I cheer for Knox and the Red Wolves, I can't shake the feeling of Tessa's eyes on me. I try to ignore it, but I still know she's there.

The Red Wolves are holding onto a slim lead, but the opposing team is pushing hard. I hold my breath when Knox steals the puck and breaks away toward the goal. The crowd is on their feet, myself included, as he closes in on the goalie. With a flick of his wrist, he sends the puck flying into the lower corner of the net. The arena erupts in cheers.

"Yes! Go Knox!" I shout, jumping up and down. Hailey and Jade are screaming beside me, also caught up in the excitement.

As the team begins to celebrate the goal, Knox turns his head, and I swear our eyes connect. With his signature, cocky smirk, he lifts his stick and points directly at me.

Like he made that goal for me.

The noise around me fades for a split second as I take this moment in. Holy shit this is intense and exciting at the same time. Then he skates away like he didn't just do that in front of everyone.

As the team celebrates the goal, I can't help but sneak a glance back at Tessa. She's still there, her eyes fixed on Knox. I quickly turn back to the ice, trying to push her out of my mind. The game continues at a breakneck pace. Levi and Asher are playing their hearts out, supporting Knox and driving the team forward. By the end of the third period, the Red Wolves have secured a solid lead. The final buzzer sounds, and the crowd goes wild.

I'm on my feet, cheering until my voice is hoarse. Hailey and Jade pull me into a hug, and we start squealing. As we make our way out of the stands and toward the players' exit, the adrenaline from the win is still pumping through my veins. Jade is chatting with Hailey about how exciting the game was and all I can do is nod along because my mind is on Knox. I can't wait to congratulate him on the win, to see his face light up with that cocky grin of his.

As we approach the exit, I spot my best friend. "Isla!" I call out, waving.

She turns, her face breaking into a smile when she sees us. "Hey, guys! What a game, huh?"

"It was incredible," I agree as we reach her. "Your photos must be amazing."

Isla shrugs as if she isn't a fantastic photographer. "I got some good shots. But enough about me, how was it attending the game as a hockey girlfriend?" she teases with a wink.

"It was...intense," I admit. "I don't think I've ever been so on edge watching a sport before."

Isla laughs. "Welcome to the world of dating a hockey player. You'll get used to it."

"I sure hope so," I mutter, glancing around for any sign of Knox.

Just then, Asher emerges from the locker room, his hair still damp from his post-game shower. He spots us and makes a beeline toward where we are standing.

"Well, well, if it isn't the Red Wolves' biggest fans," he drawls, throwing an arm around Isla's shoulders. She rolls her eyes but leans into him.

"You played great out there," Hailey tells him sincerely.

Asher shrugs. "I was alright. Knox though, he was on fire tonight. Did you see that goal in the third period? The man's a machine."

I smile proudly at the praise for my boyfriend. My boyfriend. I swear I'll get used to it at some point.

As if summoned by our conversation, Knox appears, a small cut on his cheek and a satisfied gleam in his eye. My heart skips a beat as his gaze locks with mine. He makes his way over to me, ignoring the good-natured ribbing from his teammates.

"Hey, you," he whispers, slipping an arm around my waist.

I melt into his touch. "Hey yourself," I murmur back, unable to keep the smile off my face. "You were incredible out there."

Knox's lips quirk up in that signature cocky grin of his. "Not too bad, huh?" He pulls me closer, his hand resting comfortably on my hip like it belongs there. Because it does.

I'm about to respond when I catch a glimpse of movement out of the corner of my eye. I glance over and see Tessa, lingering near the exit, her gaze fixed on us. Well, more specifically, on Knox's arm around me. Her expression is unreadable, but it doesn't take a rocket scientist to figure out what she's thinking.

Knox must sense my tension because he follows my line of sight. When he spots Tessa, I feel him stiffen slightly. But instead of pulling away, he does the opposite. In a move that's both casual and deliberate, he turns his head and presses a quick kiss to my temple.

It's a small gesture, but the meaning behind it is clear. He's choosing me, right here, right now, in front of everyone. Including Tessa.

I can't help but lean into him, but when I glance back at Tessa, she's already turning away to leave.

As Tessa disappears from view, Knox's arm tightens around me. "You good?" he says in my ear.

I nod, turning to face him fully. "I'm good. More than good, actually. I'm so proud of you, Knox."

His eyes soften, a rare vulnerability peeking through his usual bravado. "Thanks, picosita. It means a lot having you here."

I brush my fingers along his jawline. "There's nowhere else I'd rather be."

Knox leans into my touch for a moment before straightening up.

"Alright, lovebirds," Asher calls out, breaking the spell. "Let's get Levi and Wilder and get out of here."

With that announcement, Knox moves his arm from around my waist to slip his hand into mine. He brings the back of my hand up to his lips and puts a small kiss on it. And the look in his eyes tells me that is just a small taste of what is to come tonight.

32

SELENE

A quick sigh leaves my lips as I slide another book onto the shelf. Normally I don't mind my job but tonight has been boring. It's been so bad that I've spent part of the night picking at my split ends. It's then that I realize I need to get a haircut. Maybe I can convince Isla to come with and we can make it a little self-care day.

With a yawn, I pull my phone from my pocket, half-expecting a text from Knox. There is none, but I do have a notification: Knox Sanchez posted a photo.

My stomach gives an involuntary flip as I swipe open the app.

The photo is from last night's game—a shot of Knox skating down the ice with his eyes locked in on the puck.

Damn, he looks good.

I tap the heart without thinking, then scroll through the comments. I find praise from fans, Wilder hyping him up, and a few thirst comments that make me roll my eyes. But then I see this one:

TESSAM9352: GOOD SEEING YOU AFTER THE GAME. 😌 STILL THINKING ABOUT IT.

What the hell?

My pulse spikes as I reread the words, hoping I somehow misunderstood. But there they are, staring up at me from the screen.

Good seeing you after the game.

My thumb hovers over the comment as if I can erase it from his page and from my mind with sheer willpower. The emoji she used feels like a slap in the face.

Is she implying that—?

No. No way. Knox wouldn't—

Would he?

I let out a shaky breath as I scroll quickly to see if Knox replied, but there's nothing. No acknowledgment. No like. Maybe he didn't see it. Maybe he ignored it.

But it doesn't stop the knot from forming in my stomach. I lock my phone and place it on the ground near me. I keep telling myself it's nothing and she's just trying to get his attention.

Except it doesn't feel like nothing.

. . .

I'm so lost in thought that I almost don't hear the footsteps approaching. While the carpet does muffle the sound, I can still hear the person growing closer. At first, I assume it's just a student who wandered in to grab a book before the library closes in less than thirty minutes. But when I turn around, Knox is standing there, hands in his pockets, staring me down.

My mouth drops open in shock. "Knox? What are you doing here?"

"Thought you might need some company," he says, his voice low and smooth.

"What—why?"

He shrugs casually, but his eyes are fixed intently on mine. "You mentioned you were working late tonight so I thought I would stop by."

Why am I questioning my boyfriend's motives?

I shake my head, trying to recover from my shock. "Well, this is...unexpected." A small smile tugs at my lips as I step closer to him. "I swear you've been in here more recently than you've ever been in here the entirety of your Crestwood career."

That makes him laugh. "And you would be correct. Maybe I'm expanding my horizons. Or maybe I just wanted to see you." He reaches out, his fingers grazing my hip and pulling me gently toward him.

Being in his arms again makes me feel warm and cherished. However, I still feel uneasy as because there is a knot still sitting low in my stomach. I glance at him, hesitating before I blurt, "Did you see the comments on your post from last night?"

Knox tilts his head slightly. "Not really. I just posted it and hopped off. Why?"

I hesitate. *Just let it go.* But the words slip out anyway. "Tessa commented on it."

His expression shifts instantly, and I can see the coldness in his eyes. "What did she say?"

I grab my phone off the floor and scroll to the post. Knox steps closer as I hold up the screen, his eyes scanning the words. His lips end up pressed into a thin line.

"Selene, I didn't see her after the game," he says firmly, eyes snapping back to mine. "I took you back to your dorm room and that was it. I haven't talked to her, haven't even thought about—" He stops short and lets out a long breath as if he's trying to keep from swearing.

"I know," I say quickly, but my voice doesn't sound as confident as I want it to.

"She's just trying to get attention," Knox says. "That's all this is. I didn't see her. I wouldn't do that to you."

My fingers tighten around my phone as I glance back at the screen. The comment stares up at me, mocking my insecurities that I've done so well to hide. Or so I thought.

Knox's fingers brush along my jaw as he tips my face up, so I have to meet his gaze. "Hey. I'm with you. Not her. Don't let her mess with us."

I swallow, heat rising behind my eyes as I force a small smile. "I know. It just caught me off guard."

"Then forget about it," he says, brushing a strand of hair behind my ear. "Because I promise you, she's not part of my life anymore."

His thumb grazes my cheekbone and just like that, the knot in my chest starts to loosen. I exhale slowly, the stress that I felt begins to fade as I let myself lean into his touch. For a moment, neither of us says anything.

Then Knox tilts his head, and I immediately recognize the look in his eyes. I already know where this is going. I quickly shake my head before I say, "Knox..."

His lips quirk into that familiar smirk. "What? I can't visit my girlfriend at work?" I shiver when he leans in, and I feel his breath hot against my ear. "Besides, there's something kinda hot about fooling around here, isn't there?"

I giggle as I playfully shove at his chest. "You're ridiculous. And we are not having sex in the library!"

"Who said anything about sex?" Knox teases, but the heat in his eyes tells a different story.

I roll my eyes, trying to ignore the way my body responds to his. "I know how your mind works, Sanchez. But I'm at work. And as much as I appreciate the company, I can't exactly take a break."

Knox doesn't retreat, his hands settling more firmly on my hips as he backs me up against the bookshelf. "I think you can spare a few minutes," he murmurs, his face hovering inches from mine. "I saw that you have someone working at the circulation desk with you tonight. No one's going to miss you but me."

I can't shift my gaze from his because the intensity in his brown eyes has me locked in. I know I should push him away, insist that I need to get back to work. But I can't seem to make myself move.

"Knox, we can't," I breathe, even as my hands come up to rest against his muscular chest. "Not here."

"There's no one down here, and I made sure we're in a camera blind spot. It's just you and me, Selene."

I hate that I have to be the bigger person here because there's nothing I want more than for him to bend me over this book cart and take me. However, before I can protest further, he closes the distance between us and captures my mouth in a searing kiss. A muffled whimper escapes me as my fingers clench the fabric of his white t-shirt in an effort to bring him closer.

It was foolish of me to even think that I would have enough strength to deny this because I want it as bad as he does. Knox's kiss is demanding, his lips claiming mine with a hunger that makes my knees weak. You would think it was weeks since we've seen each other instead of a day and a half, but I don't mind one bit. His hands roam my back, sliding under the hem of my sweater to caress my lower back beneath it.

I know we shouldn't be doing this here, now, but I can't bring myself to care. Not when Knox is kissing me like I'm the air he needs to breathe. Like nothing else matters, period.

He breaks the kiss to trail his lips along my jaw and

down the column of my throat. I tip my head back against the bookshelf to give him better access. A low moan escapes me as he finds that sensitive spot just below my ear.

"Shhh," he warns; his breath feels hot against my skin. "We need to be quiet, remember? We're in the library after all."

I nod, not trusting myself to speak. Knox's hands slide down to my thighs and he lifts me effortlessly. I wrap my legs around his waist as he pins me harder against the shelf. I can feel him, all of him, pressed against me, and I know my panties are growing wetter by the second.

He recaptures my mouth, kissing me deeply as he rocks his hips into mine. My mind goes hazy and even though I know I should stop this, I still can't seem to care. Not when he feels this good. Not when I want him this much.

Knox's hands slide further under my sweater, and I feel his fingers skimming my ribcage before cupping my breasts through the thin lace of my black bra. I'd worn it to feel confident today and I'm now even happier that I did. I arch into his touch as a breathy moan escapes my lips. He swallows the sound with another kiss as his hands make their way to my leggings.

Goosebumps appear on my skin as Knox's fingers tug at the waistband of my leggings before pushing them down my hips. I gasp as the cool air hits my bare skin, slightly cooling me down but doing nothing to dim the heat radiating between us. Knox doesn't even bother to remove my leggings all the way or lower my panties at all. He shifts them to the side and his fingers find my pussy.

"Already so wet for me," he says approvingly, circling my clit with his thumb. "It's one of the many things I love about you."

My eyes widen at his word choice, but my brain is only able to process what he said, not comment on it. Instead, I find myself biting my lip hard to keep from crying out. And all of that is before he slides a finger inside of me. I clench around him, my hips rocking instinctively to meet his touch. All I can think is that I want more. More of this. More of him.

"Knox..." I whimper. "Please..."

He nips lightly at my skin before he replies. "Please what, picosita? Tell me what you want."

I swallow hard. "You know what I want."

"I want to hear you say it." His finger curls inside me and I'm convinced he's discovered another spot of mine that I didn't know existed. I have to bury my face into his chest to muffle my moan.

"I want you to—" I breathe as my nails dig into his shoulders through his shirt. "I want you keep fucking me with your fingers."

Knox pulls his body back slightly to give me one of his cocky smirks. That is the only warning I receive before his fingers began moving faster. I can barely think straight, lost in the pleasure he is enacting on my body. His thumb presses against my clit and I swear I see the entire Milky Way.

"That's it, baby," he encourages against my lips. "Let go for me."

A few more thrusts of his fingers and I'm flying apart at the seams. I bite my lip so hard to keep quiet as my whole body trembles with the force of my release. Knox works me through it and doesn't stop until I collapse against him.

"Holy shit," I pant, trying to catch my breath.

Knox chuckles, pressing a kiss to my temple. "That's just the beginning. I'm not done with you yet."

He eases his fingers out of me and brings them to his mouth, licking them clean. The sight sends another bolt of desire straight to my core. Before I can fully recover, he's undoing his jeans and freeing his cock. He quickly puts a condom on and grabs my legs. Before I can blink, he's yanking off my underwear and leggings and wrapping my legs around his waist. It takes what feels like an eternity before he positions himself at my entrance and with one smooth thrust, he's inside me, stretching and filling me up as if we are made for each other.

We both groan at the sensations coursing through our bodies. My eyes drift shut as Knox starts to move, his thrusts deep and steady. I cling to him because it's the only thing I can do to try to anchor myself. It's almost too much. Between him being inside of me and us doing this in the library where I work. I know we should stop, but at the same time, it's exactly what I crave. What I need.

"Knox," I gasp out, tipping my head back. "Oh my—"

He grunts in response as he finds a quicker rhythm. One hand grips my hip tightly while the other makes its way to my hair so that he can tug my head to the side to leave another trail of open-mouthed kisses along my neck. I'm so lost in everything that is happening that I barely remember my own name. The only sounds are our labored breathing and the occasional creak of the book-shelf as Knox drives into me again and again. It's a miracle no one has come looking for me yet.

Thank fuck for that.

"You feel so good," Knox groans against my throat. "So fucking perfect."

I can feel the pleasure building inside of me every time he hits that one particular spot that only he has found. I'm so close to slipping off the edge.

"Knox, I'm going to..." The words dissolve into a small cry as he reaches between us to rub my clit.

"That's it, picosita. Come for me," he urges.

And who am I to not give him what we both want? A few more thrusts and I find myself biting down hard on his shirt to muffle my cries as I come undone. Knox's hips begin to move more erratically just before he finds his release.

We stay like that for a long moment as we try to catch our breath. Knox presses his forehead to mine and I run my fingers through his hair, savoring this moment together. But reality soon slams into me. We just had sex. In the library. Where I work. What was I thinking? I can't believe I let myself get so carried away.

"Hey," Knox says softly, sensing the shift in my mood. "You okay?"

I nod slowly, but I refuse to look him in the eye. "Yeah, I just... We shouldn't have done that here. What if someone had caught us?"

Knox carefully sets me back on my feet, keeping his hands on my hips to steady me. "No one saw us, Selene. I made sure of it." He tilts my chin up gently, forcing me to look at him. "I would never let anything happen to jeopardize your job or reputation. You know that, right?"

I search his eyes before I release a shaky breath. "I know. I trust you. It's just... a lot to process."

A small smile tugs at his lips. "Well, processing is kind of your specialty, isn't it? Overthinking in that brilliant mind of yours." He taps my temple playfully.

I can't help but laugh softly as some of the tension drains from my body. "Shut up. You like my brilliant overthinking mind."

"Mmm, I like a lot of things about you," he says, leaning in to brush a tender kiss across my lips. "Especially the fact that you just let me fuck you senseless in the library."

I groan, shoving at his chest as I note that he said like this time. "You're insufferable. Now help me get dressed before someone really does come looking for me."

Knox chuckles but obligingly helps me fix my clothes. I know I'm going to have to clean myself up after these activities, but it won't be too long before my shift is over, and the library is closed for the night. Once we're both presentable again, Knox pulls me into his arms.

And there's nowhere else I'd rather be.

33

SELENE

I nearly jump out of my bed when I hear a sharp knock on my door. Who could be here at this ungodly hour? I stumble to the door, my mind already racing with ways to tell the person on the other side to fuck off. I swing it open, ready to unleash my sleep-deprived fury, but my words die in my throat. Knox stands there with a charming smirk on his face, holding two steaming cups of coffee and a bag that smells suspiciously like breakfast sandwiches from Brewed Beginnings.

"Morning, picosita," he says, his voice far too chipper for this early hour. "I figured the only way I'd keep myself out of bed after practice was with the promise of seeing your beautiful face."

I step aside, letting him into my dorm room. "You're lucky you come bearing gifts," I tease, reaching for one of the coffees. "Otherwise, I might have had to slam the door in your face for waking me up so early."

Knox chuckles, setting the bag of sandwiches on my desk. "And risk missing out on all of this? Never."

We settle around my desk and unwrap the breakfast sandwiches. I take a big whiff of the aromas of bacon and eggs as they fills the room. Between that and the smell of coffee, I'm already in heaven. I take a bite and let out a low moan.

Knox raises an eyebrow at me and tilts his head to one side. "If I knew a simple breakfast sandwich could make you moan like that, I would've been at your door every morning."

I playfully swat at his arm. "Shut up and eat your sandwich, Sanchez."

We dig into our breakfast, the comfortable silence stretching a bit longer than I anticipated, but that's probably because we are both starving.

"So what's on the agenda for today?" Knox asks as he wipes his mouth with a napkin.

I sigh, glancing at the pile of textbooks on my desk. "Psychology lecture, followed by a mountain of reading. You know, the usual glamorous life of a college student."

Knox nods and runs a hand through his hair. "I feel you. Between practice, games, and trying to keep up with my classes, I barely have time to breathe."

"And yet you still found time to bring me breakfast," I say with a small smile.

Knox shrugs. "What can I say? I have my priorities straight."

"That you do, and I'm not complaining one bit. In fact, I'm honored to be one of your top priorities."

"You should be. The guys have been giving me so much shit for being 'whipped.' They say I've gone soft."

I try to imagine Knox being teased by his teammates and can't see it. "And what do you say to that?"

"I tell them that half of them have the same issue, and the other half are just jealous they don't have a gorgeous, brilliant woman like you in their lives."

I giggle and quickly take another sip of coffee to hide my reaction. "Well, I'm glad I can be your excuse for going soft."

"Trust me, picosita, there's nothing soft about me when it comes to you."

He's right about that. And I'm sure he'll be willing to show me just how not soft he is later. We finish up our breakfast, and Knox glances at his phone. "I should probably head out and let you get ready for your day."

"Yeah, I suppose I should make myself look presentable for class."

Knox stands, gathering the empty coffee cups and sandwich wrappers. "You always look stunning, Selene. Even with bedhead and no makeup."

I roll my eyes but can't fight the smile that appears on my lips. "Flattery will get you everywhere."

He winks at me as he heads for the door. "I'm counting on it. Text me later?"

"Of course. Now go, before I decide to skip class and keep you here all day."

Knox chuckles and opens the door. "Don't tempt me." With one last look, he's gone.

I lean against the closed door for a moment, hating that he had to leave. How is it possible for one man to make me feel so giddy and nervous at the same time? It truly doesn't make a bit of sense. Shaking my head, I push off the door and start getting ready for the day ahead.

I head to my psychology lecture, still feeling the warmth from Knox's surprise visit this morning. As I settle into my usual seat in the lecture hall, I pull out my laptop and get everything ready so I can take detailed notes. But as the professor begins discussing the day's topic, my mind keeps wandering back to Knox.

The professor is explaining self-perception theory, which describes how our self-image is shaped by observing our behavior and how others respond to us.

"For example," she says, "if someone frequently compliments your intelligence, you're more likely to start identifying as a smart person."

I can't help but reflect on my own insecurities and how being with someone like Knox challenges them. Not that he is the answer to this, but he sees me in a way I'm still learning to see myself. It helps me as I navigate reworking my brain to not immediately pick my body apart.

I jot down a few key points from the slide on the board and it takes everything in me to focus on the presentation. I look at the time on my laptop and am grateful that it's almost time to meet up with Isla for a small lunch. She and I need to catch up and I want to be doing something other than sitting in a classroom.

As class ends, I gather my things and head out. I meet up with Isla at one of the dining halls on campus. She's already snagged a table by the window and waves me over with a bright smile.

"Hey, girl, how's it going?" she asks as I slide into the seat across from her.

"Oh you know, the usual. Juggling classes and trying not to get lost in daydreams about a certain hockey player..." I joke.

Isla rolls her eyes good-naturedly. "I have those same issues so I can't even laugh at you properly about it. Let's get some food and then we can chat."

After grabbing what we wanted from the variety of options that are available, Isla and I settle back at our table. She takes a big bite of her pizza and her salad before she looks at me.

"So spill. How are things going with Knox?" she asks.

I can't help but smile. "Really well, actually. He surprised me this morning with breakfast."

Isla's eyebrows shoot up. "Wow, that's dedication. Especially for a hockey player who probably values his sleep. Ask me how I know."

That makes me laugh. "I know, right? But he said seeing me was worth keeping himself out of bed after practice."

"Aw, look at you, all smitten!" Isla teases. "I'm happy for you, Selene. You deserve someone who makes an effort like that."

"Thanks, Isla. I don't know, it just feels...right with him, you know? Even though we're so different."

She takes a sip of her water. "Sometimes opposites really do attract. And you balance each other out."

"I guess so." I play with my sandwich. "But I am really happy in a relationship for the first time in a long time."

My best friend claps her hands together and brings them up to her mouth as if she's getting emotional. "You're going to make me cry."

I shake my head. "Now, you know if you cry, I'm going to cry. So please don't, for both our sakes."

"Okay then, I should change the subject," Isla says as she tucks a piece of her hair behind her ear. "I need to fill you in on Tessa."

I groan, already anticipating what's coming. "What has she done now?"

"She's been stomping around our room like the whole world betrayed her," Isla says, rolling her eyes. "Ever since she found out about you and Knox at the hockey game, she's been in a perpetual state of pissed off. Not that it is hard for her to do."

I sigh. "I assume I'm public enemy number one because I got with him when she was planning to try to get back with him. Why, after years of them being separated, she wants him back now, I have no idea."

"Because he's graduating and has a shot at getting drafted? The NIL money they are already getting isn't anything to laugh at either."

I nod along because Isla has a good point. "It could be that. I wonder when she decided that she was going to go after him again. Not that it really matters because he's with me."

Isla hesitates for a second before saying, "True. And I don't know the full story, but from what I've picked up... she and Knox weren't exactly 'together' for most of their relationship. More on-and-off. A lot of drama. And if I had to guess? She probably thought she'd always have the option to go back to him."

I frown. "So she only wants him now because he moved on to something that is more serious?"

"Sounds like it," Isla says, shrugging. "She never mentioned him much before this semester, at least not to me. But I heard her on the phone once—right before the season started—telling someone she was going to 'make it happen' this time." She air-quotes the last part. "I didn't know who she meant at the time, but I'd bet money it was Knox."

I press my lips together. Tessa's been plotting this for

months? Good to know. "She needs to find someone else because that ship has sailed."

"Stake your claim," she says as she holds up her hand to give me a high five.

I high-five Isla, laughing. "Oh, I have. And I plan to keep doing so."

"Good. Don't let Tessa's bitterness ruin what you and Knox have," Isla says "She had her chance, and she blew it. Repeatedly. This is your time now."

"You're right. I refuse to let her drama seep into my relationship. Knox and I are good together, and that's what matters."

"Exactly. Besides, from what I've seen, Knox only has eyes for you. Tessa can scheme and pout all she wants, but it won't change the fact that he's crazy about you."

I wonder if I should tell her about Knox saying the L-word while we had sex in the library. I quickly decide not to because I haven't even talked to him about it yet. "Thanks, Isla. I needed to hear that."

"That's what I'm here for and—" She stops talking for maybe ten seconds. "Wait a minute."

"What? What's up?"

Isla leans forward and grasps my hands that were resting on the table. "Do you remember I told you about that little black book I found of Tessa's? The one I accidently knocked off her desk?"

"Yes..." I say as I vaguely recall it and am now

wondering where this part of our conversation is going to lead.

"What if that was her little research book of sorts? To, like, figure out who was around Knox or something?"

My eyes widen as I process Isla's words. "Wait, you think she's been, what, stalking Knox? Trying to gather intel on him and the people in his life?"

"It's possible. I mean, think about it. She's clearly obsessed with getting him back, and she's not above playing dirty to get what she wants."

"But she seemed surprised to see me at the hockey game. Wouldn't she have known about me sooner?"

Isla shrugged. "Maybe she hadn't put two and two together about you two yet. After all, it's not like Knox was seriously dating anyone after her until you."

"I don't know.... It seems a bit far-fetched, even for Tessa. But I guess I can't put anything past her at this point."

"I might be totally off base. But I just wanted you to be aware of the possibility."

I let the idea roll around in my head for a moment before I turn my gaze back to Isla. "When's your next class and is Tessa usually in your room at this time?"

Isla checks her phone quickly. "I have class in about an hour. And no, Tessa's class or something should be beginning in about ten minutes. Why?"

I stand up and gather my garbage, formulating the

plan that's spinning in my mind as I go. "I think we should go take a closer look at that little black book. If there's even a chance it has information about Knox or me, I want to know."

Isla looks hesitant for a moment but then agrees. "You're right. Better to know what we're dealing with. Let's go."

We throw out our trash and put away our trays and head out of the dining hall. The walk across campus allows us to make sure that Tessa will definitely not be in the room once we arrive at our destination. Once we're there, Isla uses her badge to get through the main entrance and unlocks the door of her room when we reach it.

"It should be on her desk," Isla whispers, moving toward Tessa's side of the room.

"Okay," I whisper back. Why we are whispering I'm not sure, but it just feels right. I follow, my eyes scanning the desk until they land on a small, nondescript black notebook. I pick it up and flip it open.

At first glance, it looks like a normal small notebook. Then I swallow hard as I start recognizing some of the names. They are people I know from around campus and even a few professors. Next to each name are details about each person, which is weird as hell. But soon I realize that's the tip of the iceberg. As I flip further, I start to see Knox's name appearing more and more.

My fingers tighten around the notebook as I turn

another page because apparently, I can't stop. It's like watching a car accident unfold in front of me and I can't take my eyes away from the scene.

Knox's name is everywhere. His practice and game schedule is listed. Places where she might be able to catch him around campus. How did she know all of this stuff?

I flip another page and almost drop the book.

I find myself staring at my own name. I freeze. *What the hell?*

Right next to it are notes she's made. They include dates and observations she's figured were important enough for her to write down:

- Library shift: late night three days a week.

-Working out in the gym.

- At hockey game tonight. Did not expect. Need to adjust.

I think I'm going to be sick. I slam the book shut and I wish I could lie and say I wasn't shaking. "What the actual *fuck*?"

Isla, who had been leaning over my shoulder reading along, sucks her teeth. "Okay, I was *kidding* about the whole 'stalking' thing, but, uh... I take it back. I was so very wrong."

I rub a hand across my face as I try to wrap my head around what we've just uncovered. "She's not just keeping tabs on Knox." I swallow hard, forcing the words out. "She's been watching me as well."

"What's her endgame here?"

That's a great question and I don't know, outside of her wanting to obviously get back with Knox.

And that's the problem.

Because whatever Tessa's planning, she's been working on it for a while.

And that means she's not done yet.

34

SELENE

I walk up to my regular treadmill with my earbuds already blasting my go-to workout playlist. I'm pumped up and ready to go before I head back to my place to get cleaned up and wait for Knox to come by.

And I can't wait to tell him that I have proof that his ex-girlfriend is stalking him.

I crank up the speed on the treadmill, my feet pounding in rhythm with the heavy bass thumping through my earbuds. Sweat beads on my forehead as I push myself harder, determined to beat my personal best. I'm in the zone, focused solely on the digital numbers ticking upward on the display.

Thirty minutes later, I'm a sweaty mess but feeling triumphant as I cool down with a light jog. I hop off the treadmill and wipe the sweat from my face and neck.

As I grab my water bottle and start toward the area

with the yoga mats, I can't help but glance over at the free weights section again. The usual crowd of regulars are there, chatting and laughing between reps like they own the place. A familiar knot of anxiety starts to form in my stomach, but I force myself to take a deep breath.

Before I can second-guess myself, I march right up to the rack of dumbbells. I can do this without Knox being here. The first thing I do is select a set of five pound dumbbells and remind myself that I'm here for me, not to impress anyone else. I find an open spot and start my first set of bicep curls, focusing on my form and breathing.

At first, I feel self-conscious, like everyone must be staring at me and judging. But as I power through the reps, I start to find my rhythm. The burn in my muscles feels good; I would even say it's empowering. I catch one of the regulars giving me a subtle nod of approval in the mirror.

I finish my set and rest the weights at my sides and breathe out a sigh of relief. It's a small victory, but it feels huge to me. I'm not the same insecure girl I was just a few weeks ago. I'm stronger now, inside and out.

As I set the weights down and take a long drink from my water bottle, I start to think about Knox and the bombshell I'm about to drop on him. I still can't believe Isla and I found all the information she's been tabulating for who knows how long in that little black book of hers. First of all, it's creepy as hell. Second of all, why? Why go through all that trouble instead of just going to Knox?

Has she gone to Knox?

The thought makes me pause mid-sip. What if Tessa has continued to try and reconnect with Knox this whole time? The knot in my stomach tightens. I shake my head, trying to get rid of the uneasy feeling that is creeping into my body. No, Knox would have told me if she had reached out again. He's always been upfront about their history, even if he doesn't like talking about it much.

I grab my stuff and head to the locker room, my mind still coming up with questions. As I put on my outerwear, I try to focus on the positives. I faced my fear at the gym today. School is going well. I'm making progress with my diet and in the gym, not to mention, I'm getting stronger. And Knox and I have been getting closer.

I finish getting dressed and check my phone. Nothing from Knox yet, which tells me I have enough time to probably jump in the shower and prepare a little before he arrives.

I hurry back to my dorm, taking the stairs two at a time. I unlock my door and toss my gym bag near the bed. I grab all of the things that I need, head to the bathroom, strip off my sweaty clothes, and jump in the shower. The soothing hot water does a number on my sore muscles, and I love every second of it. I debate whether it's worth washing my hair before I decide it needs it. As I'm working shampoo onto my scalp, I rehearse what I'm going to say to Knox.

"So, Isla and I found something that you should probably know about..." No, too casual. "Knox, there's something important I need to tell you, and it's about Tessa." Better, but still not quite right.

I sigh and rinse the suds from my hair. Maybe I should just wing it and see what comes out. It might be better than me overanalyzing this. With a heavy sigh, I step out of the shower and wrap a towel around my body and another around my hair. I dash back to my room and get changed. Just as I'm about to start blow drying my hair, I hear a knock at the door. My heart leaps into my throat. Is Knox early?

I quickly throw on a cozy oversized cardigan and try not to care about how my damp hair is leaving wet splotches on the shoulders. Taking a deep breath to calm my nerves, I open the door to find Knox standing there, hands tucked into the pockets of his worn leather jacket.

"Hey," he greets me with that trademark smirk of his. "You're looking quite wet."

I roll my eyes, but I'm not even remotely upset. "I just got out of the shower, smartass. You're early."

"What can I say? I couldn't wait to see you," he teases as I step aside to let him in. The scent of his cologne already has me wanting to melt into a puddle on the floor.

Knox plops down on my bed like it's his own. "So, what's this important thing you needed to tell me?"

"Well there are a couple of things I want to tell you actually. Do you want to start with the good or the bad?"

Knox folds his arms across his chest. "Let's start with the good. I have a feeling I'm going to need it."

I take a deep breath and sit down next to him on the bed. "Well, the good news is that I finally faced my fear at the gym today. I used the free weights without you there to hold my hand."

Knox's face lights up and it's so weird to see him this happy for me. "Selene, that's amazing! I knew you could do it. Hell yeah!"

"Thanks, Knox. It felt really good, like I'm finally making progress, not just physically but mentally too."

"I never doubted that for a second," he says softly, reaching out to tuck a damp strand of hair behind my ear.

I clear my throat and look away. "So, about the bad news..."

Knox's expression turns serious. "Yeah, what's going on?"

I take another deep breath, steeling myself. "It's about Tessa. Isla and I found something that you need to see."

I reach for my phone, unlock it, and pull up the photos, my hand shaking slightly as I pass it to Knox. "This notebook belongs to Tessa. It...it looks like she's been keeping tabs on you. Like, obsessively."

Knox's expression grows more serious as he scrolls through the images. There are pages filled with notes about his class schedule, hockey practices, even what he ordered for lunch in some places. "What the hell?" he mutters under his breath.

"I know," I say quietly. "It's beyond creepy. And look at the last page."

Knox swipes to the final image. His eyes widen and his jaw clenches. "She has information about us in here?"

"Yes."

Knox stares at the screen, his eyes scanning over the details Tessa has and he looks almost as dumbfounded as I felt the first time I read it.

"This is..." he starts, then shakes his head. "I don't even know what to say. How long has she been doing this?"

"I don't know," I admit. I swear my stomach rolls, making me feel slightly nauseous. "But from the looks of it, it's been going on for a while."

Knox sets the phone down and rubs a hand over his face. I can see the tension throughout his body. "I thought she was finally out of my life for good. I never imagined she'd go this far. She sent me a couple more text messages after the one I told you about, but I just blocked her without responding."

I reach out and grab his hand. "I'm so sorry. I can't imagine how violated you must feel right now."

Knox squeezes my hand. Not enough to hurt me, but I can tell he's barely containing his rage. "This is bullshit. I can't believe she's been stalking me this whole time."

"Yes, and as a result, us." A chill runs down my spine at the thought of Tessa watching us. "You don't think she's been, like, physically stalking us together, do you? Taking photos or videos?"

Knox's jaw tightens and he looks like he wants to punch something. Or someone. "If she is, I swear to..." He doesn't finish the thought, but I can imagine where it was going.

This time, it's my turn to grab his hand because I swear my blood turns to ice. "Knox, we had sex in the library. What if she saw us?!"

Knox's eyes widen at the realization. "Shit. The library." He stands up abruptly and starts pacing, running a hand through his hair. "If she saw that... Selene, I'm so sorry. I never meant to put you in this position."

I shake my head as I try to push down the rising panic. "It's not your fault. Neither of us could have known she was capable of something like this."

But the thought of Tessa possibly watching us makes my skin crawl. I wrap my arms around myself, suddenly feeling exposed even though I'm fully clothed.

Knox notices my discomfort and sits back down beside me, his expression softening. "Hey, we're going to figure this out, okay? I won't let her hurt you or invade our privacy anymore. At least there's no indication that she saw that in the images you snapped."

I lean into Knox, seeking comfort in his solid presence. He wraps an arm around my shoulder and pulls me closer. For a moment, we just sit there in silence, processing what this all could mean. I break the silence first.

"I just can't believe she would do this," I whisper. "I

mean, I knew she said you were off limits when I was thinking about rebounds, but this is next level—"

"Wait a minute. Rebounds?"

I bite my lip, realizing I've said too much. "It was a while ago, before you and I started hanging out again. I was pissed at how you treated me after we fucked the first time and Isla and I were coming up with a list of guys I could be with to get you off my mind. Tessa mentioned that you were off limits because you two were going to get back together."

Knox shakes his head in disbelief. "Unbelievable. The entire thing. And there's no way I would have ever seen you with another man, Selene."

"Excuse me?" I turn to him in surprise.

As I'm trying to process whether I should be angry or not he replies, "Even when I was being an asshole and fucking things up, you were mine. You always were mine."

I stare at Knox as I try to calm the anger that threatens to be unleashed. "What do you mean, I was always yours?"

Knox's intense gaze holds mine. "Exactly what I said. From the moment we met, I knew there was something different about you, picosita. Something that drew me to you like a magnet. Even when I tried to push you away, I couldn't stay away for long."

My mind reels, trying to process this...Hell, everything over the last few hours. "But...but you never said anything.

You acted like you couldn't care less about all of this at first."

He sighs. "I know. And I'm still so sorry for that. The truth is, I was scared. Scared because I could see where this was going. Scared of getting hurt again after what happened with Tessa. So I pushed you away, thinking it would be easier than risking my heart."

"Are you trying to say—"

"I love you, Selene. And I will do everything I can to protect you and cherish what we have."

I swear I stop breathing. "Knox, I..." I start, but the words get stuck in my throat. My mind is racing, not even sure how to respond to his words.

He reaches out and takes my hand, his thumb gently caressing my knuckles. "You don't have to say it back, Selene. I know I've put you through hell with my hot-and-cold bullshit. But I need you to know that my feelings for you are real. I was just too much of a coward to admit it."

Tears prick at the corners of my eyes. "I love you too."

A grin spreads across Knox's face, his eyes crinkling at the corners. He leans in and captures my lips in a kiss that gives me no room to think about anything else.

Including Tessa.

35

KNOX

"Fucking finally," I say as I slam my bedroom door behind me and quickly lock it so we will not be disturbed.

I'd been waiting for the moment that I could get her alone. It's been days since we've seen each other and said I love you for the first time. The sound of my door meeting the doorframe means that our time alone can begin. Selene lets out a breathless laugh as I press her against the wall. I take a moment to stare at her, shook by the fact that she's here putting up with my shit. Her fingers make their way to my hair and pull me out of my short daydream just before our lips crash together.

My hand lands on the back of her neck to make sure that her lips are anchored to mine. Selene parts her lips, inviting me to explore her mouth with my tongue. I groan into the kiss as my free hand lands on the doorframe, trapping her with my body.

Our tongues play with one another as the kiss deepens. It's then that I feel Selene's hands slide under my shirt and her nails grazing my abs in a way that absolutely feels incredible. I break the kiss just long enough to reach back and snatch my shirt over my head and toss it aside. Her green eyes darken with lust as they roam over my bare chest.

"I don't... I can't ever get over looking at you," she says, and I'm not sure she realizes she said it aloud.

"The feeling is mutual, picosita," I mutter as move my hand so that I can grind my hips into hers.

She feels how hard I already am for her, and I can't help but smirk. When she moans, she lifts her leg a little, and I take the opportunity to hook that leg around my hip. She immediately pulls me closer to her. I move her away from the wall slightly so that my hands can make their way down to her ass, and I can't help but give it a big squeeze.

"Knox, I need—"

"I know what you need. Hold on to my shoulders."

She does so without saying another word and I put my hands under her thighs and then pick her up. Selene lets out a small yelp before she giggles. Spinning us around, I walk us toward my bed and toss her down gently. I can't lie and say that I didn't enjoy watching the way her breasts moved, but I don't take much time to think about it because my body covers hers as I settle between her legs.

My lips descend on hers once more before making their way to her neck. When she doesn't give as much access as I want, I grab her hair, enjoying the way those pretty red strands look in my fist and pulling her head to the side lightly so I can get to the spot that I know she loves. Her moan echoes through the room as I suck at her pulse point, no doubt leaving a mark. I don't care. I want everyone to know she's mine.

My free hand slides under her shirt, fingers grazing the smooth skin of her stomach before cupping her breast through the fabric of her bra. She arches into my touch, and I enjoy the whimper that escapes her lips.

"Knox," she pants. "Please..."

I nip at her pulse point again before soothing it with my tongue. "Please what, baby? Tell me what you want."

"I want—" She stops talking for a moment as if she's trying to regain her composure. "I want you to fuck me."

Hearing the words come from her lips is enough to send me over the edge, but I need to exercise restraint. "All in due time, baby."

I release her hair and slide my hands down her body, gripping the hem of her shirt. She sits up just enough for me to pull it over her head and toss it aside. I take a moment to appreciate the sight of her in that dark purple bra. The contrast against her creamy skin makes my mouth water.

"I didn't realize how much I loved the color purple until now," I say. I run my fingers over the lacy edge of her bra, lightly teasing the exposed skin above it. Selene shivers under my touch and when I look up, our eyes immediately lock. Her pupils are blown wide with desire and the look she's giving me is like she's pleading for more.

Good.

I dip my head and press open-mouthed kisses on the tops of her breasts before running my hands up her back. She quickly realizes where my destination is and moves her body so that I can slide my hand around to unclasp her bra. The garment falls away and I sit back on my heels to drink in the sight of her, bare and beautiful beneath me.

"Breathtaking," I whisper as I move to cup the weight of her breasts in my palms. "Every fucking inch of you."

Selene gasps after I lean forward and use my tongue to tease her nipples until they harden even more. I take my time worshipping her breasts, and I love every moan and gasp that falls from her lips.

"I need more..." she says as her fingers make their way to the waistband of the sweatpants I put on this morning after I showered.

"Patience, picosita," I respond, loving how desperate for me she sounds. When I reach the waistband of her leggings, I make quick work of them by tugging them down her legs along with her panties.

She's now fully naked before me, a sight that never fails to take my breath away. It's something I can look at for the rest of my life. I run my hands up her smooth legs, slowly inching closer to where she wants me most.

"Knox, please..." Selene says as she lifts her hips off the bed.

Unable to deny her any longer, I lower my head and drag my tongue along her folds. Her answering moan is music to my ears. I take my time, using long, broad strokes of my tongue to pleasure her. I can't deny that I'm loving every bit of her sweet taste.

"Oh my—" She cuts herself off as her hands get lost in my hair to hold me in place. As if I'd want to be anywhere else.

I focus my attention on her clit next, flicking, swirling, and sucking until her thighs start to shake around my head. I add a finger to her pussy and then another, making sure to stroke in time with my tongue. I know exactly what is going to make her explode, and I can't wait to see her fall off the edge.

And that's when I feel her whole body tense as I continue, and I can feel her tightening around my fingers.

"Knox, I'm gonna—" Her words dissolve into a moan as her orgasm crashes over her. I don't relent, guiding her through the waves of pleasure until she collapses back onto the bed, spent and panting.

I press a gentle kiss to both of her inner thighs before crawling back up her body, grinning at the blissed-out expression on her face. "You're so fucking gorgeous when you come," I say against her lips before claiming them.

When I pull back from her, she says, "I want to return the favor."

With a smirk, I roll onto my back, pulling Selene on top of me. "Be my guest, baby."

She doesn't hesitate, trailing kisses down my chest and abs, her fingers hooking into the waistband of my sweatpants. In one smooth motion, she removes them and my boxer briefs.

"Mmm, someone's eager," she says as she wraps her hand around my cock.

I groan at the sensation, but it's nothing compared to when she takes me in her mouth.

"Fuck yes," I hiss, my fingers threading through her fiery locks. She bobs her head, taking me deeper each time, inch by inch. Her hand does an excellent job of working what she can't fit in. "Selene, holy fuck..." my voice trails off because I can't find a single thing to say.

I do my best to stop my hips from fucking her mouth. She's driving me wild with pleasure, pushing me closer and closer to coming in her mouth. But as much as I'm enjoying this, I need to be inside her. Now.

"Selene," I gasp, gently pulling on her hair. "Wait, baby. I need you be inside you."

She releases me with a pop, looking up at me with a seductive smile. "How do you want me?"

"On all fours, baby."

Selene moves herself so that she can turn around and position herself on her hands and knees before me while I grab a condom. The sight of her like this, waiting and ready, nearly undoes me. I kneel behind her, running my hands over the curve of her hips and the dip of her lower back.

"You're so perfect," I growl, gripping her hips tightly. I line myself up and with one smooth thrust, I'm buried inside her tight, wet pussy. We both moan at the feeling of our bodies becoming one.

I start to move, slowly at first, but soon the intensity builds, and I have to pick up the pace. It's as if I don't have a choice in the matter.

"Yes, Knox, harder," Selene says as she pushes back to meet each of my thrusts. I comply eagerly, gripping her hips hard enough to bruise as I pound into her.

Wanting to be even closer, I lean over her back, pressing my chest to her skin, now slick with a sheen of sweat. One hand slides up to play with her breast while the other finds its way between her legs to rub her clit.

"Oh fuck yes!" Selene cries out. I love the way her body trembles beneath me as she gets closer to the edge. "Don't stop, I'm so close..."

My own release grows rapidly with each thrust as her walls clench around me. I pinch her nipple and rub her clit faster, determined to make her come again before I do. "That's it, baby, let go. Come for me," I command in her ear just before I nibble at the sensitive skin of her neck.

Selene shatters in my arms and the feel of her pussy milking my cock for all it's worth is what sends me over. I let out a groan as I explode inside her, spilling into the condom.

We collapse onto the bed and I'm aware of how heavy I must be on her back. I wait a few seconds before I pull out of her and dispose of the condom. I come back to bed and gather Selene in my arms. She sighs with a smile on her face.

"I love you," she says as she plays with my happy trail that could easily lead to a round two.

"And I love you too." It feels amazing that we just freely say those words now.

"Mmm, I could stay like this forever," Selene says, her breath warm against my skin.

"I'm not letting you leave this bed anytime soon," I reply and tighten my arms around her.

She giggles and props herself up to look at me. "Is that a challenge, Hockey Hottie?"

"More like a promise, picosita." I tuck a stray lock of her hair behind her ear. I lean up to kiss her, and soon we are trading slow, lazy kisses. Just as things start to heat up again, Selene suddenly bolts upright, eyes wide.

"Oh shit! I totally forgot, I promised to make dinner for you and the guys tonight!" She scrambles out of bed, frantically searching for her discarded clothes.

I prop myself up on my elbows, enjoying the view of her naked body as she hops around. "Babe, relax. The guys will survive us being a little late. We should probably grab a quick shower after...the activities we just did anyway."

She shoots me a playful glare over her shoulder while she's grabbing her leggings. "Shut up."

"Hey, I'm offering to help conserve water here. Purely for the environment, of course." I flash her my most charming grin.

Selene rolls her eyes but can't hide her smile. "Uh-huh, sure. Your commitment to being eco-friendly is truly inspiring." She finally locates her bra that's half hidden under my hockey bag. "But seriously, I really don't want to be late starting dinner."

I sit up and swing my legs over the edge of the bed. "It'll be fine. Let's grab that shower and then we can head downstairs. I'm sure they probably know what we were up to up here anyway."

That earned me a t-shirt to the head, but it was completely worth it.

36

SELENE

Knox and I head downstairs hand in hand, and when we reach the last step, I look into the living room. Blaise and Wilder are staring at the television, playing a video game I don't recognize. Asher isn't here because he and Isla are having a date night.

Wilder pauses the game and turns to face us with a smirk. "Well, well, well. Look who finally decided to grace us with their presence." He waggles his eyebrows suggestively. "Sounded like you two were having quite the workout session up there."

Heat rushes to my cheeks and I quickly drop Knox's hand. "You just wish the situation was reversed!" I chuckle before I continue. "Who wants dinner? I'm starving!" I call over my shoulder before I make a beeline for the kitchen.

Knox laughs, but I don't bother looking to see if he's

following me. I start pulling out the ingredients Knox bought so that I could make chicken alfredo pasta and garlic bread. It took a lot of convincing for him to believe that I actually wanted to do this after the last time I made food here and Wilder made his joke. Speaking of, I can hear them talking smack to each in the living room.

"Shut up, Wilder," Knox says. "Like you're one to talk. Remember that girl you brought home last week? We all heard you two going at it."

"Hey, when you've got skills like mine, it's hard to be subtle," Wilder replies.

I roll my eyes and focus on the task at hand. Boys. Kind of assholes.

As I start boiling the water for the pasta, I feel someone walk up behind me. Strong arms wrap around my waist, and I lean back into Knox's solid chest.

"Need any help?" he says in my ear.

I shiver slightly but manage to keep my voice steady. "I think I've got it under control. Why don't you go make sure Wilder and Blaise don't kill each other out there?"

Knox chuckles. "Nah, they'll be fine. I'd rather stay here with you."

He nuzzles into my neck, and I have to bite back a moan. Damn him for being so irresistible. I'm trying to focus here.

"Knox," I warn, but it comes out breathy. My protest is such bullshit and we both know it. "I'm going to burn the garlic if you keep distracting me."

"Let it burn," he growls, spinning me around to face him.

Just as he leans in to kiss me, Wilder bursts into the kitchen. "Something smells amazing in here!" He pauses when he sees our position and smirks. "Oh, sorry. Didn't mean to interrupt."

I quickly disentangle myself from Knox's arms. "You're not interrupting anything."

Knox shoots Wilder a glare that could melt steel, but Wilder just shrugs it off. "Hey, don't stop on my account. I'm just here for the food."

I clear my throat, trying to regain some composure. "Well, you're going to have to wait a bit longer. It's not ready yet."

"No worries, I can be patient." Wilder hops up to sit on the counter and swings his legs like he's a little kid. Which is comical given how big he is.

I raise an eyebrow at Wilder. "Are you sure about that? Patient isn't exactly the first word that comes to mind when I think of you."

Wilder clutches his chest dramatically. "That hurts, Selene. I'll have you know I'm the very definition of patience. Just ask any of the ladies I've been with."

Knox scoffs as he continues to help me with dinner. "More like the definition of a pain in the ass."

"Jealousy is a disease, bro. Get well soon," Wilder tosses back at Knox with a grin.

Then something pops in my mind that I can't stop myself from saying. "Would Jade say the same?"

I immediately regret throwing Jade under the bus. Knox looks at me, but I can't read his expression. Not that it matters much because it's too late. Wilder's grin falters for a split second before he recovers.

"Jade? What about her?" he asks, trying to sound nonchalant. But I can see the tension in his shoulders.

I shrug, turning back to stir the pasta. "Nothing, really. I just noticed you two seem...close."

Wilder hops off the counter, his usual smirk replaced by a frown. "We're just best friends, Selene. Don't make it into something it's not."

"I didn't say it was anything," I reply innocently. "Just an observation."

If someone didn't know where awkward was, it is definitely standing in the corner of this kitchen, making its presence known more by the second. Knox clears his throat. "Hey, Wilder, why don't you go set the table? Selene should be done with dinner soon."

Wilder nods, looking relieved for the out. "Sure thing, bro."

As he leaves the kitchen, I glance over at Knox. "What was that about?"

Knox sighs, rubbing the back of his neck. "It's...complicated with those two. They've been dancing around each other for years, but neither will make a move."

I frown as I drain the pasta. "Why not? They obviously like each other."

"Because Wilder is the class clown basically," Knox explains, leaning against the counter. "And I don't think Jade takes him seriously at all."

"Well, maybe Wilder needs to show Jade that there's more to him than just jokes," I say thoughtfully as I stir the alfredo sauce. "I mean, he seems like a good guy."

Knox nods slowly. "You're probably right. But I don't think Wilder knows how to do that. Being the jokester...it's his thing, you know?"

His words strike a chord with me. I think about my own tendency to use humor or the party girl image to deflect when I'm feeling insecure or vulnerable. Like earlier, when the guys were teasing us about having sex. Do I do the same thing Wilder does? I guess I do, in a way.

As I'm pondering the parallels between Wilder's coping mechanisms and my own, the garlic bread timer dings, jolting me out of my thoughts. I quickly pull the tray out of the oven, the warm, garlicky aroma filling the kitchen.

Knox inhales deeply, a smile spreading across his face. "Damn, that smells good. Thanks, baby."

I grin at him as I transfer the golden-brown slices to a serving plate. "Well, someone has to make sure you hockey boys are eating home-cooked meals once in a while."

Knox chuckles, shaking his head. "You sound like my

mom. Next thing I know, you'll be hiding veggies in the pasta sauce."

"Don't tempt me," I tease, bumping his hip with mine as I hand him food to carry to the dining room table. "I can't wait to see her and your abuela again."

Knox's face softens at the mention of his family. "They can't wait to see you again too," he says. "Mamita keeps asking when you're coming over again. I think she likes you more than me."

I laugh as we carry the food into the dining room. "Well, can you blame her? I'm a delight."

Wilder and Blaise are already seated at the table, their eyes widening as they take in the spread. "Damn, Selene, you went all out," Blaise says.

"I figured you guys deserved a real meal for once," I reply, setting down the pasta dish. "Instead of just pizza and protein shakes."

"Hey, don't knock the pizza and protein shakes," Wilder says, holding up his hands. "That's the fuel of champions right there."

Knox snorts as he takes his seat next to me. "Yeah, if by champions you mean guys who can barely skate a lap without wheezing."

"Excuse you, I am a finely tuned athletic machine." Wilder flexes his biceps to prove his point.

I roll my eyes at Wilder's antics as I sit down across from him. "Sure, Wilder. Knox mentioned you were huffing and puffing at practice yesterday."

Wilder glares at Knox. "Bro, that's fucked up." He turns back to me "And after I complimented how good the food smelled too."

Blaise chuckles as he reaches for the garlic bread. "But she's got you there."

As we all dig into the food, conversation flows easily. Despite the earlier tension with Wilder, he seems to have bounced back to his usual joking self.

"Hey, this is really good, Selene," Blaise says around a mouthful of pasta. "Like really good."

I smile at the unexpected compliment from the usually stoic Blaise. "Thanks. I'm glad you enjoyed it. I put a lot of love into it."

Wilder makes an exaggerated gagging noise. "Gross. Love? In my food? No thanks."

"Says the guy who just scarfed down two helpings," Knox points out, gesturing at Wilder's already empty plate. "I'm not even sure you tasted the food."

Wilder shrugs unapologetically. "What can I say? I'm a growing boy."

"More like a bottomless pit," Blaise mutters.

I chuckle and shake my head as Knox's hand finds mine under the table. He gives it a gentle squeeze. I glance over at him, and he winks at me. I don't even bother trying to hide my grin.

Soon the meal winds down and everything is cleared courtesy of Blaise and Wilder, who decided to clean up since Knox and I cooked. Once that is done, we all settle into the living room, the guys sprawling across opposite ends of one couch while I curl up in Knox's lap in an armchair. He drapes an arm around my waist, pulling me even closer.

"So, what's the plan for tonight?" Wilder asks, propping his feet up on the coffee table. "We could hit up downtown, see what kind of trouble we can stir up."

Knox shakes his head. "Nah, man. I think I'm good just hanging out here."

Wilder makes a whipping noise and gesture, earning a glare from Knox. "Come on, bro. Don't be lame. Live a little!"

"I am living," Knox replies. "Living my best life right here with my girl." He punctuates his statement by pressing a kiss to my neck.

I can't help but smile, but apparently that's enough for Wilder. He pushes himself off the couch and makes a grand announcement. "Well, if you two are just going to be all gross and couple-y, I'm out." He turns to look at his other roommate. "Blaise, you in?"

Blaise considers for a moment before shrugging. "Sure, why not. Beats third-wheeling these lovebirds."

As Wilder and Blaise head out, I remember my plan to throw Knox a surprise birthday party. I untangle myself from his lap, giving him a quick peck on the cheek.

"I'll be right back," I say. "I just need to ask Blaise something real quick."

Knox raises an eyebrow but nods. "Hurry back."

I catch up to Blaise just as he's grabbing his coat from the hook by the door. "Hey, Blaise, wait up a sec."

He turns, looking at me curiously. "What's up?"

I lower my voice, glancing back to make sure Knox is out of earshot. "I want to plan a surprise party for Knox's birthday in a couple weeks. I was hoping you could help me out and we can have it here?"

A slow smile spreads across Blaise's face. "That's a great idea. Knox never makes a big deal out of his birthday, but I think he'd really appreciate this."

Relief floods through me. "Awesome. I'll start putting together a guest list and figuring out decorations and stuff. Just keep it quiet, okay?"

Blaise mimes zipping his lips. "My lips are sealed. Knox won't suspect a thing."

"Thanks, Blaise. You're the best." I give him a quick hug before he heads out the door after Wilder.

I return to the living room where Knox has moved to the couch and is now channel surfing. As I sit down, he wraps an arm around my shoulder and says, "What was that about with Blaise?"

"Oh nothing," I reply, waving a hand. "Just needed to ask him about...a class."

Knox pulls back slightly, narrowing his gaze. "You and Blaise have a class together? Since when?"

Crap. I scramble for a good explanation. "We don't, but he had the same professor last semester. It's, um, an elective. Intro to...Sports Psychology. Figured it might be interesting, you know, with you being an athlete and all." I give him what I hope is a winning smile.

Knox studies me for a moment, and I hold my breath, praying he buys it. Then he shrugs and pulls me closer again. "Makes sense. You're always looking out for me." He grins and taps my nose playfully. "My little cheerleader."

I swat at his chest and laugh. "Excuse you, I am nobody's cheerleader. If anything, you should be my cheerleader and praise me, Hockey Hottie."

"I'll cheer for you anytime, baby," he replies with a wink. "In fact..." He shifts suddenly, flipping us so I'm pinned beneath him on the couch. "Let me show you just how good I am at praising you."

Before I can blink, my giggles turn into moans as a quiet evening with my boyfriend turns into anything but.

37

SELENE

I rush around Knox's house in an effort to arrange the platters of snacks that I purchased. The rich aroma of freshly baked brownies is calling my name, but I ignore it because I have a job to complete. There will be time to consume what I want later because life is all about balance and not having to constantly judge myself by the numbers on the scale.

As I step back to survey my handiwork, I can't help but grin. The once cluttered living room has been transformed into a vibrant party space, complete with colorful balloons and a 'Happy Birthday' banner strung across the far wall. It's a bit over-the-top, but it's not every day someone turns twenty-two.

Asher strolls into the living room. "Damn, Selene, you really went all out."

"Thanks. Blaise helped me pull all of this together. In fact, he should be coming back right—"

The front door opens, and Blaise walks in on cue.

"—now," I finish, smiling at Blaise as he enters with an armful of extra decorations. I can also call myself psychic now.

Blaise looks around the room and nods. "This looks incredible. Knox is going to be blown away."

I feel a flutter of excitement in my belly at the thought of Knox's reaction. I want everything to be perfect for him.

Wilder walks in from the kitchen and snags a brownie from one of the platters. "Knox better marry you after this," he jokes.

I force a laugh, hoping it doesn't sound as nervous as I feel. The idea of Knox and I together, married, makes my heart race in a way I'm not quite ready to admit out loud. "Very funny," I manage, busying myself with adjusting the snack platters again. For the fifth time.

A knock on the door stops this from getting even more awkward. Instead of waiting for any of the guys to answer, I rush over to the door and pull it open. A sigh of relief leaves my lips when I see it's Levi, Hailey, Isla, and Jade standing on the other side.

Isla steps forward and pulls me into a warm hug. "We're here to help! We brought more food and alcohol. Point us in the direction of anything that still needs to be done."

I move out of the way so they can come in. "You guys

are the best. I think we're just about set, but maybe you could help me with the drinks?" I pull my phone out of pocket. "I think Willow should be here any minute too."

"Excellent, it will be good to see her again," Jade says.

I lead the girls to the kitchen, leaving Blaise, Wilder, Levi. and Asher in the living room.

"So," Hailey starts as she unloads a tote full of various bottles, "how are things with you and Knox?"

"They're amazing. I feel like I've finally stopped waiting for something to go wrong, if that makes sense?" I answer as I start pulling out plastic cups and an assortment of mixers from another tote Isla brought in.

"That's great!" Jade claps her hands together. "Looks like we were wrong about him."

I pause for a second until I realize what she is referring to. She's thinking about when Hailey and Jade warned me about Knox before we officially met. They had been concerned that Knox's reputation would lead to heartbreak for me. Given what we went through when we had sex for the first time, they weren't wrong, but he's changed and grown.

We both have.

"We're not going to jinx it by saying anything more," Hailey adds quickly, noticing my brief hesitation. "We just want you to be happy."

I smile at them, grateful for their support. "I am. Really." I scan the counter for a second before I hold up a bottle of tequila. "Shots to celebrate? Before the birthday boy gets here?"

They all exchange glances and shrug in unison. "Why not?" Isla says.

I'm already grabbing a few shot glasses from the cabinet near the stove. I swear I know where more things are in this kitchen now than the occupants of this house do.

As I pour the shots, we chat about nothing in particular, and once we all have one in hand, Hailey decides to do the toast.

"To friendships and hockey," she says, raising her shot glass. We all clink glasses, and the sharp crack of glass on glass cuts through the hum of conversation from the living room.

The tequila burns its way down my throat, leaving a warm glow in its wake. I wince and then laugh as Isla makes a face like she just bit into a lemon. "Forgot how strong that stuff is," she says, sticking out her tongue.

We start to put together a few mixed drinks for the rest of the party when I hear another knock at the door in between someone testing out the music setup for the party. I'm convinced it's either Willow or Knox and I'm really hoping for the former. Knox isn't supposed to be back for another twenty to thirty minutes and I'm counting on that.

"I've got it!" I call out, rushing from the kitchen. Blaise catches my eye and gives me a thumbs up. I give him a small nod as I make my way to the door. I think he's telling me that everything is set, but I'm already focused on the door and what—or who—is on the other side.

I pull it open, and my excitement deflates just a tiny bit when I see Willow standing there alone. She's holding a small blue gift bag that I see white tissue paper coming out of.

"Willow! Hey!" I say too enthusiastically. I'm blaming it on the tequila. Always blame it on the tequila.

"Hey, I'm so sorry I'm late. It took me longer than I thought to finish up an article I needed to get to my editor asap."

"You're not late at all," I reassure her, stepping aside so she can enter. "We're just getting started. Come in!"

Willow hesitates for a moment, and I can see her eyes scan the room. She's looking for someone, but I'm confused as to who it could be since she knows her brother shouldn't be here yet.

She steps in slowly, and I take the gift bag from her hand. "This is so sweet. Knox will love it."

"He better," she mutters, but there's a softness in her voice that makes me think she's joking. Or at least half joking.

I start to lead her toward the kitchen where the girls are mixing drinks when I feel as if she's not right behind me anymore. I turn around and find Blaise standing in the doorway of the living room, and Willow is staring him down.

What the hell?

"Willow," Blaise says, breaking the tension. "Good to see you."

Her eyes flicker with something I can't quite read, but she forces a tight smile. "You too, Blaise."

An awkward silence follows, and I'm caught looking between the two of them. I'm still confused about what could have happened. Did they have a falling out that Knox never mentioned?

I clear my throat. "Willow, do you want a drink? We just did a round of shots, but there's plenty left."

She tears her gaze from Blaise and looks at me, her expression softening. "Sure. I'll take whatever you're making."

With that, I turn and head back to the kitchen, but not before glancing over my shoulder to see Willow brush past Blaise without another word. He stands there for a moment longer, watching her go, before returning to the living room where the guys are now arguing about sports or something.

I quickly pour another shot of tequila and hand it to Willow. "Here. Once you take it, you've been initiated into the friendship and hockey circle."

"Thanks. I can kind of do without the hockey, but I'll stay for the friendship," she says just before she takes the shot in one gulp. Isla and I share a look, and I know she also noticed how weird of a thing that was to say.

Willow sets the shot glass down with a bit more force

than necessary, and I watch as she wipes her mouth with the back of her hand.

"Everything okay?" I ask, trying to sound casual.

"Yeah, fine," she says, but her eyes are already drifting toward the hallway where she last saw Blaise. I follow her gaze and piece it together slowly. Maybe it's not something as simple as a falling out. Maybe it's something else entirely.

Jade interrupts my thoughts. "We should make a batch of something. Maybe spiked fruit punch?"

"Sounds perfect," I say, pushing the thought of what could be happening between Blaise and Willow out of my mind for now. I'll ask Knox later.

With all hands on deck, we easily finish the rest of the party prep in what feels like seconds. I check my phone and use my party voice to yell, "Hey! Knox should be here any second! Find a hiding place, because we won't have much notice. I'll answer the door since I told him I'd hang around so we could have a quiet evening here."

Everyone starts to look around, trying to find places to hide. It's almost comical watching a group of grown men and women try to make themselves invisible behind furniture and in doorways. I turn back to the kitchen and see that Isla is whispering something to Willow, who nods but doesn't smile.

"Thanks for this," Willow says to me as she starts to walk toward the living room.

"Of course."

I watch as she enters the living room and Isla holds me back for a second. "Do you think Willow and Blaise...?" Isla starts, but I cut her off.

"They wouldn't. Knox would kill him," I reply. "Now you have to go hide."

We make our way to the living room, where Willow is lingering near the doorway, clearly unsure where to go. I point her toward a corner where a tall potted plant offers some halfhearted cover. She shrugs and moves in that direction, but not before casting another quick glance at Blaise, who is crouched behind a sofa with two of the guys from the team.

My attention is drawn to the front door when I hear a knock. Knox wouldn't knock on his own door, so who is that? I look around the room, and everyone freezes in their hiding spots. I tiptoe to the door, my heart pounding, but it's not from fear. It's the excitement of springing this surprise on Knox. I open the door and this time, it's my turn to freeze in place.

"Tessa," I say, trying to keep my voice neutral. "What are you doing here?"

She glares at me and lets out a long breath. "I need to talk to Knox."

I fight the urge to roll my eyes and step outside, closing the front door behind me. "He's not here. Is there something I can help you with?"

Tessa crosses her arms and taps her foot, clearly agitated that I'm blocking her. "It's none of your business."

"If it has something to do with MY boyfriend, I think it's my business. Now what can I help you with?" Was it petty of me to say that? Sure, but I could careless right now.

Tessa's eyes narrow, and for a moment I think she's going to explode. "You know that you're such a bitch for sinking your claws into him after I told you not to."

I take a deep breath, trying to steady myself. The last thing I need is a scene right in front of Knox's house, especially with everyone inside. "Knox makes his own decisions, and he chose me."

Tessa's lips curl into a smirk that is pure evil. "For now," she says. "But we both know he's just biding his time."

"Is that what you tell yourself?" I shoot back. "That he's just waiting for you? Because from where I'm standing, it looks like he's moved on. Just like you should have."

She takes a step closer, and for a moment I think she's going to slap me. My body tenses, ready for whatever comes next.

Instead, Tessa stops and tilts her head, her smirk growing wider. "You really don't get it, do you? The reason I'm telling you all this is because I've been where you are. I know how it feels to think that he's in it for the long haul."

I've had enough and she's doing nothing but wasting my time. "But you're the one that cheated on him and broke his heart so what's your fucking point? Other than you're being a weirdo who has to come and see her ex-boyfriend on his birthday. Or did you already know he wasn't here because one of your favorite pastimes is stalking him and writing details about it in your little black notebook?"

Tessa's face drains of color, and for a split second I see something like fear in her eyes. Then she recovers and I can see the anger on her face. It all happens quickly, but it clicks immediately that she's going to attack me. And I was already ready.

Tessa lunges, her hand aiming for my hair, but I side-step, and her momentum carries her into the door. The thud is loud enough that I worry it might alert the people inside. She recovers quickly, turning to face me with a wild look in her eyes.

"You think you're so clever," she spits out. "You think you have it all figured out. But you don't know shit, Selene."

I hold my ground, not moving an inch closer to her. "Enlighten me then."

But instead of responding, she tries to attack me again, but I see a flash out of the corner of my eye. A strong hand grabs Tessa's wrist and pulls her back. It's Knox and I don't think I've ever seen him look this angry.

"What the hell, Tessa?" he barks. "Are you out of your mind?"

Tessa looks up at him, and for a moment all the fight drains out of her. She almost seems small and vulnerable, but that only lasts for a minute.

"I just need to talk to you," she says, her voice trembling slightly as she breathes heavily.

Knox doesn't let go of her wrist immediately. Instead, he looks at me, and I can see him scanning my face and body. "Are you okay?"

I give him a quick nod, but I can still see that he's double-checking. When he sees that I'm unharmed, he turns to face Tessa and loosens his grip.

"Talk," he says, crossing his arms.

Tessa rubs her wrist and glares at me as if all of this is my fault. "Not here. Alone."

"No," Knox says, his tone leaving no room for negotiation. He crosses his arms over his chest. "Anything you have to say to me, you can say right here in front of Selene."

Tessa hesitates, her eyes flicking between Knox and me. I can almost see the gears turning in her head, trying to come up with a way to manipulate the situation to her advantage.

"Fine," she says, her voice flat. "Happy birthday, Knox." She pauses, as if expecting him to thank her or at least say something. When he remains silent, she continues. "I'm sorry for everything. For how it ended, for not being there when you needed me. For...for hurting you."

Is this her play? An emotional appeal? She can't be serious, and with me standing right here?

"Is that it?" Knox says.

"That's it. I wanted us to get back together, but now

I'm not so sure about that," she spares a glance at me. "You know how good I am for you. How good we are together."

Before I can react, Knox responds. "We were good together, but that was a long time ago.

And like I've told you, I'm leaving the past in the past. Now leave."

Tessa's eyes widen, as if she's been slapped. "So that's it? You're just going to throw everything we had away because you've found some new toy?"

I feel a surge of anger at her calling me a toy, but I bite my tongue and wait to see what Knox will say. This is his battle now.

"You threw it away when you cheated. Don't try to rewrite history. Now apologize to Selene for the name calling and get off my porch and out of my life. If you don't, I'm going to the dean about your stalking habits."

Tessa stands there, stunned into silence. I can see the wheels in her head spinning, trying to grasp at any last thread that might save her. But there's nothing left for her to hold onto. Knox has made it brutally clear where he stands.

"Selene," Tessa starts, her voice much weaker than before. "I'm sor—"

"Save it," I cut her off. "Just go."

She hesitates for a moment longer, as if she can't quite believe this is how it's ending. Then she turns on her heel and walks down the steps, not looking back. I watch her until she's out of sight, half expecting her to turn around and try to run into Knox's arms.

When she's gone, the tension in my body releases all at once and I feel like I might collapse. Knox reaches for me and pulls me into his arms. I enjoy the hug and quick kiss that we share.

"Are you sure you're okay?"

"I am. Thank you for handling that and happy birthday, baby. I'm sorry you had to deal with that on your special day," I say as I put my hand on the doorknob.

"It's nothing. I'm just happy that now I get to spend the rest of the evening with you."

I let out a deep breath. It takes everything in me to control my face. I push open the door and step aside to let Knox in. "Yeah, I'm looking forward to—"

"SURPRISE!"

Knox steps back in shock as the room explodes into cheers. The look on his face is priceless. Even after the altercation with Tessa, seeing him so genuinely surprised and happy almost brings a tear to my eye. I glance around the room and see Isla waving frantically from the makeshift DJ booth in the corner. She catches my eye and mouths, "Is everything okay?"

I nod subtly, not wanting to ruin the moment.

Knox turns to me, and I swear he's still in shock. "You planned all this?"

I shrug, trying to play it cool. "With a little help from your friends."

He pulls me into a tight hug, and I can feel his gratitude radiating through his body. "This is amazing. Thank you."

"Let's go have fun. We can talk later," I turn to walk away, knowing he would follow me.

But his hand catches mine. "No, I don't want to have whatever that," he gestures to the door. "was sitting on our conscience all night."

His thumb brushes lightly over the back of my hand. His gaze searches mine before he speaks again.

"Seriously, are you okay?" he asks with a low voice.

I hesitate. I could lie, wave it off, pretend it didn't shake me as much as it did. But he'd see right through it.

So instead, I squeeze his hand back. "I will be."

He holds my gaze for a second longer before nodding, like he's accepting my answer even if he doesn't fully buy it, but he doesn't push any harder. Instead, he says, "Tessa doesn't get to ruin anything for us."

I swallow hard, my throat suddenly goes dry. "No, she doesn't. But now it's time to party."

"Wait there's something else I need to do."

"What—"

Knox leans forward and gives me the biggest kiss. It's enough to earn even more cheers and whistles from our friends. I can't help but grin when we break apart to catch our breath. "I love you, picosita."

"And I love you too," I say with a smile that I don't think will ever be wiped from my face.

EPILOGUE
KNOX

Thereee Years Later

"How much further do we have to go?"

I shake my head at how impatient my girlfriend of just over three years is. It's something I'm used to, but I can't help but find it amusing. Not to mention I don't necessarily blame her since she is blindfolded and I'm leading her to our destination.

"We're almost there, I promise," I say, squeezing Selene's hand a little tighter. The cool air of the rink is a stark contrast to the warm summer night outside.

Her lips pout, but I can tell she really wants to smile. Surprises aren't her favorite because she likes to be in control and know what's coming. Still, she's been a good sport about this one.

I stop us just short of the ice and take a moment to

stare at her. Her red hair is slightly longer than it was when we were in college, and I never miss an opportunity to see her green eyes and count the freckles on her face. She's beautiful and it still knocks the wind out of me, even after all this time.

"Okay," I say, "You can take it off now."

Selene hesitates for a beat and then slips the blindfold over her head. She blinks and takes in the empty rink, the polished ice glinting like a diamond under the lights. Her mouth forms a perfect 'O' from being shocked.

"You wanted to surprise me with ice skating again!"

Add another point to the scoreboard for me.

"Knox, did you rent the whole rink out just for us?"

I shrug. "Maybe I did. Maybe I didn't."

Selene's eyes sparkle with joy and I know every bit of effort this took was worth it. "You're ridiculous," she says, but I can tell she's thrilled.

I take her hand and walk her over to the bench. I had everything set up before we arrived thanks to help of the coordinators here. Things have become really easy to schedule these days because I'm now in the NHL, playing for the DC Titans. With how crazy things have been between my career and her being in grad school to get a master's degree in psychology, this felt like the perfect date-day activity that allowed us to ignore the outside world for a little bit.

"I'm way better at ice skating than I used to be."

I look up at her as I get my skates out of the duffel bag.

"I know that, and I also know it's, at least in part, thanks to me."

She playfully rolls her eyes at me. "Don't let it go to your head. I practiced a lot and watched a lot of YouTube tutorials."

We switch out our shoes for skates, and I can't help but think about the first time we did this together. She was nervous but tried her best not to show it. Hell, she went from borrowing Isla's ice skates to purchasing her own. I grin as I watch her lace her skates with the confidence of someone who knows what she's doing.

"Ready?" I ask, standing and offering my hand.

"Hell yeah," she says, taking it.

We wobble together toward the ice, and I brace myself for her first few unsteady moments. Selene surprises me by gliding out with a grace that I wasn't expecting. She's come a long way, and I couldn't be prouder.

"Show-off," I mutter, but I'm smiling.

She spins around to face me, skating backward with ease now. "Maybe you'll have to start watching out for your job," she teases.

I burst out laughing. "Oh yeah? You think you can take on the pros now?"

Selene shrugs as if she doesn't have a care in the world. However, her grin is huge, telling me that she's joking even though I knew that she was. "Give me a few more YouTube videos and who knows?"

That makes me belly laugh to the point where it even

takes me by surprise. I speed up to catch her, and she lets out a mock scream, turning just in time for me to grab her around the waist. We slow to a gentle glide as I hold her close.

"Seriously though," I say, kissing the top of her head, "I'm really proud of you."

"For my skating?" she asks, tilting her head back to look at me.

"For everything," I say. "For putting up with my insane schedule, for killing it in your program, for still finding time for us."

Selene's expression softens. "Knox, you know this works because we both put in the effort. It's not just me."

I release her gently and we skate side by side in silence for a moment. She's right. We've both worked hard to balance our dreams and our relationship. It hasn't always been easy, but standing here now, it's clear that every sacrifice has been worth it.

"Remember when you tried to teach me how to stop?" she says after a while.

I chuckle. "Which time? The second lesson where you crashed into the boards, or the third one where you took me down with you?"

"Both. You were so patient."

"I had selfish motives," I admit. "Any excuse to spend more time with you."

"Well, it worked out pretty well for you, didn't it?"

"Yeah," I say softly. "It really did. And I wouldn't change a thing."

Selene slows down, causing me to circle around her. She bites her lower lip, a telltale sign that she's deep in thought. I come up beside her and take her hand again.

"What's on your mind?" I ask.

She looks at me, then she looks away before her gaze meets mine once more. "Knox, I've been thinking..."

Oh fuck. Here it comes. The big "we need to talk" moment.

"...about how lucky we are," she finishes, squeezing my hand.

Relief washes over me so intensely that I almost laugh out loud again. Instead, I just nod, trying to play it cool. "We are pretty lucky, yeah."

"I mean it," she continues. "Not everyone gets to pursue their dreams and keep the person they love by their side."

I pull her a little closer as we continue to glide. "Are you saying you love me, Selene?"

She smirks. "After three years together, I'd hope so."

"Well, that's good to know," I say, kissing her cheek.

We skate in comfortable silence for another few laps, just enjoying each other's company. It feels good to just be on the ice with the love of my life, not having to worry about the pressures that come as a result of my career.

"Race you," Selene suddenly says, shooting off like a rocket before I can even react.

"Hey!" I shout after her, laughing as it takes me maybe a split second to chase her.

She's fast, I'll give her that. Her form looks nearly perfect from where I am. I hold back just enough to let her think she has a chance, enjoying the sight of her determination and the way her hair flows behind her.

I can't wait to have it clenched in my fists later while I'm fucking her.

"Come on, slowpoke!" she yells over her shoulder, her breath visible in the cold air.

I put on a burst of speed and close the gap between us. At the last moment she swerves, and I almost plow right into the boards. I manage to stop just in time, turning to see her laughing.

"Thought you had me there, didn't you?" she says, panting slightly.

I skate over to her slowly, stalking my prey if you will. "You know I could've smoked you if I wanted."

"Sure," she says, sticking her tongue out at me.

"But," I add, stopping just inches from her, "it's more fun this way."

She leans in as if to kiss me, then pulls back quickly. "One more lap. The finish line is where we entered the rink. Winner gets to live out one of their sexual fantasies."

Before I can protest, she's off again. This time I don't hold back. I lower my body, digging into the ice with each stroke of my skates. All I can focus on is the finish line and Selene's figure cutting through the air ahead of me.

Halfway around the rink, I catch up and we're neck and neck. She glances at me with a mix of fear and excitement. I can tell she's giving it everything she's got. I'm torn. Part of me wants to let her win just because I love seeing her so happy, but another part of me—the competitive part—wants that prize.

We cross the imaginary line together in a blur, both of us immediately trying to slow down without wiping out. Selene grabs onto the boards, and I do a quick stop that sends a spray of ice into the air.

"That was... wild," she says between gasps for air.

I skate over to her, my heart pounding not just from the exertion but from the rush of the race. "Call it a tie?" I offer, extending my hand.

She takes it and pulls me closer. "A tie means we both win."

"I can live with that," I say, just before our lips meet in a kiss.

We break apart slowly. "So, which fantasy do you want to start with?"

Selene laughs, a sound that warms me more than any winter coat ever could. "Oh, we'll have to make a list. We have all night, after all."

"All night?" I raise an eyebrow. "I thought you had a paper due tomorrow."

She waves me off with a flick of her wrist. "It's done. You're not the only who keeps surprises, Hockey Hottie."

"Well, color me impressed," I say, "You really are amazing, you know that?"

"I know. Now kiss me."

I pull her to me and give her a kiss that could literally set the ice ablaze. Because there's no way I could deny her. Ever.

If you would like to read a bonus scene featuring Selene and Knox, you can grab it here.

Willow and Blaise's story will be the next book in this series.

ACKNOWLEDGMENTS

Writing about Selene and Knox was such an amazing experience, and I'm sad that this is the end of their story. Well... it's not really the end because they will appear in future books.

TK and CB, I'm truly grateful for your friendship and support throughout this journey. Also, thank you, CB, for giving me insight into Mexican culture. It is such a privilege to learn about a culture that is not my own.

Andra, you've hit it out of the park once again. Thank you for creating this—I couldn't have imagined Selene and Knox any other way.

Ellie, thank you for keeping my hot mess in check. I can't wait to work on the next release with you.

Chrisandra and Elizabeth, I can't thank you both enough for jumping on this project and being so patient with me. Your hard work is immensely appreciated—thank you.

Kim, thank you so much for your thoughtful comments about this book. Your feedback was amazing and truly made the story better.

And of course, I can't forget to thank every single reader for picking up this book. The fact that you took time out of your day to read my words means the world to me.

Thank you.

ABOUT THE AUTHOR

Emery Paige is a dreamer, a word crafter, and a wine lover. She has been a writer and reader for as long as she can remember. Being able to call herself a romance author is a dream come true.

When she's not pouring her soul into her next romance, Emery can be found indulging in her love for music or watching YouTube, where she enjoys everything from travel vlogs to fashion and cooking.

If you would like to keep in contact with her, please visit her website (www.emerypaigebooks.com) or sign up for her newsletter to receive the latest information about her and her books.

She's also on Instagram and TikTok.

www.ingramcontent.com/pod-product-compliance
Lightning Source LLC
Chambersburg PA
CBHW020011120726
47903CB00004B/1231